MW01488964

AWAKENING TOUCH

THE DIVINE TREE GUARDIAN SERIES

LARISSA EMERALD

Awakening Touch
The Divine Tree Guardian Series, Book Two

by Larissa Emerald
Copyright © 2016 Castle Oak Publishing LLC

ISBN-10: 1-942139-09-8
ISBN-13: 978-1-942139-09-6

http://www.larissaemerald.com

This novel is a work of fiction. References to historical events, real people, or real locales are used fictitiously. Names, characters, places, and incidents are the product of the author's imagination and are not to be construed as real. Any resemblance to actual events or locales or persons, living or dead, is coincidental.

Published in the United States of America.

BOOKS BY LARISSA EMERALD

Paranormal Romance

DIVINE TREE GUARDIAN SERIES

Awakening Fire
Awakening Touch

VAMPIRE

Forever At Dawn – short
Forever At Midnight – short

ROMANTIC SUSPENSE

Winter Heat

BAREFOOT BAY – KINDLE WORLD

Come Sail Away – short

For my daughter, Rachel,

*There are good days and bad days with any endeavor,
but anything is possible when you put your mind to it.*

I'm proud of you and love you always.

THE STORY

Paranormal Investigator, Grace Wenger, seeks the truth behind a recent French healing miracle, and if true, hopefully obtain the curative potion for her inoperable disease. While on her quest, she set out to unearth a ghost or two in the gorgeous wine country, but nowhere in her wildest imagination did she anticipate falling for a mysterious shapeshifter, guardian to a magical tree, and battling a Reaper demanding the tree's secrets.

Immortal Ian Hearst, a Divine Tree guardian, avoids human involvement. A master at distancing people from the tree, he's failed to keep Grace from repeatedly trespassing onto his land and trying to get to his Divine Tree. She tests more than his protective duties, when he falls prey to her sassy, open nature. But by opening his heart, she allows the Reaper a path for evil deeds to multiply. Soon Ian finds his love for her puts him at direct odds with his duty.

THE LEGEND

In the beginning of ancient time, the massive Tree of Life stood tall, with heavy branches and mile-deep roots, holding within knowledge of the universe. But after the division of good and evil, this sacred tree needed to be protected against exploitation and the Archangel Seth was charged with the tree's protection.

Realizing one such tree was far more susceptible to destruction than several, the angel split the tree into twelve that took root around the globe; if one tree should fall, the knowledge of the universe would prevail within its colleagues.

The archangel created a brotherhood of powerful immortal guardians to safeguard the mighty trees. These twelve brothers, from the Isle of Skye, formed the league of the Divine Tree Guardians.

Awakening Touch

1

"Why are you dying?" Ian Hearst plucked another fistful of dried leaves from an ill grapevine. He shook his head and dropped the leaves to the ground, then walked over to his horse, mounted, and rode away.

Custos felt his immortal Guardian's lingering frustration. Yes, Ian was dedicated to his winery hobby. He was enthusiastic about everything he did, actually. His extensive attention to detail showed in everything at Chêne Sacré from the hand-carved railings and elaborate stonework at the château to the manicured lawns and colorful garden that led to the rows of vines.

Custos stood within the heart of a sprawling vineyard on the outskirts of Provence, France. He was a Divine Tree, one of eleven unknown around the globe, an ancient oak stretched tall and full, and this expanse of land was his refuge from the world with the protection of his Guardian.

He swayed and bent as the lavender-scented breeze coming from the south rippled over his bark and stroked his limbs. In the shadow of the Alps, he wiggled his roots even deeper into the ground and drank the moisture from the rich soil, allowing thirsty wood fibers to absorb the life-sustaining minerals held deep within the French earth.

The spring rains had let up, and this May morning the sun warmed his branches and the wind gently teased his rich green leaves, which were beginning to thicken with the commencement of summer. Today captured the perfect essence of existence—joyous, peaceful, and harmonious. The wisdom of the ages coursed through the vast catacombs of Custos's being like electricity zinging through wires, igniting each synapse and particle of knowledge and history with renewed life. Days such as these should be cherished.

He sighed, only slightly worried that Ian might be too distracted from his Guardian duties by his vineyard and winery. Even though contentment should be flowing easily through every sliver of wood, a vibration of unease couldn't be denied. His Georgia complement—one of ten around the world—was finally showing signs of real life after a lengthy dormant recovery period following an altercation with the demon Io.

The demon had used Ian's brother and his soulmate's magical ability to poison a Divine Tree. Thank heavens they'd found a way to thwart the evil fiend and save the sacred tree.

As the day burned brightly around him, the ancient oak turned within, sorting and filing and restructuring the indefinite quantity of files, the knowledge of the universe he held within. It was what he did to overcome that feeling of being…alone. He supposed that Ian did the same with the winery in his own way. The land had been this Guardian's friend from the beginning, the very thing that had sustained Ian over the millennia.

Custos had enjoyed the company of the twelve

brothers—one gone now—who guarded him. He pushed the thoughts of loneliness aside, shifting the black hole energy farther down into a leeward root.

And so it went, moving and shuffling the secrets of the universe until something prompted him to stop and take heed.

With an internal yawn, the Divine Tree became aware of unusual activity within the vineyard. *People.* No, there was but one human. The other was something else. He reached out with a tendril of energy, testing what he found.

A reaper.

With a sharp gust of wind, heavy gray clouds eclipsed the sun, and a shadow covered the ground. But the Divine Tree didn't need eyes to know this creature was the Dark Realm's spawn. Although death was a natural part of the circle of life, there was nothing natural about reapers. They took individuals before their times and claimed their souls.

Custos could sense it all. A little girl, no more than seven years old, ran desperately, moving as fast as her tiny legs could carry her. She squeezed through a small opening in the grapevines, and with a frantic burst of energy, she stumbled forward, planting her palms against the ancient oak's massive trunk. She hugged the bark as if she knew it was her only hope and tilted her head way, way back, looking up into the branches. Perhaps she was considering climbing up, with thoughts of a safe haven, but Custos wasn't sure.

A tingling sensation shot deep into his roots then. A special quality emitted from the child. And when she laid her cheek upon the old oak, images of the future and the potential role the little girl played in it rolled over him.

Her breaths came in ragged, labored exhales. More tortured than what a child's breathing should have been, even under the circumstances. She started to cry and gasped sharply for air. She glanced over her shoulder, her vivid blue eyes round and frightened, and her silky, light brown hair sticking to the wetness on her cheeks. Coughing, she stepped over roots as she scrambled around to the other side of Custos's massive trunk. With a few strangled wheezes, she collapsed to the ground, her breathing shallow, growing even more labored with every inhale. Her eyes slowly closed, then fanned open before closing again.

The reaper bounded over the top of the vines and landed squarely on both feet. He angled his head, taking in the situation.

Custos moved his roots upward through the earth, encircling the child and pulling her closer. "You cannot have this little one."

The reaper laughed. "No?"

"Go find a deserving soul."

Someone as wicked as you are.

"Now where's the fun in that?"

This time, at the sound of the reaper's voice, the sweet girl moaned. The reaper leaned in. Placing his index finger to his pursed lips, he whispered, "Shh."

With the girl's back tucked snuggly against his trunk, Custos felt her heart slowing, stopping, dying. He heaved upward, dislodging deeper roots that had been in place for centuries. Moving one and then another, he wrapped her up and drew her down into the earth, where he opened a porthole and took her inside the catacombs of knowledge to safety.

"No," the reaper bellowed, the eerie sound echoing across the land.

"She is not for you," Custos snapped.

"It is her time. Could you not hear her struggling?"

Custos shook every branch in fury. "She lives. I have the power to make it so."

Beside himself, like a dog that had just lost a well-anticipated bone and was still salivating over the prize, the reaper stomped around in a circle and glared at the Divine Tree. Finally, realizing he had no immediate recourse, he changed into a scraggly vulture and flew to a nearby cork oak, where he resumed his reaper form and sat perched high in the evergreen branches, scythe in hand.

Knock yourself out, Custos thought, knowing the reaper would soon grow bored and go searching for easier targets. The critical task at hand was to find the right grain of knowledge to cure this sweet child of the killer illness named cystic fibrosis.

In the meantime, his Guardian needed to know the reaper had some evil business afoot.

Ian lifted the saddle from the gelding and set it in the tack room. His ride among the vines had been invigorating and reminded him why riding horseback remained one of his favorite activities. It reminded him of the life he'd lived over the centuries since he'd left Scotland, before modernization with fancy cars, mega computers, and phones that demanded an instant response.

The gelding tossed his head as if to say farewell. Ian paused to run his palm along the animal's neck. The horse had taken quite some time to accept Ian, for he'd sensed the shape-shifter forms of bear and eagle residing inside the Guardian and hadn't been able to relax due to a natural fear of becoming prey.

As Ian raised his hand for another pat, the branches of the tree tattoo on his back warmed. Custos was summoning him.

The layout of his estate was built around his needs to attend the oak. There were underground passages hidden in several of the buildings, the nearest one tucked within the massive wine cellar. Although he could approach aboveground, he rarely did if he perceived a true threat. The clandestine location enabled the best surveillance of the situation. And sometimes the element of surprise was key.

The cool fifty-five-degree temperature of the wine cellar brushed his face as he entered. He picked up his pace, moving past the new batch of oak barrels waiting for the cellar master to test and approve for structural integrity. Inside a private room, stairs rose to a private, rarely used, split-level wine-tasting bar. Ian flicked a switch on the wall and the staircase tilted upward, guided by mechanical lifts and hinges. He trotted down a second set of stairs beneath the first, which led to the underground passages. At the bottom, he hit another lever and the upper staircase descended, closing the opening and returning everything to its original position. From here, he had a number of directions he could go, including to the château straight ahead or to the Divine Tree. He hustled toward the oak, the thud of his footfalls echoing through the stone.

The passage ended at the subterranean entrance to the tree where a threshold comprised of twisted and gnarled roots formed a golden arch over the doorway. At the top, knots of wood created the images of bear and eagle, his shape-shifter beings. Ian completed the anointing ritual, allowing sap to drip from a thick, wet root onto the tree of life tattoo on the inside of his wrist.

"Benison," Custos whispered.

"Blessings," Ian returned. "My strength and loyalty are yours."

After acknowledging the Divine Tree, the door opened and he entered.

Inside, on the far side of the hand-carved furniture of the watch room, he was stunned to find a little girl curled up sound asleep on the floor. How had she gotten in here?

He narrowed his eyes, noting her convenient location to the invisible porthole to the outside. "What is this?" Ian whispered aloud so as not to wake the child.

The neighbor child, Maely Dubois. I brought her inside, Custos answered within Ian's head, the Divine Tree's voice like dry autumn leaves rustling across the ground.

"Which is even more shocking. What of our code of secrecy?"

The girl will not know. She sleeps.

"But why? Why did you bring her in?"

Look about to the south and you will find a reaper. He was pursuing the child. She had an illness that he planned on taking advantage of.

"Had?"

I'm capable of healing, so I chose to do so.

Ian rubbed the backs of his knuckles along his jawline and shook his head. This act of compassion would cause them trouble. He could feel it. He peered outside through the magical properties of the tree bark, and sure enough, a reaper reclined in a treetop, his fiery eyes trained on the ancient oak, his soul-extricating scythe resting across his thigh. "What does he want?"

That hasn't been revealed to me yet.

"Does he have a name?"

A rustling noise indicated the Divine Tree was thinking, sorting through his infinite stores of knowledge. *The reaper calls himself Death.*

"Of course he does," Ian muttered. As usual, the Dark Realm was predictably unoriginal.

"But Death can't have the girl," Custos announced, this time out loud.

"Agreed." Ian stepped closer to Maely. "I'll take her home."

He bent and lifted her slowly and gently into his arms. She snuggled her cheek against his hard chest and placed her palm over his heart. Protectiveness surged inside him, eliciting a moment when he feared for the child's safety. He sighed, releasing the anxiety.

She will be fine.

He wondered, not for the first time, how the Divine Tree could be so sure.

Maely weighed barely anything. He carried her back the way he'd come, except this time he took the route that led him to the forest near her parents' property. He exited aboveground at a ledge of rocks. The girl stirred as they came out of the tree line and traveled into her father's vines. She blinked her eyes open.

"Bonjour, *petit agneau*," he said in French. "Did you get lost? I found you asleep, and I'm taking you home."

She attempted to rise up. Ian stopped, adjusting her so that she rested on his forearm in an upright position. "Merci, monsieur," she said, then hugged his neck. "I had a lovely adventure this morning."

"Really? Tell me about it." He began walking again.

"The mean, ugly man chased me. And then the magic tree saved me and took me inside its trunk. It was the coolest thing ever."

"That sounds like a wonderful dream."

Her expressive eyes grew wide as an owl's. "Oh, it wasn't a dream at all."

"Why, it must have been. Trees can't take people inside them."

"This one can. Plus, my breathing problem is better. Look." She inhaled deeply for effect. "See? No more coughing."

"I'm glad to see the fresh morning air and sunshine has done you good."

She wriggled in his arms. "No. It was the tree. I think he made me better."

Ian stopped and set her feet on the ground. They were close to her house now, and some of the workers were heading toward the attached winery for lunch. He knelt to her level. "I'm glad you're feeling better, *petit agneau*. But I doubt my old oak had anything to do with your improvement." He stood. "Come, let's find your maman."

She didn't argue or say anything more, but simply slid her tiny hand into his very large one, tilting her head up to look at him with a bright smile. Ian thought he caught a special spark within her beautiful blue eyes. It made him wonder what he was missing as they continued on.

When he was young, before he'd been called to his role as an immortal Guardian, he'd been smitten with a young lass. He remembered one rainy day in particular when they'd built a fort out of a drying cow hide and played pretend games, as kids sometimes do, of being parents and having a family and a farm and predicting their naive version of the future.

His life had turned out nowhere close to his imaginings. The lack of family was a sore spot for him, one he often managed to push aside. But in moments like this, when he'd longed to have a child and family of his own, well, it sucked to be immortal. Eventually, everyone passed on and left him alone. He had long ago stopped trying to have a normal life, refusing to go through the pain of losing anyone again.

If he'd had a child, though, he fancied she'd be much like Maely—sweet, intelligent, caring, and adventurous.

He approached Madame Dubois. "I walked your daughter home. I found her asleep beside my old oak. She seemed to be having a bad dream."

Her mother gasped. "Maely, I thought you were playing with the kittens!"

Running into her mother's open arms, the child laughed. "I was! Then a horrible man came and chased me. I ran and ran until I hid behind the tree. The tree saved me. And look!" She placed her hands on each side of her ribs, drawing air deep into her lungs and releasing the breath. "The rattles are gone!"

Madame Dubois eased her hands onto the girl's back. "I don't feel any vibration of fluid." She gave a puzzled frown. "Your lungs seem clear."

"They are." Maely pushed away and twirled around. "What's for lunch?"

"Thank you for bringing her home," Madame Dubois said to Ian. "It was very kind of you."

"Not at all." He frowned as he watched the child dance over to the food. "She certainly has a vivid imagination."

"Yes. She does."

Ian crossed his arms, putting on a stern expression. "Perhaps you could speak with her about not roaming onto my property?"

Madame Dubois straightened her spine. "I'm sure Maely meant no harm."

"Nonetheless. I worry about my vines."

"Of course. I'll encourage her to be more careful and to remain near the house."

"Excellent. We understand each other, then." And hopefully the child would not get any more inquisitive about his Divine Tree.

2

Three months later

"Dammit, I've tried everything. The vines keep dying," Ian said. He tore a dead, shriveling leaf from the thick woody stalk of the sick grapevine and gently smoothed it flat against his palm, unfurling its sickly, curled edges. His inner beasts thrashed in his chest, restless, as if they sensed something he did not yet discern. "It's like something is devouring the vine from the inside out, leaving a paper-thin skeletal outer layer."

François Lagarde, a fellow winegrower and friend, leaned over Ian's outstretched hand. "The blood-red coloring is most unusual," he exclaimed. "Most unusual, indeed."

The sun had crested the surrounding trees and shone a bright golden glow on all it touched, making everything, even the dying vines, look healthier in its radiance. Ian knew better. These vines weren't coming back.

He inhaled the scent of rich soil and ripening grapes. "So what do you think is killing my plants? A fungus? Bacteria? Some microscopic insect?"

His friend stepped back, moving his hands behind him and stretching his torso. "It's not the fruit fly that spread acid rot in parts of the northern Rhône, that much I can tell you." He shook his head. "Perhaps the vines are being poisoned."

"What?"

"Remember the Burgundy threat in 2010? Someone held the Romanée-Conti vineyard for ransom, threatening to poison the vines. Perhaps this is something like that."

Ian straightened. "I don't think that's what's happening here. I haven't received a ransom note. And as you can see, my vines are already suffering."

"Just the eight vines?" François asked.

"Yes, but I've been removing dying vines for the past three months. Now there are more and they're situated practically in the middle of the vineyard. If it spreads, the damage will be done in only a matter of days. My vineyard will be wiped out by the time we reach harvest."

"Well, my best recommendation is to keep removing the affected plants. Then have them tested to determine the cause."

Ian sighed. "I'd thought the same but had hoped you'd be able to identify the problem." He directed his friend back to where their horses stood. "I'm at a loss."

They mounted as the horses sidestepped anxiously, seeming to pick up on Ian's tension.

François grasped his reins with a firm hold. "Your situation is a concern to us all, my friend. This could behave like an epidemic and strike every plant in the area."

"I won't allow that. The plants will be eradicated by this evening. I will personally see to it." Ian set his horse in motion and led the way back to the house and stables.

Minutes ticked by as they passed vine after vine draped

with young bunches of grapes. Beyond and to the north, Ian could see the expansive canopy of the Divine Tree rising above everything else. A slice of unease cut through him. Could whatever was attacking the vines hurt the tree? It was a plant after all, albeit one with magical abilities.

Back at the house, the stable hands were at the ready to see to the horses. "Would you like to join me for some refreshments?" Ian asked François before sending him on his way.

"Thank you, but not today. You have work to do, my friend. And I won't keep you from it." François gave Ian a meaningful stare, one that relayed his concern.

Ian nodded. "Another time, then. Though I will see you at my gala Saturday evening, no?"

"But of course."

He walked François around to the front drive where his friend slid behind the wheel of his Ferrari and drove away.

Immediately, Ian pulled out his phone and sent a text to his foreman, instructing him to bring over the necessary equipment and manpower to remove the vines. He'd meant it when he'd told François that he'd personally remove the sick vines.

Bernard, his *delegato,* the assistant provided to him by his Divine Tree to be his intermediary with the outside world beyond his home, came out of nowhere, as he frequently did. "May I be of some service?"

"Perhaps," Ian responded. "I need to remove some vines."

"I'm sorry to hear that." The man's voice expressed his sincerity.

"I've called the foreman, but as you see, he hasn't arrived yet. Will you drive the truck down that row?" He pointed to which one he meant. "You can't miss the dead vines. I'll meet you there."

The Divine Tree had chosen to root in this plot of land, and it wasn't long before Ian had discovered that grapes, and just about anything he could think of, thrived in the soil. The land had become a part of him, almost as important to him as the ancient oak. It was his family, the only thing that had been with him over all the centuries he'd lived here.

He was about to put his phone back in his pocket, when it thrummed and vibrated. He swiped his finger over the screen. His foreman was set already? Viewing the message, he blinked, hard. No, it was not the foreman. It was his brother, Venn.

Dismay coursed through him as he read the text.

Our train is being rerouted because of a landslide. Will be delayed.

Venn and his wife—by God, Ian still wasn't sure how that had happened—were coming to France to visit. But now he wondered if they would ever get here. First their plane had needed to be changed out, and now the train from Paris to Avignon was having issues?

His heart rate increased. Thankfully they were safe.

He hadn't seen *any* of his brothers face-to-face in the hundreds of years since they'd all become Guardians. Sure, they used today's technology to see each other on screens now. But that was all he'd had. No handshakes, no claps on the shoulder, no fierce bear hugs. He swallowed a hit of emotion, his throat tightening.

They had so much to discuss, so much to catch up on. Not only was Venn now married but evidently, Seth, that crazy archangel who'd changed he and his brothers into Divine Tree Guardians, had agreed to watch over Venn's Divine Tree for a spell. Who knew that was even possible? But they had delayed their trip until his tree had grown strong enough after some sort of trauma. Even now, that tree still couldn't communicate with the other Divine Trees.

Ian thumped his fist to his chest a time or two as he forced his feet to walk toward the vineyard. Venn had alluded to some scary shit going down at his Divine Tree in America that he wanted to discuss. Ian wondered what that was about. He knew the Dark Realm was behind the near death of Venn and his Divine Tree, but there were more details yet to discover.

He needed to get this situation with the vineyard under control, though, so he could devote all his attention to the Thousand Days until the Age of Atonement. He'd recalled Seth had spoken of a coming of the Age of Atonement, when the doers of evil would answer for their deeds. But life had a way of linking one day to the next and he had grown complacent, forgetting the conflict was on the horizon. Perhaps he had involved himself too deeply in his vineyard.

Either people believed in supernatural phenomenon or they didn't. That's what Grace Wenger had discovered while producing her TV show, *From the Far Side*. Sometimes she found it best to test the waters before jumping into the real reason she was visiting a place. Otherwise, people turned her away before she could even say hello. Ghosts, spirits, and unexplainable occurrences weren't your average topic of conversation. And when the events involved a child... Well, that called for even more caution and finesse.

As the late August day warmed, she introduced her assistant Skylar and herself to the Dubois family they were about to interview, claiming to be random travelers just stopping in for lunch at the small winery.

Grace found the Dubois family of four charming. The couple was much younger than she'd imagined, closer to her own age of twenty-eight. Perhaps they were even into their midthirties, given their two adorable children—a boy around four and a girl named Maely, who was a year older.

Monsieur Dubois conversed enthusiastically with a group of vineyard workers at an outdoor table on the veranda overlooking the vineyards. Madame Dubois, with a riot of long, curly, brownish-red hair was more subdued.

With a smile and a "Merci!" Grace accepted the crusty bread and glass of rosé Madame Dubois offered in hospitable welcome. The view was gorgeous, and Grace could have sat there for hours all alone and taken it in; however, she didn't have that luxury.

"Are you staying in town?" the young mother asked.

"Yes, for the time being. But I'd like to extend my stay, so I'm looking for just the right place," Grace said. Small mom-and-pop wineries like theirs dotted the area, many offering bed-and-breakfast accommodations, as well as workaway projects to supplement their vineyard operation and attract extra workers.

"We have a room available, if you're interested." Madame Dubois paused, her eyes assessing. "Sixty-five euros per day."

"That's fair." Grace looked off across the fields of grapes. "Is that the Chêne Sacré Winery over there?" She nudged her chin toward the grand estate a good distance away and up the hill, pondering its English translation, *Sacred Oak*.

Madame Dubois raised a perplexed brow. "You've heard of it, *non*?"

"There was some discussion in the village. A miracle, they say."

Actually, there were whispers in town about the healing of a child. But that wasn't how Grace had come to learn of it. She belonged to an active underground network of believers who kept her updated about new and unusual paranormal events. Usually, they were thrilled if she chose to investigate a ghost sighting or such for her program. But this story had piqued her interest immediately, and she'd come all the way to France to learn more.

Madame Dubois narrowed her eyes, clearly growing cautious. "Do you believe in such miracles?"

Grace searched the woman's eyes. "Yes, I do."

The woman glanced across to her little girl, whose light-brown hair just touched her delicate shoulders. As if sensing her mother's apprehension, the child fled her father's knee and skipped over to them from the head of the table. She had the clearest, brightest blue eyes Grace had ever seen. She danced along carrying a dilapidated handful of wildflowers that flopped over her tiny hand.

Grace stifled an inhaled breath. She hadn't expected to meet the little girl so soon.

"Your daughter was the child in the stories…wasn't she?" Grace asked softly.

A long moment passed as Madame Dubois seemed conflicted, possibly weighing manners and a mother's protective instinct. "Maely, this is Mademoiselle Wenger. She might be a guest for a little while."

With childish abandon, the girl held out her small hand. "Pleased to meet you," she said as she dipped in a curtsy.

The instant Maely's hand touched Grace's, tingles rushed up into her arm and through her chest. Maely smiled, appearing aware of what had transpired between them yet at the same time remaining innocently unfazed.

She looked up at her mother. "I told Fletcher not to pick these, Maman. Now look at them." The child heaved a sigh.

"Hmm, let me see." Grace leaned in, stroking the foliage. "Go put them in some water. They'll perk up."

Even after Grace's slight touch, life bloomed in the flowers in the girl's hand. The child looked from the flowers to Grace's eyes, yet she didn't question the sudden deepening of color of the cut plants. She only grinned. Then she glanced at Skylar, seeming to consider the purple streaked highlights. A hint of uncertainty touched the child's gaze. Given the sheltered country life out here,

Grace suspected the girl had never seen such unusual hair coloring.

"I like your hair," Grace said.

Skylar set her glass on the table. "Thank you."

Maely spun to face her mother. "May I go play with the kittens now?"

"Yes, *ma petite*. For a few minutes."

"She's so sweet," Grace said. "I'm happy to hear she is cured of her illness."

"Who are you?" Madame Dubois inquired, stiffening now.

Grace finished the last bite of her bread and wine. They were both delicious. *Another reason to be eager to stay at the Dubois's place,* she thought as she deposited the glass on a nearby tray. She clasped her hands together low in front of her, knowing full well that she might not be welcome when she finished what she had to say.

"I produce a television program in the United States about unusual things," she began. "Such as the extraordinary healing of a child who had a terminal form of cystic fibrosis yet is left today with no sign the disease ever existed."

Madame Dubois opened her mouth to speak, then pressed her lips together. She made the sign of the cross and glanced around.

From the corner of her eye, Grace noticed Monsieur Dubois close his knife and stand. The other guests followed suit. The pointed look in his eyes said he'd overheard her explanation and that he was going to turn her away.

"Non, non," he interjected with a shooing motion. "We've had enough of reporters. Please, you must leave."

His eyes darted from hers to the other guests, and she knew he didn't want a scene. Actually, Grace didn't want one, either. News spread rapidly in quaint areas such as this, and she didn't want the locals clamming up before she'd had a chance to really begin her investigation.

"Very well," she said, taking a step back. "My interest is more in the location where this miracle took place, anyway. At Chêne Sacré, if my information is correct. Perhaps I should begin there."

Seeing that Grace was immediately willing to give in and leave, Monsieur Dubois turned from them, mumbling, "Good luck with that."

"What did he mean?" Grace inquired, as Madame Dubois ushered her toward the exit.

The woman lifted a shoulder. "Monsieur Hearst is the most inhospitable man I've ever had the displeasure of meeting. His place is guarded as if his vines were made of gold. Don't expect to find a tasting room at that fancy winery. There isn't one. Very few people even know what the man looks like."

"I had heard he was an eccentric recluse. I wasn't able to find any photos of him, and only a few of the estate with regards to Maely's...incident." She pictured a grumpy old Scottish expat who lived in a moldy, crumbling château while indulging in an expensive hobby.

They came to a stop when they reached the driveway, where Grace had left their rented Peugeot. Skylar slid in behind the steering wheel while Grace hesitated, looking back over her shoulder.

"Please understand, Mademoiselle Wenger. We must protect our daughter."

Grace touched the woman's arm and leaned in. She felt a connection to this woman, in the way one knew they'd enjoy someone's company. Call it instinct, intuition, a vibe that they shared. "I get it." Grace smiled. "But I have a personal stake in this. Whether the piece ever airs or not, I need to find out how Maely was made well." It was her only chance for healing her tumor. And a long shot at that.

Madame Dubois turned away. "I'm sorry. I can't help you."

Grace didn't press. Another time, perhaps. "Thank you for lunch, at least."

She got in the passenger side, and Skylar drove off.

The road wound and turned as they headed back toward Puits, the village where they had stayed the night before. As Skylar slowed for each bend, Grace was glad she'd paid a little extra to rent the automatic transmission.

At least they drive on the right side of the road here.

Along the way, Grace kept sight of the acres and acres of land that made up Chêne Sacré, which was easy to spy with its grandeur and high elevation. Actually, the beauty of the place far exceeded her shabby expectations, although she supposed it could still be neglected up close.

"That's Chêne Sacré up there," she said to Skylar. "There's a small vineyard-guesthouse combo up the road to the east. Let's try there next for a place to stay. It would really help to be as close as possible to Ian Hearst's estate."

"Sounds good to me."

Grace caught sight of what she presumed was his home staring down at her from a crest at the highest elevation. Even from a distance, the château resembled an ancient castle on a hill. When the Peugeot rounded a curve, the château disappeared, only to reappear around another bend. They seemed to be moving in a downward circle around it, and she kept tabs on it as they drove.

"What was it about this place that cured Maely?" she asked, not expecting an answer. Her thoughts began to wander. Could it have been the soil? Something in the vines themselves? A ghost or spirit? What? Why? How?

Her mind tried to wrap around such a phenomenon capable of altering the very nature of the cells in the girl's body. That's essentially what would have taken place as there no longer seemed to be even a trace of the disease the child once carried.

Skylar navigated a sharp bend in the road, instinctively clutching the wheel and easing off the gas. The car smoothly came out of the turn, and Grace was vaguely aware of how few vehicles she passed. Not like in the States.

Maely. She pictured the girl's bright blue eyes.

The narrow road opened up into a small valley. Something white blocked the road immediately ahead. Were those...sheep?

"Look out!" Grace yelled.

Skylar slammed on the brakes, and the car veered to the right.

Oh shit.

Out-of-control now, the car bucked up and down over the rough terrain and pitched front-end first into a small ditch.

When her vision and nerves finally settled, Grace heaved a long, calming breath. Thank God not a single sheep had been hit.

She looked at Skylar. "Are you all right?"

"Yes."

Slowly, Grace opened the car door, stepped out, and surveyed the damage. The front end was buried to the bumper. "No way we're getting out of this on our own."

Looking around, she took stock of their location. It wasn't that bad, she supposed. She dug her phone from her pocket, snapped a picture of the car, and then engaged Google Maps. The Dubois's small winery was around eight miles back, and the Hearst mansion was straight up the hill, though it probably wasn't a good idea to just show up there.

"Guess we walk the rest of the way." With a shrug, she reached into the car and grabbed her backpack, which contained her wallet, iPad, and water bottle. A walk to the next guesthouse didn't faze her in the least. She'd faced far worse challenges in search of a story—the shack she'd investigated along an alligator-and-snake-infested bayou outside of New Orleans came to mind. Now *that* had tested her resolve. But the place had been haunted big-time, so it made the airboat trek and all the other yuck factors worthwhile.

Grace led the way to the road and stopped. "It will take over an hour to make it to the guesthouse, I'd guess. Maybe we'll be able to hitch a ride. And hopefully they'll have a tractor or truck that could get the car unstuck." She looked up and down the road. The sheep had almost cleared it. She passed one last straggler and shooed it along. "See the trouble you caused us?" she said to the laggard.

Grace walked along the poorly paved road, thinking of her next move. When they found a nearby place to stay, then what? How would she gain access to a recluse's property?

Deep inside an ancient underground storage cave, Death lounged, his back against a large rock. The deep-rooted death-vine buried itself in the ground, all the way into Hell. He'd secured it here in case he needed it to hold his clients. He chuckled out loud at that.

The cord flopped and wiggled up from the earth on the other side of the room. Any victims he chose would find themselves bound until he marked their time and their soul.

He'd just returned from the Dark Realm where all the talk had been of the Age of Atonement. Apparently, the hourglass counting the Thousand Days until AOA had been set. Every beast within that fiery hole was trying to figure out how to save themselves before Atonement arrived. It didn't matter if they were demon or reaper, siren or gargoyle, when that time came, they'd all be frozen in time, never to wreak havoc on the world again. Never to adulterate, fornicate, hate, envy, murder, embellish with sorcery, or dance in drunkenness or reveling again. Never to *be* again.

He threw a rock at the vine. It quickly seized the chunk and wound around it.

Good thing the demon Io had solicited his help. Now, from what he'd learned about the Divine Trees, he might just have an out. And wouldn't it be great to really live again? He thought of all the things he'd missed by being owned by the Dark Realm. Pretty women, most of all.

This time he tossed the vine a handful of grape leaves. Within seconds, they were dust.

He adjusted the bones in his ribcage, bones he'd collected from the people he'd taken. He'd added them to his skeletal frame, making his structure larger and more formidable. Souvenirs, so to speak. He cracked his neck, enjoying the sound. And he wouldn't mind adding a few more before the tree helped him change. No, that's as it should be...

3

Ian tossed the final bag of damaged vines into the rear of the winery truck. He'd personally dug up a dozen grapevines, the eight dead plants and two more on either side for good measure. He'd triple bagged each one as he went, and then when he was finished, he burned the equipment he'd used during the task. Given the potential destruction the diseased plants might be capable of, he intended to take every precaution, not just for his vines but for his Divine Tree.

The sun hung high overhead and darted out between clouds that cast shadows across the land. He drove away from his estate and toward Lourmarin, where he planned to turn the vines over to agricultural specialists. Getting rid of the affected plants made him feel better already.

He trundled along the road that he'd taken since before it supported automobiles, back in the days of horses and carts. Coming around one of the sharpest bends, he spotted a car stuck in a ditch. He slowed his truck to a crawl, checking out the other car as he drove past. He zeroed in with his eyes, as well as his senses, allowing his beasts to join in and help him gather information.

The vehicle was empty—no movement or sound coming from it, no sign of blood. He inhaled deeply, catching a perfumed scent. Decidedly female. He sniffed again, noting dual aromas. Perhaps someone had already picked them up.

Resuming his speed, he drove on. A few miles up the road, he spotted the women, one short and average with dark cropped hair, one tall and slender with long blond hair that bounced over her shoulders where it wasn't trapped beneath her backpack. His gaze lingered on the tall woman's long tanned legs, shapely calves, and firm backside.

Suddenly, as if she was aware of his truck, she spun around and waved her arms, stepping slightly into the road. She was stunningly beautiful.

He tensed, and for an instant, he warred with civility and survival instinct. Should he offer them a ride? Without intention, his foot let off the gas.

He shook his head. No, he didn't pick up strangers on the side of the road. He didn't allow people to meddle in his business. He didn't mingle with society because the fewer connections he had, the less he had to explain why he didn't age or die. He had very few friends, and he liked it that way.

He steered the truck to the far left, giving the women a wide berth. They seemed just fine walking along. Then the blonde eased dangerously farther into the road.

He pressed on his brakes, stopping. "Hey, are you trying to get yourself killed?"

She paused and stared at him, as if she were processing an intrusion into her thoughts. Her gaze scanned the estate's logo. She leaned into the window, her delicate brows pinched together contrasting her smiled. "How about a ride? We're just heading a few miles up the road."

Ah, her accent revealed her to be American.

Before he could respond, she tugged on the door handle and swung the door wide. He could hardly tell her to get out now, could he?

Without saying a word, he nodded. In answer, she slid into the passenger seat, and then over her shoulder, she called, "Come on!" to her friend.

"That's my rental car back there. We swerved to miss some sheep crossing the road. As a result, the vehicle turned out to be the injured party."

"I see. I'm heading to Lourmarin. I can take you that far if you'd like." He put the truck in gear and resumed driving.

"Actually, you can drop us at the B&B up the road, if you don't mind. Hopefully, they'll have a room available and a truck to pull my car out."

Again, he gave a brusque nod.

She glanced out the window at the scenery, then back at him, letting her eyes roam over his dirt-covered clothes. "I noticed the logo on the truck. Do you work for Monsieur Hearst?"

He couldn't help smile. "Yes."

A hint of enthusiasm flashed in her eyes. "I guess this is my lucky day," she murmured under her breath.

"How is that?" he asked, since he could hear her perfectly fine with his Guardian hearing. He suspected she hadn't intended for him to, though.

"Oh, nothing." She licked her pink lips and searched his eyes before lowering her lids and then bringing them up again in a bashful stare. "I'm Grace Wenger. American tourist searching for an awesome experience in French viticulture."

"You've picked the best time of year for it," he said.

"That was pure luck. I've heard Chêne Sacré has the

most exquisite wine around these parts. Folks in town claim it even has medicinal qualities. Is that true?"

He shrugged. "Some claims are over-exaggerated. There are people who'd like to profit from our popularity."

She raised an eyebrow. "So you're saying your wine isn't special?"

"Our wine is exceptional. The finest quality for centuries. But it doesn't heal."

"And what of the child who was cured of a deadly disease at the winery? Did she drink Chêne Sacré wine?"

"That's preposterous," he snapped a bit more sharply than he'd intended.

She flinched.

"Those are just rumors," he added, forcing calm into his tone as she looked out the window.

Ian wondered at the shadow he glimpsed in her eyes before she'd turned away. What was troubling her? The car stuck back there? Something else? Every thought and emotion showed on her beautiful face.

With a firm hand on the steering wheel, he let his concerns abate. None of his business. Besides, he had problems of his own in the bed of the truck, and since the agricultural center closed at 2:00 p.m. on Wednesdays, he didn't have time to deal with Mademoiselle Wenger. Or her odd questions.

Her face brightened suddenly. "Does Chêne Sacré house guests?" she inquired with a hopeful lift in her voice.

"No. Our vineyard is not that sort of establishment."

"Oh," Grace said.

He didn't miss the way her bottom lip jutted out in the teeniest pout.

"What? No tourist attraction?" Skylar interjected.

He glanced at the unusual woman in the rearview mirror. Out of character for him, he was inclined to explain. "Our focus is singularly on creating superb wine. The tourist trade isn't part of Chêne Sacré. We are award-winning winegrowers. That's it." He paused, hearing himself, and winced at how boastful he sounded. It was merely the truth, though. Still, he continually struggled to be sensitive and relate to the human experience. "Forgive me. I get carried away with what I do."

She nodded. "I can relate to that."

He turned into the drive of the guesthouse and stopped the truck. "There you go."

Her striking dark-blue eyes met his and held. "Will you wait just a minute while I check and see if someone can get my car out?"

He hesitated. He really should be on his way. But then he found himself muttering, "Hurry."

She turned with a skip in her step as she walked toward the quaint, vine-covered entrance. Her friend dashed after her to keep up.

Ian pushed his back into his seat, feeling tension shoot through him that he hadn't experienced in a long time. Maybe even since before he'd become a Guardian. He forced a rush of air between his teeth, fighting the desire to get to know Grace Wenger better—much better. That she was a visitor from another country made it seem like the perfect opportunity for a sexual dalliance. No long-term emotional attachment that would be a problem for an immortal. But she asked far too many questions, didn't she? He ran his palms along the steering wheel until they reached the top where he gripped the leather firmly.

A few minutes later, she flounced back to the truck in long, relaxed strides. She opened the door and tilted forward, leaning her palms on the front seat. She smiled. "Everything is good. They have a room, plus someone will go get my rental car. I can't thank you enough for your help."

"No problem," he responded, at the same time wondering how he could see her again.

She stepped away, placing her hand on the doorframe.

Her tongue barely wet her lips, and then her top teeth raked over the corner of her lower lip. "Maybe you wouldn't mind showing me your vineyard sometime?"

"We don't give tours." Then as if of their own accord, he heard unprecedented words escape his mouth. "But perhaps for you, I could make an exception."

"That would be awesome."

She eased the door closed, and he rolled down the window, saying, "By the way, I'm Ian Hearst."

So that is Ian Hearst. Interesting.

She wanted to shake herself to make sure she wasn't imagining things—something she always had to question in her line of work. Hosting a television show, even one as small as *From the Far Side*, gave her plenty of opportunities to hobnob with the rich and famous. She'd met hunky stars, notable producers, and lots of important, wealthy men. But never had she experienced anyone with Ian Hearst's charisma and powerful presence. *Oh. Man.*

And he'd been sweaty and in work clothes, straight from the fields. God, what would he be like when he was cleaned up? With a wave of her hand, she fanned her neck and face because she suddenly felt damned hot.

For a long moment, she stared down the road in the direction he'd driven away. Once her heart rate settled enough that she could think, another impression settled over her: Ian Hearst had an old soul. In some unexplainable way, he seemed as ancient as the ruins she'd visited on the Isle of Skye. An odd flash of memory whipped around her, and the whispers of an old legend seemed to fit with his unmistakable brogue. She chuckled to herself. She'd never imagined a Frenchman with a Scottish accent before.

My goodness, there is a lot to learn about Ian Hearst.

And if her physical reaction to him was any indication, she'd have to work super hard to maintain her objectivity.

"That good, huh?"

Skylar's voice startled her. "Oh, yeah."

They turned together and headed into the building. "A tour of his winery would be ideal, the perfect opportunity to scope out my next move…and refocus on the task at hand. He had kind of agreed to it already, too. Hadn't he?"

"Sounded that way to me," Skylar agreed.

"This might be easier than I'd hoped." Encouraged, she traipsed beneath an arbor entrance and into the guesthouse. Inside, she finalized the arrangements for two rooms—one for herself and one for Skylar.

The owner, a man of medium stature with a groomed beard, beamed at her as he said he could take her to get her car right away. He instructed her to wait within the vine-covered entry while he brought his truck around.

"Do you mind if I go to the room? The car isn't that far, you can handle it," Skylar said.

"Sure." She stifled a yawn, suddenly realizing she'd been running on adrenaline for the last twenty-four hours. She hadn't grasped how exhausted she was after the transatlantic flight, renting a car, and finding a place in Lourmarin. True, she and Skylar had had downtime last evening when they'd arrived, but they'd spent dinner yesterday asking questions to discover what the local resident's knew about Maely's miracle. Unfortunately, it appeared the Dubois family had done an outstanding job of covering up what had happened to their daughter. People were full of speculation, but no one knew for certain much about Maely or the incident.

However, they'd had a lot to say about the reclusive Ian Hearst. A local celebrity of sorts, he apparently only socialized within the elite viticulture of the exclusive wineries in France. But she had managed to meet him face-to-face. Definite progress.

A search on her iPhone brought up a cover story of Chêne Sacré on *Wine Scene* magazine. Chêne Sacré had garnered accolades for its wine's almost medicinal power. Some claimed it made them feel younger and healthier.

Grace thought the town's people were a little too caught up in their own hype. She didn't think Ian Hearst was the type to create an elaborate marketing campaign. From what she'd learned of the man, he appeared to be a recluse. Still some locals did suggest the wine's popularity was only propaganda buildup to boost sales. One gentleman wondered what Ian Hearst was hiding, since his was one of the few wineries that didn't offer tastings. Still others insisted the claims were true and that they'd experienced the healthy wine firsthand. Was there some sort of weird connection between the winery's reputation and the healing of the seven-year-old girl?

Some of the talk seemed far-fetched even to Grace…and she believed in ghosts.

It took around forty minutes for the guesthouse owner to drive her to the stuck rental and free it from the ditch. She gazed out at the landscape with its rolling hills of vines in neat rows, getting an even better feel for the lay of the land that made up Ian Hearst's winery.

With the car back on the road, the kind, helpful man unhooked the chains from beneath the front bumper of the Peugeot that he'd used to pull out the car, saying, "There you go."

"Merci," Grace said.

He brushed dirt from his hands. "Are you returning to the house now?"

"No. I have to drive to Lourmarin to pick up my equipment." She'd need to stop and pick up Skylar, something she'd forgotten earlier.

With a nod, he began to turn away, then paused. "My wife will be fixing roast lamb this evening." He kissed the tips of his fingers and flicked them away from his lips. "*Magnifique.* You must be back by supper."

"Yes, we should be back in time."

He gave her another one of his warm smiles before they went their separate ways.

Two hours later, she and Skylar had collected the equipment from the hotel and they were settling into the farmhouse—in time for dinner. Heavenly aromas of rosemary and garlic drifted up from the downstairs kitchen.

There came a knock at the door, and then it opened a fraction. "I'm starving," Skylar murmured, dipping her head inside. Her purple-highlighted, coal-black hair fell across one eye.

"Come on in." Grace waved a hand. "I'm looking over a map of the area."

"Planning for something?"

"Yes. This place rents bicycles, so I thought that would be a cool way to start. What do you think? Would you like to go for a ride tomorrow and do some scouting?"

"Sure. For how long?"

Grace shrugged. "I haven't decided."

Skylar brushed her hair to the side and out of the way of her dark-brown eyes. "Brandon promised we'd Skype tomorrow. So I wanted to hang close to the computer, at least for a bit, if that's okay. It'll be our six-month anniversary."

With effort, Grace refrained from rolling her eyes. She recalled that every month for the five months Skylar had worked for her, there was a monthly celebration of when they'd met. Way too mushy in Grace's opinion.

"No problem. You can stay here while I investigate the area and come up with a plan."

Salt and pepper is what Grace's mother had dubbed them when Grace had brought Skylar to the family farm for a Memorial Day cookout. Mom had also pointed out the girl was Grace's latest stray. She might be right, but Skylar had endured a hard life. In her late teens, her dad had killed her mom and then committed suicide.

Skylar offered a shy grin. "You're the best."

"I'll figure this out later," Grace said, setting the map aside. "Let's go eat."

They both moved out into the hall, and Skylar's stomach made a loud gurgle as the door closed. They chuckled in unison, Grace's sounding light against Skylar's deep, throaty laugh.

Grace thought of all the animals she'd taken in over the years and how she'd started a "care farm" to take in abused animals. They'd collected horses, llamas, pigs, goats, and chickens. School kids and social organizations made trips to help care for the rescued animals. Grace was proud of what she'd started, even though some of her efforts didn't work out so well. Like the time she'd taken in a blue jay that infected the entire house with bird mites. What an ordeal it had been to get rid of itchy mites. She sighed. Even her mistakes didn't stop her.

4

Today is the day, Grace thought as she grabbed her backpack to head out. The anticipation of uncovering a hidden secret within the Chêne Sacré vineyard nipped at her. For six years, she'd been running after the unexpected and unexplained. Orbs had floated up beside her and kissed her on the cheek. Voices from the other side had whispered in her ear. Ghosts had followed her through the streets. She'd had this talent for finding such things her entire adult life, since the year she'd graduated from college and learned she had an inoperable brain tumor, slow growing but deadly nonetheless.

Grace ambled across the tile floor and out into the courtyard where the bicycles were stored. A worn turquoise one with a front basket caught her eye. The tires looked new, as did the seat. She pulled the bike from the rack and guided it to the road.

Overhead, clouds eased across the sky. She wasn't afraid of a bit of rain, but how long or how far her ride would go remained to be seen and depended on the fickle weather.

A small zing of anticipation twirled through her at the thought of seeing Ian Hearst again. An intriguing man, with intense silver eyes, he had the chiseled, handsome looks to go with his money, although it was difficult to accurately judge him fully since he'd been tucked behind the steering wheel. Still, her pulse sped up.

She climbed on the bike, rode down the short driveway, and onto the street toward Chêne Sacré. She had a map, as well as her iPad as backup. However, she'd learned on other out-of-country cases that accessing map programs wasn't possible unless good Internet service was available. She propped the map on top of her backpack in the basket, keeping the screen in view.

In the hundreds of paranormal events she'd researched, she'd begun at least a third of them without the property owner's permission. Usually those cases involved public property, though, and this morning she was well aware that she was pushing the boundaries of legal investigating. Wasn't French law more lenient than in the United States? She hoped so.

Ian Hearst's last words to her teased her: *But perhaps for you, I could make an exception.* It was almost the same as if he'd given her permission. She was going to accept his words as an invitation and hoped in thirty minutes to be knocking at his door. She pedaled harder uphill, then veered off the road at a spot void of fencing, continuing along a well-manicured lane between the vines toward the mansion. Fragrant rows of grapes framed each side, closing her in.

This seemed an excellent time of year to visit the area. The vines were heavy with grapes, and every now and then, she saw a few bunches that were starting to turn red. The Hearst mansion was visible over the tops of the vines, growing larger as she approached, the entire landscape package creating a breathtaking view. The château sat at the top of the hill in glorious splendor, rising three stories and probably large enough in perimeter to fill a football field. It was framed by large trees.

The grapevines, which were marked off by poles, clipped by at a regular pace as she road past them. It reminded her of driving past telephone poles along a highway with the way it created a rhythm and tempo.

She slanted her head, peering again at Ian Hearst's château, when an unusual but familiar smell hit her nose, warning her that one of her seizures was coming. Then everything went black.

The curtain of darkness peeled away as she opened her eyes. She blinked and turned her head from side to side, noting that she was on the ground, utterly confused, with the bike resting over one leg.

A sweet voice called her name. "Mademoiselle Wenger! Are you okay?"

It took a moment to realize the question had been asked in French.

Maely.

"How did I…?" Grace glanced about, answering in the same language. "Where am I?" It took several more seconds for the situation to register. She must have had a seizure and crashed the bike.

"You fell. And you were twitching and wouldn't wake up," the girl explained. She placed her delicate fingers to Grace's cheek.

"I'm all right. That happens occasionally… I pass out."

Grace pushed to her elbow and groaned as the soreness of her muscles set in and extreme fatigue overwhelmed her. The usual seizure aftermath. She tried to stand, but her thighs didn't cooperate and she sat back on her heels.

"You're ill," Maely said, her eyes meeting Grace's in the most unusual way, as if she could see inside Grace's body. The child's tiny hand clasped onto Grace's larger one. "You need to go to the tree. It will heal you."

Grace blinked. What was she talking about?

Maely tugged her forward. "Come with me, I'll show you," her angelic sweet voice urged in a way that touched something inside Grace.

With her mind still fuzzy, Grace pushed to her feet and shuffled along after the seven-year-old. And as she put one foot in front of the other, the relevant facts of the situation began to solidify. Yes, she was in France. She was here for work. She was trying to discover what miracle healed this beautiful child. But what had she said about a tree?

Maely led her through the vineyard to a massive oak. She left Grace where the roots began jutting from the earth and continued in light happy steps to the tree, where she spread her arms wide across the bark in a hug. The tree dwarfed the little girl, its trunk the size of five normal trees combined. Grace had never seen such a beautiful tree.

"His name is Custos," Maely said, still embracing the oak. "He saved me from the evil man and took me inside him."

"What evil man?" Grace inquired.

"I think he said his name was Death," she said innocently. "But the tree called him a reaper. I was running away from him."

A gulp of air rushed into Grace's lungs on her sharp inhale. If she were in any other line of work, she would be wondering what kinds of sick things this child had been exposed to and she'd be seriously questioning her parents. But she'd witnessed many strange occurrences before.

She knew one's beliefs governed what one could see, or not see.

Grace didn't think the child spoke of an agricultural reaper, though. And there was only one other kind of reaper that she could think of—a conveyor of death.

She eased closer to the tree. Her fatigue from the seizure was making her woozy, so she sat on a large bend of gnarled root. "How did you escape?" she asked the girl in a calm tone.

Maely twisted around, letting go of the tree, her vivid blue eyes searching Grace's. "You believe me?"

Grace nodded. "Yes. I know there are some things in this world that can't be explained."

The girl smiled. "Maman and Papa think I'm imagining things. The tree did it. I fell asleep, and when I woke up I was inside the tree."

Grace understood why the girl's parents would be skeptical. Even she had difficulty understanding. How could an oak have that kind of power? She wondered if it was a tree at all and not some otherworld creature taking the form of a tree. She supposed there were shifters and chameleon-like beings that weren't what they seemed. Her heart began to beat faster.

"So do you think Custos made Death go away?" Grace asked.

"Yes. And the tree made me better. I don't have my breathing problems and I don't cough anymore!"

Which confirmed the information Grace had gleaned— the child had been healed of cystic fibrosis. Looking at the sweet child before her, Grace was so thankful for that miracle.

She smiled at Maely. "I'm glad you are well."

"He can heal you, too. That spot in your head."

"How did you...?" Grace hesitated, shocked that Maely was able to sense her tumor.

The child lifted both shoulders to her ears and let them fall. "Sometimes I just feel these things."

No wonder her parents wanted to keep her protected

and away from reporters. So many people would stop at nothing to exploit such a gift.

"Come. Put your hand on the tree," Maely advised.

Grace moved closer and did as instructed. As they stood facing each other, Grace bent down to Maely's level. She ran her palm over the child's shoulder with comforting strokes. "I'm glad he made you well, sweetie," she said again.

Maely's striking blue eyes were wide and serious for such a young child. "He can heal you, too. I know he can."

5

Ian marched upon the scene with the full intention of pummeling the culprit that was disturbing the Divine Tree. The tattoo on his back warmed and pulsed, a sure signal that something bad was happening. In warrior mode, with his knife tucked in a sheath at his hip and a Glock hidden at the back of his waistband, he advanced into the clearing surrounding the tree. He stopped abruptly, unexpectedly stumbling upon Grace and the neighbor's girl sitting and admiring the tree.

At first he sighed in relief since the threat wasn't near the level of danger he'd anticipated. There were no demons or gargoyles. However, sweet packages could be just as dangerous by drawing unwanted attention to the oak. Interest had obviously already spread from Maely to Grace.

"What are you doing here?" Ian barked, his voice louder than he'd intended it to be. For the second time there was a lack of control to his reaction when he was near Grace that he couldn't comprehend. He was tempted to stand closer to her in order to inhale her alluring scent.

Maely jumped at the sound of his voice. Two feminine sets of eyes settled on him.

"I'm sorry," he said, calming his voice. "I didn't mean to startle you. But you shouldn't be here."

As before, he sensed the child wasn't afraid of him. "Bonjour, Monsieur Hearst. I brought Grace to visit Custos. He can heal her," she said in a matter-of-fact tone.

Ian was taken aback by her use of the name only a Guardian knew. It spoke volumes of the relationship Maely must have with the Divine Tree. Ian wondered at the changes occurring in his world; things he never thought possible were happening. Was it because the Age of Atonement was approaching?

Conflicted emotions warred within him, but his first duty was to protect the tree. The child had already overstepped the boundaries when she'd encountered the Divine Tree and Custos had healed her. That act alone confounded him. It went against the law of no interference wherein no Divine Trees would meddle in this world. So why this child? Was it because she'd laid hands on the oak? Was it because she was special in some way? Was it because the reaper had wanted to claim the girl?

And what had Maely told Grace Wenger? The lovely woman looked confused and uncertain.

Ian knelt to the child's level. "Maely, your vivid imagination will get you in trouble. You should not be here."

"But she needs Custos's help to heal her."

His gaze slid to Grace, and he noticed the scrape on her knee and elbow. "What happened?"

She waved a dismissive hand. "I just fell. The bike looks worse than I do. I'm afraid the bed-and-breakfast owner won't be very happy with me," she said with a chuckle, a defensive note in her voice.

"Everyone falls off a bicycle now and then," he said to Maely.

Rising, he held out his hand to help Grace stand. "Here, let's go to the château and take care of your injuries." He glanced at Maely. "Come along. I'll take you home and help Grace retrieve her bike once we have her fixed up."

Maely gave an impish smile, as if she knew something he didn't. If he'd been in his beast form, he had the distinct feeling the bear and eagle would be rallying around the child, all reasoning be damned.

Death flew from where he'd been perched, watching. As he landed, his feet touched the ground in his natural skeletal form. His bones rattled with every frustrated step he took as he advanced on the ancient oak. One way or another he would get what he wanted.

"Old tree," Death proclaimed, "wake and acknowledge me."

No word or sound came to him except for the soft rustling of leaves in the slight breeze. The snub grated on him. "You speak to the child but not to me." He released a sickening howl of anger. "I know you hear me."

A wood mouse scurried out from behind a fallen log. The reaper swung his scythe and severed its head. Then he picked up the furry body, lifting it high, and he tipped back his head, allowing the blood to run freely into his open mouth. When the treat had run dry, he tossed it into the bushes and smacked his teeth together.

"Whether you speak to me or not, I know you listen. How can you not? You healed that silly child. You know I have the ability to sense these things. Now I'm prepared to bargain. I'll leave the girl alone. All you have to do is tell me how I can return to the living."

Again silence.

Death took to pacing, swinging his soul-splitting scythe back and forth in front of him in the air. "I was tricked into the Dark One's service all those years ago. I'm sick of it. I want to live, and feel, and experience it all again. And I need this change most assuredly *before* the Age of Atonement."

A rumble of deep laughter shook the tree. "You can't go back. Only forward. Only where your heart is clean."

"Clean. Yes. As soon as I'm human again. Then I'll live a spotless life. Just like your precious, noble Guardian." He sneered. "And you're going to help me if you want to save…them." He nodded his head in the direction the trio had gone.

Grace's opinion of Ian changed during the day's stunning turn of events. The incident worked on her nerves, and now he appeared more mysterious than ever. She strolled alongside him, unable to match his long strides. She'd never met a man of such contrasts in her life. Sophisticated, yet he had the hard physique of a warrior. His large muscular shoulders towered over her.

Grace forced her gaze away from him.

Once again, Maely entwined her hand with Grace's. Every now and then, the child included a skip in her step in order to keep up. Inexplicably, Grace wondered who was comforting whom—the child had an uncharacteristically mature air about her for a seven-year-old. Her calm seemed almost eerie. Perhaps that came from dealing with a severe illness her entire life.

Ian led them up a number of tiered landings with flower beds housing yellow, purple, and pink blooms framed by neatly clipped evergreen hedging. She inhaled the delicate fragrance as they came to an open patio, this

one far different from the one at Maely's home, which
exuded family and friends working together. Here,
everything seemed staunchly in place. Luxurious, gorgeous
grounds, but lonely.

When they arrived at a wrought iron table, he turned
and pulled out a chair, saying, "Sit. I'll go get some medical
supplies."

"Thank you," Grace said, though an uncomfortable
tension wound through her at his gruff tone. She couldn't
blame him for being upset, she supposed, since he had
caught them trespassing. What were his options, though?
To call the authorities? Did they run intruders off at
gunpoint in France as they did in the States? On the other
hand, perhaps he was trying to pacify her with a bit of first
aid in order to send them on their way and hope they
didn't return.

Her imagination kicked in, conjuring up the many illicit
things he could be hiding on his estate. A healing tree
sprang to the top of the list. She definitely needed to get
on his good side in order to learn more.

The average person might have passed off the out-
there scenario the child offered as simply a story, but
Grace wasn't average when it came to the supernatural.
She interpreted incidents on a case-by-case basis.
Investigate, collect evidence, validate, and then either
accept or denounce the claim according to what she'd
found. But she'd seen enough weird stuff to make her a
believer, whether her audience bought it or not.

"He really is nice," Maely said, interrupting her
thoughts.

Grace gave a worried chuckled at the girl's guileless
youth. He was being nice to a little girl, yes, and he
guessed that earned him brownie points, but the
challenging look in his eyes that she occasionally noticed
directed at her gave her pause. If she'd been alone, he'd be
behaving differently. She was sure of it.

Ian exited the château carrying a small first aid kit. A short, rotund man with wiry hair and a thin mustache—the hired help, she surmised—followed on his heels with a tray of refreshments.

Bernard, she learned after introductions, set out the goodies on the table, and with what she thought was great ceremony, opened a wine bottle with the Chêne Sacré label. He poured a sample and held it out to her. "Our estate wine."

Grace accepted the goblet, wetting her lips. Should she drink alcohol so soon after a seizure? She knew alcohol was on the list of things to avoid, but this wine... She swirled the glass, admiring the dark rosy color of the liquid. This wine people had professed to have healing abilities.

Grace hadn't told *anyone* the real reason she'd jumped on this assignment. She hadn't even totally admitted it to herself, but deep down she hoped that the girl's healing miracle would be true, and perhaps she could share in some of the magic. Her seizures were getting more pronounced, which could only mean one thing: the tumor had grown to a point where it was interfering with her normal brain function.

"We produce a deeply colored, richly flavored red, as opposed to the popular rosés of our neighbors," Bernard said, puffing out his chest.

Figuring she had nothing to lose—she was safe now, after all—she took a tentative sip. This wine was the pride of the town, even if they weren't thrilled with its owner.

She peered over the rim of the glass, her gaze meeting Ian's as he stepped back, watching her. She was far from a wine expert; however, she had done her research on wine etiquette prior to heading for Provence. Raising the goblet, she examined the color and clarity, then circled the rim beneath her nose, inhaling the fragrance. Finally, she took a sip and held it in her mouth.

Both Bernard and Ian looked at her expectantly, with

expressions similar to parents wanting their child's approval. Wine made up a significant part of the French identity and culture, and they liked to talk about it. A lot.

"Mmm, fabulous. A sweet and toasty aroma, complex flavors, with nuances of vanilla and…" She repeated some of the descriptions the people she'd interviewed had said, then arched a brow. "I'm not sure of the other flavor."

Ian's mouth drew up on one side, and along with the cleft in his chin, it made him look damned irresistible. "It's most likely the tannins," he said in a deep, rich tone.

She took another sip and emptied the taster. Look at her, drinking wine before lunch.

Warmth wove through her insides and calmed her twitching nerves. She angled the glass toward Ian, lowering her lashes, then looking at him once more. "May I have a little more?"

His jaw tightened, yet he obliged her by replenishing her glass. His hard gaze ran over her. Without a doubt, he wasn't happy she was still here.

Bernard stopped her wayward thoughts when he spoke to Maely. "And for you, *ma petit*… Some fresh grape juice."

She smiled at the girl as she eagerly took a sip of her drink. Grace started when she felt a hand on her arm. She looked down and saw Ian placing gauze over her skinned elbow. She watched his strong fingers secure it with medical tape. The light brush of his fingers made her even more aware of him, though his gentle touch didn't match his brusque tone at all. She wondered which was his true personality. Or could it be both?

A ping of adrenaline shot through her as if her body anticipated and longed for his touch.

Wow. She hadn't anticipated the flutter within her stomach. She blinked. What was happening to her?

She took a long gulp of wine to calm her sudden spurt of nerves. Her first reaction was to flee, to push away her feelings of desire, but then she decided to slow down, drag this moment out. She was right where she wanted to be in the first place. On his property. Better take advantage of her good fortune while she could.

Ian stood and took the remaining glass of wine from the tray. He raised it up. "The finest wine in all of France," he said, then drank a sip.

She lifted an eyebrow, lowering her chin at the same time. "Not modest at all, are you?"

"Attitude has nothing to do with it." He glanced at her from beneath hooded brows. "It's the truth. Drink up."

After a few more sips, she had to agree with him. "I'm no expert. My usual choice at home is California white merlot." She shrugged. "Chosen predominantly for the price, of course. But I have to admit, your wine is exquisite."

He angled his head back as if contemplating the ceiling, the sexy cleft in his chin even more noticeable. He pivoted to face the vineyard, looking out at the rows and rows of ripening grapes. "This is my favorite time of year. The land is full with the expectant thrill of the harvest. It will start in just a few weeks."

She finished the last of her wine and left the glass on the table. She rose and stood alongside him—not too close, for every inch she took the draw she felt toward him became more powerful. Which totally baffled her. He was anything but her type of guy. Too rich, too arrogant, too uptight, too handsome for his own good.

She was a down-home, Southern-cooking kind of girl and liked her men easygoing and accessible. Ian Hearst appeared all gloom and doom, with perhaps an apparent soft spot for one particular sweet little child. In that she could join him. Maely was an adorable girl.

Grace could also relate to the beauty he found in the vineyard. Hills, dips, and a blend of green and gold stretched out in front of her with the occasional thick crop of trees here and there. "The vineyards are gorgeous."

Her gaze paused on the old oak, practically in the middle of the property, the one Maely had led her to. Could it possibly possess healing abilities like she'd claimed? And if so, *how*?

"I can see the tree from here. It's enormous," Grace said. "I'd like to go back there if it's okay."

"No," he said quickly. "I need to take the girl home."

Catching him staring at her, she asked, "Was the tree here when you bought the property?"

His eyes bore into her, watchful. "It was here when I arrived, yes. The property has been passed down in my family for generations."

"Then it—what was it Maely called it? Custos?—must be extremely old," she said, awed.

"You ask a lot of questions, you know that?" He turned from her and motioned to Maely. "Come, let's take you home."

"May I go home by myself?" she asked. "Maman is going to be upset with me."

"You should have considered that before you strolled onto my property." He glanced at Grace. "And you, as well."

She bit her lower lip to keep from saying anything. One thing was for certain, Ian didn't want them anywhere near that tree.

6

Ian directed Maely and Grace to his Land Rover. In a matter of minutes, he delivered Maely home to her unhappy parents. He gently, yet firmly, made it clear for a second time that he didn't appreciate the child rambling onto his property. And he said as much to Maely. "You must not trespass onto my property. I can't be responsible for what happens if you do."

Madame Dubois's eyes kept darting from Maely to Grace. He didn't know why, but he sensed a level of animosity there. Grace had just arrived in the area, so he couldn't comprehend how that could be, though.

Then Maely threw herself at his legs and hugged him.

Ian stiffened, shocked and uncertain how to react. His inner beasts welcomed the child, as if they sensed something more beyond her sweet smile. Gradually, his tension eased. He felt unexpectedly touched by the child's embrace.

She tipped her head up. "I'd like to learn more about Custos, Monsieur Hearst."

He tightened his jaw, unsure how to respond. He was beyond his depth here. "Perhaps one day," he replied, thinking it was best to pacify her.

She gave a sheepish grin. "Tomorrow?"

"No. I have many things to attend to," he said. If he put off the date, maybe she'd forget about the tree and move on to other things. He could hope.

She nodded sadly, and then they said farewell before Grace and Ian climbed back in his vehicle.

"Where did you leave your bicycle?" he asked, navigating the Rover out of the drive and onto the street.

She bit her lip and flashed an eye-roll, as if she was hesitant to tell him. "Not far." She waved a finger to the left. "It's among the vines over there, I think. They all look the same to me."

Ian tried to rein in his irritation. Even still, his voice came out sterner than he'd intended. "On Chêne Sacré?"

She hesitated. "Yes."

"Feeling brave, huh?"

"What do you mean?"

"I prosecute trespassers."

He heard the seat protest as she fidgeted. Good. She should be nervous.

"I knew you were just putting on the nice act for Maely's sake. You're not really that agreeable at all." As soon as the words were out, her lips smacked together.

He wondered if she had an ounce of censorship between her brain and that delectable mouth of hers. "There is little to be agreeable about when people don't respect your wishes."

"Wait a minute." The finger she had just pointed with did a sassy swishing side-to-side movement. "You invited me. You said you'd 'make an exception' and show me around. I was merely riding over to follow up on your invitation and arrange a time for a private tour."

Now it was Ian's turn to close his mouth. Unlike her,

he thought before he spoke. With the exception of yesterday. He should have kept his mouth shut then. What he recalled from their conversation centered around how delicious she'd looked in her tight-fitting blue jeans and the thin top that flounced low over her lovely breasts. He fought his way past those thoughts, even as he stumbled over her use of the word *private*.

"Why Chêne Sacré?" he asked. "What is your interest in us?"

"The bike is down there," she said, directing him off the road. "I turned by the broken fence."

He drove onto the grassy path and stopped, cutting the engine. Then he dropped his hands to his thighs, staring at her. "Well?" he pressed.

She moistened her lips, seeming to be stalling. Her hesitation triggered his suspicion. Every other thing she'd said signified impulsiveness, so did the pause mean she was concocting a story?

"I'm a ghost hunter," she said reluctantly, "and I've heard tales of supernatural events, or haunting incidents, occurring at your château."

He shook his head. "That's preposterous. How would you have heard that? Who would have spread such false rumors?" He opened the door and exited the vehicle. She did the same. They met at the front of the Rover. "We don't have ghosts."

She raised a questioning brow.

"It's true. Why on earth would anyone waste time and money searching for ghosts, anyway?" The idea defied reason.

"The bike is this way." She started off, talking as she went. "I believe there are things in this world that happen that can't be explained. Supernatural beings are one of them."

Ian didn't question that there were weird entities in this world. He was one himself, and he'd had to personally deal with a lot of crazy evil stuff. He wondered what her experience with such unusual instances might be. Knowing what he knew, there were a lot of worse creatures on the prowl than ghosts—demons and reapers, for instance.

A slice of fear for her shot through him. At least right here, right now, she was safe. It had been over two months since Death's incident with Maely. Custos hasn't said a word, but there never was a certainty where the Dark Realm was concerned.

He scowled. "Perhaps you should leave well enough alone and not go looking for trouble."

"My, that sounds like a believer to me."

The bicycle was about fifty yards ahead. "It doesn't matter what I believe. But I can tell you, there aren't ghosts here. So you may as well go home." He paused, thinking. "Tell you what. I'm having a gala Saturday evening for local winegrowers. You and your friend are now invited. Then you can see for yourself that there is nothing unusual about my winery."

"That sounds intriguing," Grace said slowly, a slight raise to her brow. "I'll see if Skylar is interested."

Ian approached the bicycle first and stood it up, giving it a quick perusal. "It looks fine. Do you want to ride it back to the farmhouse, or would you like me to drive you?"

She eased into him, taking hold of the bike. Her arm brushed against his ribs, her hair caught in the stubble on his chin. He inhaled her flowery scent. The aroma combined with touching her was so powerful, so consuming, he instantly sprang back so he wouldn't crush her to him.

What the hell?

She glanced back at him. "I think I can ride it just fine."

Ian coughed and angled his body away, adjusting his stance in order to conceal his erection. If she only knew what had crossed his mind. He wondered what she'd think of that.

When she hiked her leg over the seat and settled her bottom onto it, he suppressed a groan. *Merde,* she was sexy and hot, and was made even more so because she didn't even realize the effect she had on him. Or did she? His bear growled inside his chest.

In the nearly 900 years since he'd taken this Guardian stint, he'd never experienced such an instantaneous rush of desire. Now every nerve in his body was on alert, amplifying the throb that settled in his crotch.

What exactly did he want? A date? A kiss? Her body rubbing against his so he could feel her breasts nudging his chest and slide his hands down to cup her ass? A meaningless sexual encounter?

He inhaled slowly.

She began to pedal, riding between the vines, moving farther from him.

Call her back, his bear advised.

"Thanks," she shot over her shoulder.

He didn't uttered a word, just watched her leave, frustrated beyond measure as he tried to recall techniques to pursue women. It had been that long. Not that he'd ever wanted to before.

No. What an absurd idea.

Besides, he couldn't afford to get close to her and have her poking around and finding out about what happened to Maely—and Custos by extension.

Sadly, she was not for him.

Back at the guesthouse, Grace ambled into her room and plopped into the chair next to the window. She gazed out at a terrace lined with a border of clay pots filled with a rainbow assortment of flowers. She sucked her bottom lip between her teeth in indecision and bounced her leg, heel tapping against the floor, knee hopping like a pogo stick having an anxiety attack. She needed to go back to the Hearst estate and investigate that amazing tree. And Ian Hearst had given her the perfect opportunity. There had to be a way to gain irrefutable proof.

Darn it all, Ian Hearst had showed up and stopped the whole learning process. Maely might have shared a lot more if they hadn't been kicked out. He'd been somewhat gracious about it, but his disapproval rang clear and the message had been amplified with every scowl on his gorgeous, chiseled face. *Stay off his property.*

Well, his grim gaze wouldn't stop her. Something about that tree made the child better. The unspoken words and secretive behavior of Maely's parents was a major indicator that there was more to learn. Sometimes it was what people didn't say that held the principal clues.

Grace wasn't sure if it was actually the oak or perhaps a being residing within the tree. A fairy, nymph, troll, or witch could possess the healing magic Maely had experienced, Grace supposed. Actually, she was grasping at straws at this point, expanding the bounds of her imagination.

A light rap sounded on the door. Skylar popped it open and stepped halfway in. "You're back. I thought I heard you. So did you discover anything interesting?"

Where to begin?

Grace stilled her leg movement and motioned Skylar in. "Well, I had another run-in with Ian Hearst."

"Holy guacamole. He's hot."

"You think? He did clean up nice, too," Grace said with a playful smile, then turned serious. How much should she share with her assistant? Although she'd taken the eccentric young woman in, so to speak, since Skylar had been homeless when they'd met and Grace had given her a job and a place to live, their relationship was more mentor and student rather than a close friendship. They each had their quirks, but Skylar was dependable and gradually became her assistant and chauffeur, so the relationship worked. And she was very caring about Grace's seizures.

With a haphazard finger-combing of her hair, Grace swept the strands around from the back to the front, fixing it over her right shoulder as she turned her attention to her assistant. "We hit the jackpot with this one, I think."

"That good, huh?"

"Maely took me to where she claimed she was healed. I want to take the equipment back there to monitor it."

"But?" Skylar prodded. "There's something more. I hear it in your voice."

Grace hesitated. "Ian Hearst caught us and has ordered me to stay away."

Skylar's brow crinkled as she made a dramatic face and chuckled. "Oh boy. My kind of case."

"And here I was trying to guide you to the straight and narrow."

They both laughed.

Skylar rubbed her hands together. "So when do you want to go?"

"He actually offered us the perfect opportunity. We're invited to his château for a winegrowers gala Saturday evening."

"Wait." Skylar held up a hand. "Let me get this straight, he tells you to stay off his property, then turns around and invites us to a gala? That doesn't make sense."

"I know, right? I think he wants to prove he has nothing to hide. Either that or he's using the"—Grace made air quotes with her fingers—"keep-your-enemies-close tactic."

"Then we shouldn't miss it."

Grace smiled. "I couldn't agree more."

On Friday, Grace realized neither she nor Skylar had

packed any clothes that would do for an evening event like a gala. Since she wasn't about to miss the opportunity, she declared a day of shopping. Grace did some quick Internet researches on her iPad before they left the guesthouse, and Skylar drove them the hour drive to Avignon, which was a bigger city and would offer more choices.

As always, shopping in a strange new place gave her a thrill. Avignon epitomized ancient, lively, cultural France. Exploring made her feel like a college student again. She chose the area southeast of the Place de l'Horloge—Rue Rouge and adjoining streets were full of clothing shops.

Skylar was like a kid in a mall, dashing from one store to the next. Grace could tell who had the younger feet, because she had a hard time keeping up.

"Look, I can juggle," Skylar said as a street performer drew her into his act.

"I didn't know you were so talented."

Grace's shoes slapped on the brick road to the next store. The squares were free of automobiles and allowed for venders to set up shop beneath tents. Many sold art. She would have loved to explore more, but until they had found proper attire for the gala, that remained their main objective.

In the third shop, Skylar cracked her up by selecting a red-and-purple ensemble that could have been seen at a Red Hat Society luncheon. She did a dance in the middle of the shop. Thankfully, they hit pay dirt at store number four—lots of cute, sexy dresses. Grace selected a black one while Skylar chose midnight blue that looked stunning with the purple streak in her hair.

"Let's eat and then find shoes," Skylar said.

Around the corner, they found a quaint restaurant, Hiély Lucullus. Grace sat next to a second-floor window that looked down on the street.

"My goodness, it feels great to sit," Grace muttered. And boy, did it. The food was superb, too; however, by the time they left, Grace was worried that it may have been a mistake. It would have been much quicker to have grabbed something from a café along the street.

For a couple of blocks, there wasn't a shoe store in sight. Then they hit several in a row. Skylar matched her free spirit with equal energy and enthusiasm for all things new and different. She tried on zebra heels, wedged boots that came to the knee, and crystal stilettos with pink ribbons around the ankles. Grace couldn't remember how long it had been since she'd just goofed around like this.

In the end, Skylar purchased heels that were the color of her dress with a cluster of feathers on top. Much fancier than Grace's classy black heels.

By the time they returned to the guesthouse, they were happily exhausted.

And the only time she'd thought of Ian Hearst the entire day was when she'd chosen the black strappy dress for the gala and wondered what he'd think when he saw her in it.

Ian reviewed the wine list for the evening with Bernard. It wasn't his intention to serve his best, just to make them think he was serving his best.

"We've done this hundreds of times," Ian said. "I trust your judgment."

"Thank you, sir," Bernard lined up the bottles in a custom-made display. "And what of the young woman from Thursday? She actually accepted your invitation?"

"Surprisingly, yes. And she's bringing her assistant."

"But I thought you simply wanted her to go away?"

"I do," Ian said. "But she *won't*. I assure you. She has that journalistic twinkle in her eye. There's something about her... I just don't think she'll give up until her curiosity is satisfied."

"Is there anything in particular you want me to do?"

"Yes. Keep an eye on her."

"I'll do my best, sir."

"I know you will."

The doorbell rang, and Bernard went to answer it. The first of the guests had arrived. Ian tugged at the cuffs of his shirt. He hoped inviting the young Americans didn't turn out to be a mistake. But if she learned about his winery through his peers, well, that should prove Chêne Sacré was a winery and nothing more.

Thirty minutes later all the guests had arrived with the exception of Grace and Skylar. Everyone mingled and chatted, but it was customary to wait until all had arrived before opening a bottle.

Ian flexed his jaw, wondering at their delay. He wasn't used to being kept waiting. He wasn't used to dealing with nosy foreigners at all.

7

Skylar and Grace pulled up to the Hearst estate in their rented Peugeot. "Holy moly!" Skylar exclaimed, pointing at the various cars. "Can you imagine the money sunk into those?"

They stepped from their less than elegant vehicle and wove among some of the auto industry's finest. Grace recognized a Porsche and the three Bs—BMW, Bentley, and Benz. She also took note that this was a trifling gathering with only eight cars total.

The place was gorgeously lit with candles everywhere—on the terrace, in the shrubbery line, on ledges, and in every nook and crevice. As they walked up the steps, Bernard greeted them and escorted them inside before handing them off to Ian.

Ian introduced them to several couples and two single men. A round of cheek kissing ensued. It appeared they had been the last to arrive. Bernard and a few helpers brought out bottles of wine and waited off to the side. Ian poured Grace and Skylar's glasses. Bernard followed suit with the other guests.

Evidently, the custom was to hold off serving the drinks until the final guest arrived. She felt a little embarrassed that they had held up the festivities. She sighed. Formal parties were undeniably not her thing.

Ian was a gracious host, guiding her from one guest to the next. The topic of discussion for prominent winegrowers was wine, of course. They were talking about the age of the vines, and according to the conversations, Ian had the oldest vines around.

"Old-vine wines deliver textural richness and layered flavors that build rather than trail off after the up-front fruit fades away," Monsieur Lagarde expressed his opinion.

When they had left the group, she murmured, "Perhaps we should've spent the day researching the wine instead of shopping and getting mani-pedis." She gave a soft laugh and so did Skylar.

Ian narrowed his eyes at her, and she glimpsed the solitary loner in him from the other day. Then his face brightened slightly. "Come. I'll show you around."

He guided Grace and Skylar throughout the massive downstairs, stopping at a smoking lounge and a game room, where Skylar's eyes lit up at the beautiful pool table. "I'll stay here for a while." She eased past them. "See ya."

Grace shot her assistant a thumbs-up. That was one thing she and Skylar had in common, they both took off on their own, knowing the other person had the same tendency toward independence.

Down the hall and through what would be considered an American-style family room, Ian guided her out a door onto a large patio, different from the one where he'd bandaged her knee. The fragrance of flowers floated in the air, and even here the place was dotted with candles. The full moon had risen high overhead, illuminating the vineyard so that she could make out the rows of vines and the great oak tree.

"I'm surprised you kept the huge tree in the middle of your vines. I imagine most people would have removed it. All the more room for grapes."

"It's been here from the beginning of the vineyard."

"Still, I commend you for keeping it. How old do you think it is?"

He cocked his head and shot her a quizzical glance. "Why are you more interested in the tree than the vines?"

Had she been pushing too hard? She shrugged. "It's the thing that doesn't fit." Which was true. There were other clumps of trees, but they hugged the perimeter that framed the vines.

"I suppose you're right… I couldn't bring myself to cut it down. My one soft spot, I guess."

"Well, it is a magnificent oak."

He took a step closer to her. She matched him, bringing them toe to toe. He possessed a gravity unlike anyone she'd ever known. An unnamable tension coiled in her stomach.

He touched her cheek and, placing his finger beneath her chin, tipped up her face. His mouth dipped closer to hers. Her breath caught in her throat. If she didn't know better, she thought he was going to kiss her.

But instead, as if coming to his senses, he stepped back.

Grace swallowed, her throat dry. She remembered the wineglass in her hand and took a sip. "You don't have to stay out here with me. Your other guests await your company."

He nodded. "Make yourself at home," he said, his voice rich and heavy in the cool evening air.

"Thank you."

With a slight bow, he turned and walked into the château, tall and straight, the fabric of his jacket taught across his muscular back.

Grace's knees wobbled, and she nearly stumbled as she inched closer to the French doors to peek at him as he interacted with his guests. He certainly seemed the powerful male, in control of his surroundings.

For several minutes, she remained on the porch, hesitant to go inside. She wanted to learn more about the tree, not wine. Finally, she turned and stared out over the vineyard. Her feet moved a few steps toward the tree, then a few more. It was if some kind of force was summoning her.

Taking the last swallow of her wine, she set the glass on a patio table. She licked her lips. Ian was busy with his guests… Could she sneak to the oak and back unnoticed?

She just wouldn't stay long…

The vines were spaced wide enough apart for a vehicle to move between them. The moon was her flashlight, and it—along with an app on her iPhone—illuminated the path, making it relatively easy to find her way. Not far into the vineyard, she realized that her strappy heels weren't suited for traversing soil, as each step hung up. Finally, she paused, then bent and removed her shoes before continuing. But after a few steps she realized the terrain was too rocky for bare feet as she winced with each step. Damn. She slipped her shoes back on and this time kept her weight on her toes as she walked. That way the spikey heel didn't sink in and grab the soil.

Her heart beat hard in her chest throughout the fifteen-minute trek, not so much from walking but from the covert nature of her visit. Not to mention she was again breaking paranormal investigator's number-one rule—never go alone.

The metaphysical dangers were real. While most ghosts and spirits were harmless, an altercation with an evil spirit or demon allowed the entity to attach itself to the investigator, potentially for a long time. She'd witnessed exorcisms before, and they did not seem fun…

When she reached the massive oak, she paused beneath the canopy that shaded her from the moon's beams and cast deep shadows all around her. For a long moment, she stood frozen in place, even controlling her breathing so she could absorb the energy put off by the tree. A breeze brushed against her cheek.

Since she didn't have her digital and analog audio recorder to capture any electronic voice phenomena, she used the next best thing, her iPhone recording app.

She considered the story Maely had told her about a man named Death chasing her and the tree taking her inside. With a sweep of her eyes, she glanced around. She saw nothing. She heard nothing. But the radiating sensation inside her chest communicated that something resided nearby. What, she couldn't tell. She tapped the "record" button and waited, hoping it would capture sounds she couldn't hear.

"I'm not here to hurt you," she said to the tree. "I just want to learn and understand."

Suddenly, a huge bird winged past and landed on a protruding clump of tree roots. It whipped up its head, staring right at her. An eagle, she thought. It expanded and contracted its large wings.

"Go away," she whispered. "You're interfering with my investigation. Shoo."

Darn it all, the bird would override everything else on her recorder.

"Shoo," she said again, stepping toward the eagle.

When she got really close, the bird took off and she lost sight of it. She dismissed the intruder, returning her focus to the oak.

The feeling inside her intensified.

"Tell me about healing the girl. How did you accomplish that?"

A long stretch of silence ensued. She held the phone out in front of her.

Then Ian marched out of the shadows and stood between her and the tree. "What are you doing here?" he asked, disbelief obvious in his voice.

She gasped and dropped her phone.

Ian stepped forward and retrieved it. Glancing at the screen, he hit the "delete" button.

"Wait! No!" She launched forward, trying to take the phone from him.

"I don't appreciate you taking pictures of my property."

"I wasn't taking pictures." She held her hand out palm up. "That's mine."

He ignored her. "You're a long way from the gala."

She folded her arms in front of her with a sharp exhale. "I... I felt restless." Her mouth did a cute little tugging movement to the side, and she slanted a glance at him. "Can't a girl go for a walk?"

With indifference, he insulated himself against her charm. "You weren't just going for a stroll. You were talking about the things that kid told you."

"You heard?" Her chin lifted higher. "I'm a paranormal investigator, a ghost hunter. It's what I do."

He scrutinized her. "You said you were interested in hauntings at my château. If that's true, why are you out here?"

"Are you going to give me my phone back?"

"I should keep it, but that won't persuade you to confide in me." He handed her the phone.

"Thank you." She held the phone cupped in her palm, as if sensing something. Her eyes searched his with silent curiosity.

"My guests will miss us. Shall we go?" He indicated the way with an outstretched palm.

"Your guests won't miss *me* at all."

"You underestimate yourself, chéri."

She turned quickly, brushing up against him. They both paused, suddenly transfixed by the intimate contact. In a flash of undeniable attraction, she leaned into him as he bent toward her. Their lips met, and he kissed her with pronounced tenderness, sampling her intoxicating sweetness.

Mon Dieu, what was happening?

He ended the kiss even though he desired more. Much more.

Her fingers went to her golden tresses, the way they did so often when she was nervous, he'd noticed. "I— Perhaps it's the wine," she stated.

"It's *not* the wine, I assure you. As I said earlier, you underestimate yourself."

They walked a short distance, and then she stumbled.

"Watch your step." He placed a hand at her elbow. To his surprise, she allowed him to assist her.

"Thanks. It got cloudy all of a sudden. I can't see quite as well as when I came out."

"Good heavens. And you're wearing high heels."

She chuckled. "Of course I am. It's a formal occasion."

"Another reason you shouldn't be traipsing through my vineyard." He stopped and looked at her, ready to warn her about what he was about to do. "I'm going to carry you so you won't break your leg."

Before she could protest, he swooped his arms beneath her knees and back, lifting her and settling her against his chest.

"You don't need to do this. I got out here just fine. I can get back."

"You're on my property and, therefore, under my protection. I won't allow you to get hurt." Even if she was the most reckless woman he'd ever met.

"Well…that's very nice of you."

She wrapped an arm around his neck, probably to steady herself, and within him, his beasts stirred and pawed for her attention.

Ian set Grace gently on the ground when they got to the château.

"Thanks," she said, then slipped on her shoes. The glass she'd left on the patio table had been cleared, so she guessed she'd been away long enough for the staff to clean up.

Neither she nor Ian said a word about the unexpected kiss. Grace shoved it out of her mind as he held the door for her. Deep in her innermost being, she knew he was hiding something, and she promised herself to uncover the mystery.

As they moved into the living area, all eyes turned on them.

"I was beginning to think I'd have to leave without saying good-bye," said a thin man wearing his hair long and pulled back. François Lagarde, she recalled from introductions.

"Forgive me for my delay," Ian replied.

François raised a brow in approval. "But of course, a beautiful young woman is more interesting than an old relic. That's as it should be."

Grace acknowledged the compliment with a shy tip of her head, feeling her face heat.

Monsieur Lagarde placed a peck on both her cheeks before departing. She still wasn't used to the affectionate exchange but understood it was part of French culture.

Lagarde's departure generated an exodus of the guests. Skylar broke free from a handsome young man with blond hair, reluctantly scooting close to Grace.

"Are we leaving?" Skylar asked, whispering, a hint of

sadness in her voice, and stealing moon-eyed glances at the young man.

Grace nodded. She couldn't tell her that she needed to put some distance between herself and Ian Hearst, to get her bearings and put things in perspective. That even in his enormous house, she could feel his presence everywhere.

When it was their turn to say farewell to Ian, Grace went first. And even with the recognized custom of cheek kissing, it felt different with Ian. She felt a flurry of sensations wash over her simply due to his close proximity, and his light touch on her arm… Oh, how it warmed her.

When they headed for their rental car, Grace could feel Ian's eyes on her the whole way.

The door closed behind him after he saw the last guest out. He spun on his heal and marched over to pour himself a snifter of his best brandy.

"The evening didn't go well?" Bernard asked.

"Hell no."

"I'm sorry to hear that."

Ian drank, then paused, savoring the liquor's burning effect. "It was a gamble, and I lost. The little firebrand hiked out to the oak. In heels, no less."

"Is that so bad? There's nothing she can see," Bernard pointed out as he cleared the empty glasses around the room and set them on a tray.

"True. But she's used to dealing with paranormal events. One, I don't know much about how that works. And two, Maely Dubois gave her information about the tree. I overheard Mademoiselle Wenger speak of it this evening—of a relationship between the tree and healing."

"If she finds nothing she'll go away."

He took another swallow of his drink. "But if she discovers more?"

"You will know how to handle it. Just like everything else."

The following morning Grace slept in and lounged beneath the covers for a while. She had Ian Hearst on the brain. He was the last thing she'd thought of before finally dosing off last night, and he was now her first reflection of the day.

Of course, he *was* the reason she'd come to France. No, that wasn't quite accurate. It turned out the tree may have been the real reason she was there.

She rolled out of bed, retrieved her phone from the other side of the room where it had been charging, and returned to the covers. She propped her pillows against the headboard, sat, and then brought up the recording app on her phone.

Mentally, she thanked the ghost hunter colleague who had introduced her to this particular app. It operated like some e-mail platforms where a message was stored in a deleted folder for a time, during which it could be retrieved until deleted permanently. The backup function saved the investigator much aggravation over an accidental delete. This wasn't the first time she'd appreciated the application's forethought, either.

The recording from last night displayed at the top of the list. She restored it and took a breath, wondering if it held anything from last night. The room seemed extra quiet as she hit "play."

Grace closed her eyes and listened, allowing the scene to replay in her mind. Scientists have discovered that the process of hearing happens more in the brain than in the ears. So she relaxed and didn't try too hard to force recognition.

Sound could be a weird thing. Ambient background noises and other natural sounds needed to be distinguished and filtered out. The soft whoosh of the wind was prominent, as was her voice when she asked questions. Though behind the swish of leaves, she heard something else. Deep gravely voices, like the rubbing of coarse sandpaper in a distinguishable rhythm of words, of conversation. It sounded as if an old man had said, *Leave her alone. She's harmless.*

Grace's eyes popped open. Who was that?

She sat forward, swinging her legs over the edge of the bed. Next time she'd take all her equipment *and* Skylar.

Grace got out of bed and dressed. Then a knock came on the door.

She went to the door and let in her assistant. It was routine for Skylar to check in with Grace mid to late morning to get her orders for the day. Skylar entered and made herself at home on the edge of Grace's bed.

"I'd like to take the equipment to the tree tonight and set up a vigil," Grace said. "I captured some EVPs on my phone last night. Listen."

She set the phone on the table in front of Skylar and started the recording. "It would have been so much better had I caught it on video instead of simply capturing vocal responses."

Skylar pushed back in her seat. "There's definitely something there. I'm excited!"

"Me too."

"Do you want me to load the equipment into the car?" Skylar asked, standing.

"We can do that after dinner before we leave," Grace said. She appreciated Skylar's enthusiasm. "I forgot to ask about your Skype session the other day. Everything okay at home?"

A frown crossed her assistant's face. "We never connected. Either he didn't call or service was poor."

"Oh, that's too bad. Maybe you can try again later. It could be a matter of the time-zone difference, too."

"Yeah." Skylar hesitated, as if she'd forgotten about that. "You may be right. What's the difference between France and Florida?"

"They're six hours behind us."

Skylar appeared to be doing the math. "Uh, that means it's just seven there now. No wonder he hasn't called yet." She traipsed to the door and turned, her purple-streaked dark hair falling forward to cover one eye. "Do you want to grab a bite to eat?"

"Yes. Give me a few minutes to finish getting ready."

With a thumbs-up, Skylar made a clicking noise in her cheek, then exited.

Grace scooted to the edge of her seat, resting her elbows on her knees. She contemplated the bandage on her arm, recalling the way the brush of Ian's fingers over her skin sent a rush of anticipation zinging through her. It wasn't logical to want a relationship with *any* man, given her medical situation; however, good sense wasn't one of her specialties, and one last wild fling with a hunky guy like Ian... Her heart sped at the thought. Perhaps it was exactly what she needed to banish the feeling that her life was incomplete. How did that song title go? "Live Like You Were Dying"?

She stood and shrugged. It was something to consider. But could an uptight French winery owner even truly be attracted to a flouncy Florida gal? She trotted into the bathroom to put on a dab of makeup.

Only one way to find out.

8

At eleven thirty that night, Grace and Skylar had the car loaded and were ready to go. For some reason, paranormal beings showed themselves more after dark. Skylar drove and Grace pointed out the location she'd noticed that first day when Ian had rescued them from their broken down car. It was a maintenance entrance, she thought, with enough access for a vehicle to enter and travel all the way to the tree. There was a gate, but when she got out and checked, it wasn't locked.

The makeshift roadway provided a rough ride in their little Peugeot, and it tossed them in their seats. Grace winced at every pothole they hit. She slowed to a crawl and the ride was far less bumpy. They putted along with the parking lights guiding the way.

She cut the engine and lights once she came to a spot hidden between the vines, and they got out. They met at the trunk and divvied up the equipment. Grace took the digital recorder, voice recorder, and night vision goggles;

Skylar was in charge of the motion detector and EMFs, electromagnetic field detectors. They each slung a folding chair over their shoulders—they'd purchased them upon their arrival—and finally, Grace tucked an iPad beneath an arm. It was a good thing none of the items weighed more than five pounds since they would have to carry everything the remaining distance to the tree.

Grace also grabbed a backpack that contained extra batteries and a couple of flashlights.

"Well, no one followed us onto the property. That's an excellent sign," Skylar pointed out.

"Let's hope it stays that way."

Grace led the way to the oak. "Record the video over there." She indicated where the grapes stopped and the clearing surrounding the oak began. "And put the audio sensor right on the tree."

"Got it."

When everything was set, they stepped back to assess the situation. Grace nodded her approval. "I have a good vibe about this one." She grinned at Skylar, who gave her usual minuscule, half smile back.

They positioned their chairs and began their watch.

An hour passed without so much as a blip on the electromagnetic field detector. Grace tried to remain positive as she checked the equipment again. Yes, the batteries still held a charge.

"Anything?" Skylar asked.

"No. But you know these things take time." For many investigations, it took days or weeks to discover anything meaningful. The force always waited until it was ready to reveal itself. Even knowing this, Grace tried to hide her disappointment. She had expected more in this case.

Skylar turned fidgety. She was checking her phone often, and Grace couldn't blame her. This could be lonely, boring work. Her assistant caught Grace watching and said, "If he calls, I'll head to the car to talk."

Grace nodded. She was prepared to hang out the entire night. As she twisted to grab a granola bar from her satchel, the EMF detector displayed a sudden rise in activity. Yes. Seconds later, the numbers went off the chart. Grace slipped on the NV goggles and looked around, her vision skipping from the ancient oak to the surrounding trees and vines a little farther out of their immediate perimeter. A vulture, large and incredibly ugly, landed on a thick oak branch with a menacing flap of its wings. Grace involuntarily grimaced.

The hideous bird's gaze darted between Grace and Skylar, totally creeping her out. Fifteen feet or so separated her from Skylar, a pronounced need to put herself between the vulture and the young woman caused her heart to race. Could that bird be the cause of the unprecedented activity?

She stood to move toward Skylar when, overhead, an elegant eagle swooped downward and around the tree, sleek and strong and beautiful in form and execution. The EMF and EMP signals doubled on the monitor. The eagle dove at the vulture, trying to unseat the creature. Grace placed her hands over her ears, the screeching sounds of the vulture having grown unbearable. She wondered what parts these two played, if any, in Maely's healing. Were they supernatural creatures?

After several attempts by the eagle, the vulture evacuated its perch and flew to the ground. And then the vulture changed into human form right before her eyes. A scream caught in her throat.

A shape-shifter? Her first such encounter. *OMG!*

He stalked toward them right out of his transformation. He had a thin, angular face with one brow angling down and the other brow upward in a dubious slant. Grace stepped closer to Skylar, ready to grab her hand and run.

Then equally shocking, the huge eagle swooped low and transformed into... Ian Hearst. She gasped, and the ground seemed to shake beneath her feet. What the hell was going on?

Her mind raced. Her gaze shot from one man to the other. Without a doubt, the epitome of good and evil stood before her.

She'd gotten far more than she'd bargained for this time.

"Wha-what's going on?" Skylar muttered.

"Shut up," the evil man said.

Ian's hands balled into fists. "Go back where you came from, Death."

Grace blanched at the name. Maely had mentioned this evil creature had chased her. Grace moved closer to Skylar, whispering, "Go back to the car."

Skylar spun around, taking Grace by the hand and tugging her along.

"No," Grace protested. "You get out of here." She glanced sideways at Ian. Beads of sweat broke over her shoulders and abs and along her arms. "Do you know how to deal with this?"

"There is no good way," he bit out. Then his menacing look turned to one on steroids. "I told you to stay away."

"I'm not a very good listener."

"Go!" he shouted. He jumped in front of Death and changed into a ferocious bear before presenting the evil fiend with a hardy wallop to the throat and gut, sending him back several feet.

Death cracked his neck as he stood, a total look of enjoyment crossing his hard features. "If Custos won't give me what I want, then one of these lovely ladies' death will be on him."

The tree swayed heavily to the right, its branches seemed to circle in a sweeping motion.

The bear images fluctuated in and out of form as Ian's

words bellowed forth. "Wish and demand all you want, Death, but you will *not* have your way."

Even as he told her to go, Ian couldn't explain his need to protect Grace. He'd never set eyes on her until two days ago. She should have the same pull, or lack thereof, that any other woman he'd met had possessed. To his maddening frustration, that wasn't the case. He grew shaky, and a knot formed in his stomach simply being near her.

What was that about?

Now Death had some massive bug up his butt, and he notoriously succeeded at being a persistent SOB. Hadn't this reaper had a hand in Ian's brother Euler's death in Germany all those years ago?

Ian's eyes were on Grace when evil made his move. Like a clansman rushing the front line on the moors, the guy launched himself forward. At the same time, he altered to his true skeletal reaper form, raising his scythe over his head.

Ian initially moved in tandem with the dark one, but his arms encircled Grace first, moving her out of harm's way. But damn, he couldn't save both women. He turned his head in time to see the reaper's glowing scythe descend and slice across Skylar's neck from one side to the other, the young woman's eyes instantly fixed in death. Grace screamed as blood splattered her shirt. The cut was so quick and hot, Skylar's head was fused back in place instead of toppling from her shoulders. Her limp body crumpled to the ground.

Fury didn't begin to describe what Ian felt. Hot rage, knotted muscles, pounding heart… His emotions were whirling out of control. This was his property, his tree, his responsibility. He couldn't finish that thought for the sense of failure and guilt slamming him hard. He moved on toward Death, ready to tear his black heart from his chest.

The reaper evaded him, leaping to the right.

"Leave, Death." The Divine Tree's quiet voice stopped them all. "I have the woman's soul for safekeeping. Continuing this will do you no good."

"Bring her back. Heal her like you did the child. Show me your magic," Death ordered, taunted even.

"No second chances for you," Custos said, his voice a roar of cracking leaves and brittle snapping sounds.

Death swung his scythe in the air. An eerie whistling whipped around them. Ian hated the way Grace cringed. He hated the fear in her eyes. He hated that she was touched by unadulterated evil.

Grace dropped to the ground, shaking, her face buried in her hands. She shivered violently and repeated something so softly the human ear wouldn't be able to make it out, yet he could with the super-hearing of a Guardian.

"It's my fault," she said over and over. The sad thing was that, on some level, it was. If she had done as he'd instructed, they wouldn't be here right now and Skylar wouldn't have died.

Ian knelt and gathered Grace in his arms. She rested against his chest, limp, nearly unconscious. She needed to go to his house now and stay within a proximity in which he could protect her. Death rarely allowed witnesses to live. He had a thing about loose ends.

"What about Skylar?" she murmured.

"Custos will take care of her."

"How?"

"Don't you worry. I'll show you later."

The dirt beneath Skylar shifted and moved along with heavy roots. As if she were in quicksand, her body sank until she disappeared completely into the earth.

Death went ballistic. He sliced the scythe at the roots repeatedly. "Fuck you." *Chop, chop.* "What are you doing? Give her back." *Chop, chop.* "She's mine." He fell back, hard. "Is this how you healed the child? Is it?"

But the Divine Tree remained silent, yet distinctly unhappy.

Ian stepped in the direction of the house. The tree would not give in to Death's demands. No way.

Death must have sensed that also, for he followed Ian. That is until the Guardian turned and ferociously growled at him, which halted the angel of death in his tracks.

"Go back to Hell. Get out of my sight." Ian moved on, holding Grace tighter to him. She moaned. He glanced down at her blond hair, which was spilling over his arm. She was so incredibly beautiful. So incredibly fragile. So incredibly vulnerable.

Oh shit. How was he going to deal with her? When she came around and fully realized what had happened, she was going to be hurt and furious.

His mind raced as he tried to figure out what to do with her. He wasn't used to dealing with women. Especially sexy, attractive women such as Grace Wenger, who made him feel things he shouldn't given he was immortal and she was not.

When they got back to the house, he took Grace to the kitchen and set her in a chair at the breakfast table. She tried to stand, and he placed his hands on her shoulders, forcing her to sit. She beat his hands away.

This woman had fire in her, too, he realized as she recovered from the shock she'd just been through. Her face was pale, but her eyes flashed daggers at him. "What *exactly* just happened?" she demanded.

"I think we both have explanations to offer." When he thought she'd stay put, he traveled to the kitchen, then looked back over his shoulder at her. They both needed a strong drink. Silence filled the kitchen as he worked. He worried how she would deal with the situation. He tossed some items onto a tray: coffee, cream, sugar, cups, and bourbon.

She crossed her arms over her chest and hugged herself as he returned to her. When he stepped closer he saw her flinch. Perhaps a reaction to everything that had happened in the vineyard.

"Where's Bernard?" she asked.

"All the staff has today off." He didn't add how he enjoyed having the place all to himself.

When her hot-toddy and his double bourbon were ready, he delivered her drink to her and took the seat across from her. As she took the cup and sipped, he realized that he'd given her a mug that he would have used, and it looked so large in her petite hands.

After her first taste, she took two large swigs. "Easy now," he warned. "We don't need you under the table. We need to talk."

She glared at him, set the cup on the table, then swiped a hand around her head catching her hair and arranging it over her shoulder. Her eyes held his. "What happened out there?"

"Why did you have all that equipment?" he fired back.

"Is Death who…or what I think he is?" She stood and moved around, taking a few steps and then turning back.

"You should have listened and stayed away. Why did you return?"

The war of questions ended when she advanced on him with a wave of her arm. "This is your fault." Her voice ripped from her throat as she gulped air. "This is my fault." Clutching her head in her hands, she caved inward with a whimper. "I've seen a lot of weird shit, but nothing…nothing like this."

She put her fingers over her lips, and he thought she was going to break into tears, but she didn't. She inhaled long and hard, and stared at him. When he stopped thinking how attractive she was, even in her upset state, he realized she was waiting for him to explain.

"Okay. You deserve answers, I get that," he said grimly. "You are correct. I am to blame for allowing this to happen. But why were you there in the vineyard to begin with?"

She sidled over to the table, retrieved her cup, and drank. The way she held the cup with two hands made him think she held on to it for support. He waited, the epitome of calm for her to answer his questions.

"I can't believe she's dead. Is she really?" Her eyes held his, hopeful though glassy with unshed tears. "Is it possible the tree can bring her back? Do something, anything, to undo this? Like with Maely?"

He swallowed hard. "I don't think so," he said softly. Actually, he didn't really know. There was no previous incident to reference.

She stomped her foot, threw her head back, and gave a heartsick wail.

He gave her time to release her pain and anguish. There was no playbook on how to handle a horrible situation like this.

Finally, he asked, "What were you trying to accomplish with the equipment?"

"I told you—I am a ghost hunter. I have a paranormal television show in the States, and I received information about a little girl being healed and came to investigate."

"You intend to make this public?" His voice rose with the question.

"Not necessarily, no. Not everything I discover develops into an episode. The equipment out there is just my way of documenting evidence."

Ian left her and marched over to pour himself another drink. God, she was impulsive and irresponsible. How could she even think of coming onto his property once he'd forbidden it? He downed the liquor, and even his beasts enjoyed the burn as it hit his stomach.

Fuck. How was he going to handle this situation? This beautiful human knew far too much and now had a dead friend residing within the Divine Tree...

9

Grace had anticipated Ian's anger at her investigation. She just couldn't deal with it right now. At the moment, all that mattered was what had happened to Skylar.

Oh God... She swallowed hard. "Do you think the tree can bring her back? Kind of like the way he worked a miracle for Maely?"

He shook his head. "I doubt it."

"But you know where she is?"

"Custos has taken her in."

Finger-combing her hair over one shoulder, she twisted it like a rope. She tried to process what he was saying, but it was beyond her understanding. How did an oak *take someone in?*

"I can't believe she's dead. No. She's going to walk through that door any minute and confess this was all a bad joke."

He must have understood her confusion, for he walked over to her, placing his large, warm hand on her shoulder.

"You started this, Grace. Now you're going to have to trust me. There will be no easy answer."

"I want to see her," she said, her voice trembling.

"I can't promise you anything, but I'll see what I can do. This is new to me also."

Her eyes opened wide. Had she opened Pandora's box? The entire ordeal was so far beyond anything she'd expected.

She tipped her head back and stared at the ceiling. It was vaulted, covered with pressed copper tiles that appeared unreachable. In a distant, removed sort of way, she wondered how anyone would clean them. He probably had staff to do that. He was obviously rich. Not only had she landed in a catastrophic paranormal situation, but she was dealing with a man the likes of whom she'd never met before.

But was he a man? She snapped her head back down and peered at him, as a memory surfaced and pushed aside the shock, numbness, and pain, the hurt at what had just happened to Skylar. "You're a shape-shifter. You flew in as an eagle and changed into a bear."

His jaw flexed. "Yes."

"I live for experiences like this. At least I thought I did." She paused. "It's just… I never thought anyone would get hurt." That was the truth, she realized. In all the years she'd been searching for ghosts, she'd never come across *anything* truly dangerous. Which had made her complacent. A huge mistake.

"I can see that." He took their cups and placed them in the sink.

"Now what?" she asked.

He paused, his eyes skimming over her, and even in her unwieldy state, she felt something spark inside of her at his perusal.

"I'll find you something clean to wear so you can spend the night."

She glanced down the front of her blouse, about to protest, when she saw the splattered blood dotted across her top. The sight made her physically ill and she placed her palm over her stomach.

"Tomorrow, I'll take you to the guesthouse to check out. You can get your things then. You will need to stay here so I can keep my eye on you. I doubt that Death is finished."

"You mean, he could be after me next?"

"It's a good possibility," he said, seeming all gloom and doom.

Her breath caught in her throat as she considered his response. Perhaps she should listen to the man—but he wasn't that, was he?

"Come, I'll show you to your room."

She followed him through his gorgeous, massive home. It reminded her of one of those "Living Like a Millionaire" shows. But of course, he no doubt *was* a millionaire.

She noted the furnishings she'd overlooked the other evening at the gala, since Ian and his friends had held her attention then. Almost every room had a grand archway that led into another fabulously decorated room. In the living room, huge art pieces covered the walls, making her feel as if she were in a museum or perhaps an art gallery. They ascended a staircase that wound around in an enormous spiral. She got her exercise by the time they arrived at the second floor.

He showed her into a suite with a seating area and fireplace. "The bedroom is through that door. It has its own bath."

"It's lovely," she said, too depressed to show the appreciation the place deserved. A sad sigh escaped her lips. She found herself wishing she could show it to Skylar. A heaviness squeezed in her chest. Then anger swelled inside her and she clutched her hands closed tight. They should have done something to save her. Beyond her ability to cope, she lashed out at Ian. "You should have protected her. Like you did me." She beat her fists against his chest.

Ian simply stood firm, absorbing her wrath. "I know," he said, his voice weary and heavy. He allowed her to exhaust her fury, then gathered her into his chest.

After a long, silent moment, he sighed, his chest rising and falling, all firm and controlled. "The room and bath have everything except clothes. I'll be right back with something you can change into."

When he drew away, coldness set in and she shivered. As soon as he'd disappeared through the door, she wanted him back. A sense of safety and security had gone with him.

She groaned and then strolled through the suite, checking it out. The bedroom had a king-size bed. The teal comforter and pillows probably cost more than her weekly salary. She moved on to the spacious bath where two widely spaced floor-to-ceiling windows occupied the left wall as she entered. Almost the entire room—floor and walls—was covered in marble tile. In the center, sat a Jacuzzi tub that she could walk around, which she did. A ginormous walk-in shower was off to the right. It didn't even have a door it was so big.

When she came out of the shower, she passed the toilet room and went over to the vanity with double sinks. She placed her hands on the cool, black granite countertop and leaned in, examining herself in the mirror. Her features were the same familiar ones she always saw, except now they were dulled by sadness.

She kept replaying the scene by the tree over and over again in her mind. Oh how she regretted the course she'd chosen. She was the worst person ever. She wished she'd known about the danger, though. She would have never put Skylar at risk if she had. And perhaps she would've been able to take precautions. Was there anything one could do to ward off a reaper like Death? In the way garlic and a cross would send a vampire running, that was. She should find out. The only thing she'd do differently, though, was to leave Skylar behind. Yes, it didn't matter if she was in danger,—with her illness she was destined to die anyway. But Skylar had been on the road to getting her life straightened out. Grace bit down on her lip. What a tragedy.

"Grace?" Ian called.

She left the mirror and her thoughts, and found him in the sitting room.

He held out a small stack for her to take. "I'm sorry, I only have men's clothing. When you change, I'll put your things in to wash."

"Thanks," she accepted them, hugging the items to her chest.

"Take your time. I'll return shortly."

Ian figured Grace needed some alone time in order to process everything that had happened. She'd probably react in one of two ways: either she'd come to terms with her loss, accepting her mistake in entering his property, or she'd wreak havoc on him, blaming him for this evening's events.

Holy shit, he still couldn't believe what had just happened, that a young woman was murdered on his watch and that the Divine Tree had essentially been attacked. But for what?

There was little he could do except wait it out, stand guard, and see what Death did next.

While Grace got settled in the guest suite, he decided to return to the oak to retrieve her equipment and check on Custos. There were a couple of entrances into the tunnel from the house, and he chose the one near the kitchen due to its sharp incline and direct access. Since no one was in the house except Grace, he expected it to be a quick trip there and back without the possibility of having to consult with the staff.

Once inside the passageway he shifted into his bear form. For his massive size, he could run remarkably fast, plus his senses were more acute in his animal body. An ability that would be beneficial if Death was still hanging around.

The tunnel lights engaged as he passed along the corridors until he came to the tree entrance. The door opened immediately, as he didn't have to complete the anointing ritual while in his animal form. He tromped inside, sniffed and looked around. His nose led him farther down into the catacombs of knowledge within the root system of the tree. There, resting on a bed of roots, he found Skylar. She wasn't posed or reclining in any structured way, instead she looked as if she were stretched out sleeping. A clean raise of flesh encircled her neck where she'd been cut; however, the wound appeared fused together as if cauterized, which in fact it had been by Death's scythe. Ian approached her.

"Do not touch her," Custos warned. "She's in a place of limbo right now. I believe we can save her from Death's claws. As long as she's under my protection, her soul will remain with her. Out of reach for Death. I merely need a little more time to research the answer."

With a nod, Ian retreated a step and dropped his weary body into a chair. "I'm relieved Death wasn't able to claim her soul for the Dark Realm. Grace should appreciate that also. Thank you for your efforts."

"I don't believe this is over with Death. He's more persistent than I've ever seen him." The Divine Tree's raspy voice echoed within the chamber.

"What does he want?" Ian asked.

"Resurrection out of hell."

Ian whistled. "Is that possible?"

"It's doubtful."

"If that's the case, Death will stop at nothing to get what he wants." Ian paused. "And Maely's miracle given by you shows such healing is possible."

"In Death's mind it does; however, it's not the same thing at all. He has been dead thousands of years. He made his choices. There's no going back for him."

"Then I have some convincing to do to direct him back to the Dark Realm for good." Ian peered through the oak's layers of wood and bark, checking the perimeter outside. Grace's equipment was sitting exactly where they'd left it. He exited the tree through a secret porthole. As he gathered each item, he noted its purpose and wondered what intel it had collected. Had the video caught all the action? Were their voices recorded? What else would show up on her monitors? At first he thought to take the equipment back to her car, but then he reconsidered. Perhaps it was best to store it at his house. He wouldn't want anyone to come across it if discernible evidence had actually been recorded.

With his arms loaded, it was a good hike back to the château. Now he worried about how long he'd been gone and if Grace had missed him. That thought stopped him in his boots. He couldn't remember when anyone had actually missed him. It had definitely been since before he'd become a Guardian. Sure, there had been employees and even occasional lovers over the years who he'd been fond of and perhaps had even developed a relationship of sorts with, but someone who genuinely cared for him, loved him…no. He sighed. No, love was not for him.

Death watched the Guardian move from the tree and collect that woman's equipment. Which meant if Ian was here, then who was with his sweet Grace?

Foolish Guardian. Either he didn't have a clue to the lengths Death would go to renew his life again, or the man didn't give a shit about the people near and dear to him.

He'd seen the way the Guardian had looked at her with that intense longing in his eyes. And being the intelligent badass dude that he was, Death wondered how he could exploit that...

Immediately, he took to his vulture form and flew to the château.

When the cats away, evil gets to play.

He materialized on the veranda in his human form. As he scanned the area, he had to admit he appreciated the Guardian's style—pure elegance and finesse. Nothing gaudy or cheap about this place. He noted right away that each of the doors had a state-of-the-art touch combination lock. Smart. But that didn't help him, dammit. So he moved on, quickly checking for another entrance. He found what he was looking for in a chimney.

He transformed back into his skeletal self—thereby able to fold and bend his bones in ways that would allow him easy access—and he dropped down into a spic-and-span hearth. He had to hand it to Hearst's cleaning crew. They were top-notch. The fireplace was a huge old-fashioned type, large enough for a man to easily stand inside, which proved to be the case as he turned human once more, at least on the outside.

The room he'd landed in turned out to be a class A smoking lounge—humidity controlled, the works. One long inhale confirmed the expensive tobacco merchandise. Despite wishing he had sufficient time to enjoy all that was there, he wove a strategic path through the room, angling between a seating arrangement of four dark leather chairs. In a cut-glass ashtray on an end table, perched a snuffed-out cigar. He paused to lift it and run it beneath his nose, breathing in the aroma of the Cohiba Behike cigar.

Jealousy welled inside him. Here he'd been, hanging his

ass in a damned fucking bush watching the Divine Tree, while Pretty Boy lounged in the lap of luxury. Death tucked the cigar in his shirt pocket. His gaze skipped to the perimeter of shelves filled with exquisite hand-rolled masterpieces and a fine lineup of pipes displayed behind panes of glass. Another area housed liquor, and still another, wine. He headed for the smokes, reached behind the glass, and plucked several out to slide carefully into one of his empty pockets.

Realizing he'd taken more time than he should have, he booked it out of there and into the main entrance hall where he peered up at the multiple floors above. Her essence came to him from the second floor off to the right. He followed her scent, which seemed awash with something else. If his hearing rang true—he was never sure given the screams and yells he tried to tune out in the dungeons of Hell—then the sound of running water meant she was in the shower.

Grace turned off the hot water and stepped out of the shower with a towel wrapped around her. She'd been in there so long, the room was filled with a thick cloud of steam. Kind of like her brain. She shivered as the cool air danced over her body. It felt wrong to feel anything at all when Skylar was dead.

She rubbed the towel briskly over her skin, wishing she could scrub clean the last twenty-four hours. At the sink, she dressed in the light-blue T-shirt Ian had given her and then layered a long-sleeve button-up on top, thankful for the choices. Neither shirt by itself worked—the T-shirt showed her puckering nipples and the button-down alone seemed too sexy.

Leaning a hip against the counter, she paused, staring out the bathroom doorway, lost in thought. This was like reliving her cancer diagnosis all over again. There was a fear that went bone-deep, and it was hard to think about anything else. She was scared, uncertain, angry, and confused. How could this have happened? It wasn't fair. Skylar hadn't deserved this.

Pushing her thoughts aside the way she always did, she pulled open several drawers, which revealed every kind of toiletry anyone would need, including packaged toothbrushes. She plucked the hairdryer from its cradle and grabbed a circular brush, and went to work drying her freshly shampooed hair. She wiped the completely misted-over mirror with her towel to make a space to see and then hit it with some hot air for a finishing touch. She bent forward, flipping her hair upside down to dry it underneath, alternating brushing and drying.

An odd smell wafted through the air. Burning hair caught in the dryer, perhaps? She'd begun to lift her head when she noticed the tips of a man's black shoes.

Ian? In her bathroom?

Cautiously, holding her breath, she slid her gaze up to the figure in front of her. Black fitted pants, a black shirt, some kind of tweed blazer with a pattern of black and red *z*'s. She wanted to shut her eyes before she came to his face, because based on the less than classy garb, she knew this wasn't Ian Hearst.

By the time she was ready for the reveal, she was out of oxygen, out of nerve, out of her mind with fear. She gripped the hairdryer so tightly her hand went numb. And then her eyes took in his face.

Death.

Oh God, oh God, oh God.

"He can't help you now."

Holy shit, could he hear her thoughts?

Is he talking about God or Ian? her foolish mind questioned. In rapid succession, she inhaled several breaths, the last one exhaled on a scream.

Death brought his index finger to his lips. "Shh." He stepped closer, his black eyes holding her transfixed. "We can do without the drama."

Grace pulled the hairdryer forward between them, yanking the cord from the wall. She wielded the clump of plastic as if it were a weapon, and wished to hell that it were possible. Was there something that could stop a reaper?

He advanced on her, reaching his hand out. She knocked his arm aside with the dryer, then swung it side to side in front of her, trying to keep him back. Worry sliced through her as she searched for his scythe.

An evil smile split his lips. Then, with lightning speed, he was toe to toe with her.

She could smell cigars and that other sickening stench again. Dead bodies, rotting corpses, she realized, her eyes going wide. She quickly tried to hide her fear. "I suggest you leave before Ian gets here."

He laughed. "There are so many ways to kill a person. The choices are almost endless." He slid his fingers over her collarbone with nauseating delicacy, gliding his hand up to her throat.

She shivered, then wildly fought to escape. *Run. Get Ian.*

But Death grabbed hold of her neck and squeezed with masterful control. "Your friend was lucky. She never saw it coming. Never experienced the terror. One instant she was breathing, the next—" he lifted a shoulder and lowered his voice "—she wasn't."

The scream Grace emitted this time came all the way up from her curled toes.

10

Ian had just passed the vineyard's perimeter when he heard
a scream.

Grace?

In a fit of burning anger, he dropped the equipment
he'd been carrying, ignoring the splitting and breaking
sounds of plastic as it hit the ground. He sprinted as fast as
he could to the entrance closest to him. He entered the
security code and rushed inside. As he bounded up the
staircase, another desperate cry sounded. He gritted his
teeth and pushed harder.

There could be only one thing that would make her that
frightened, that would match the desperation in her voice.

He'd honestly never thought Death would enter his
house...

Bursting into her room, he saw nothing, but he
followed Death's stench into the bathroom. That the evil
fiend had confronted Grace here within this private space
infuriated Ian even more.

It was time for Death to meet his own *permanent* demise.

Ian curled his fingers into hard, powerful fists. When he rounded the bathroom entrance, one glimpse of the reaper with his hands gripping Grace's delicate jaw sent him into an unmatched fury. The cork that kept his beasts bottled up exploded, and he transformed into bear in mid-stride. With a vicious growl, he raised both massive paws and then clawed down the length of the reaper's back, shredding clothes, skin, and the substance that took the place of muscle.

Nothing he'd experienced in all his days as Guardian came close to the intensity of the rage he was feeling in this moment. It was as if the control he'd carefully cultivated over the years had never existed. And he sensed this change had everything to do with some unexplainable pull or connection to this woman.

Death released his hold on Grace. Ian raised his paws again, this time to cut an arc and knock the Dark Realm's monster across the room. He paused to search Grace's aquamarine eyes. *Are you okay?*

She nodded, a perplexed expression on her face. "Yes. Just shaken." She paused, then whipped her head around. "I can hear you."

"Yes."

Ian was thankful he managed to arrive in time; however, it didn't relax him. Who knew what Death had in mind—steal, kill, destroy, deceive—that's what his miserable existence was all about? Plus, it also depended on how available his target was and how bad he wanted it. In general, he went for the easy victim, often expelling the least amount of energy and talent.

Well, he would have to up his game today.

Ian advanced, and as he did so, Death changed into his skeletal form and raised his scythe. The weapon was most effective at a distance, though, so Ian dodged a few blows in order to get in close and cozy. Offhandedly, he heard Grace yell, but he kept his eyes on the reaper. A grazing blow sliced across his shoulder, cutting to the bone. He spun in, opening his jaws wide, then chomped down on Death's weapon arm. The radius and ulna of his forearm snapped and broke, and the scythe fell to the ground with a clank, a bony hand still gripping the handle.

Death howled in agony, for even though he was devoid of actual sinew, muscle, and skin, he still experienced pain, the specialty of the Dark Realm.

His face twisted in an ugly grimace, and his eyes glowed red. While executing a full run, the reaper retrieved his fallen limb and kept going out the balcony door and then took a flying leap off the balcony.

Ian's ribs heaved in and out with each oxygen-packed breath he took. That was damned close. The monster could have killed her. After a reassuring few seconds, he glanced over his shoulder at Grace, her face ashen, her eyes large and wary, and her hair still damp. Even after what was possibly the most traumatic event of her life, she looked stunningly beautiful.

Sadly, she was not for the likes of him. A handful of reasons why he should cool his desire for her flickered through his mind. His duty to the Divine Tree was at the top of the list. How could he ask anyone to play second to that responsibility?

Although he was tempted…damned tempted.

She glided toward him, her steps soft and light compared to the mayhem that had just transpired. "How bad are you hurt?" Her voice quivered as she spoke.

"It's not as bad as it looks. A benefit of being a shape-shifting Guardian. We heal quickly."

Her eyes widened. "I should have figured you weren't the only one of your kind."

"You're pretty accepting of all this."

"I investigate paranormal activity for a living. I have a

head start on your average person." She attempted to smile, her color almost back to normal.

"And here I thought you were simply brave. Or crazy."

She pulled a towel from the rack. "Here. Put pressure on it with this. I think we should dress it to staunch the bleeding until it heals."

He accepted the towel and pressed it over his wound. No sense grossing her out. "I have bandages in my room."

"I can help. It's in an awkward location."

He paused, ready to decline her offer, then shrugged. "Suit yourself." He strolled to the balcony door, shut, and locked it, satisfied when he heard the bolts click into place.

"I wonder how he got inside the house."

Grace wrapped her arms around her middle. "I don't know. He was just there. I noticed the odor of cigars, I think."

Ian gave that some thought as they progressed toward his room. Imagining Death in his home made him furious. He contemplated her clue about the cigar odor. There were no external entrances to the smoking lounge. So perhaps the reaper stopped in there when he was searching for Grace.

As he led the way out of the room and down the hall, she glued herself to his side, brushing up against his good arm. She was still frightened; he could sense her emotions and smell the sharp scent of her unease.

Inside his room, the first item his gaze landed on was the fireplace. That was it! There were so many of them in the house. The bastard had entered through a chimney and into a fireplace, maybe even in the smoking room. Ian would check all the flues and put measures in place to seal them so no monster would ever enter that way again.

He progressed straight to his bathroom, where he kept another set of rarely used medical supplies. It had been so long since he'd needed them that they were probably expired. But then he recalled how Bernard meticulously stocked the place, and he realized his assistant did his job extremely well. Ian removed a large box from a cabinet and began rummaging through it, finding bandages, tape, and scissors, and setting them aside.

He unbuttoned his shirt and grimaced as he peeled it off.

Grace immediately took charge, pushing his hands aside. "I can do this. You've done enough by saving me."

His back and abs tightened as her fingers brushed over his skin, and it felt incredibly good. He couldn't remember the last time anyone had touched him, cared for him, shared even a small amount of his pain. She cautiously dabbed antiseptic over his wound, which although it hurt like hell, had already healed considerably during their walk to his room.

He glanced over his shoulder at her intense expression. With her lower lip drawn between her teeth, she looked vulnerable and delicious. A moan escaped him.

Her gaze met his. "You do heal quickly."

He wondered if healing was what she was really thinking about as she smoothed the tape ever-so-carefully over his skin. She seemed to take pleasure from running her fingers along his muscles, her hands moving in wider swipes with every pass. Finally she stilled and stepped back.

Her mouth did that hesitant sucking motion that she often did, the one that drove him wild, and her eyes met his, almost shyly. "May I stay in your room tonight?" Then she added in a rush, "I don't want to be alone."

"I can't blame you." He wanted to hold her, comfort her. But he didn't dare, for fear of what else he desired to do with her. More as a distraction than anything else, he moved into his large closet, with mahogany dresser and grabbed a T-shirt and pants and slipped them on. Returning to the room, he paused just outside the closet door, far enough away that he wouldn't reach out and touch her.

"Yes, you may spend the night with me," he said. "But I must warn you, I don't sleep on the floor."

She absorbed his words, glancing at the bed. "I'm okay with that. It's a very large bed."

He held out his hand palm up, saying with a tight smile, "After you." He knew in today's world many men and women were in bed together at the end of their first date. Muscles tensed in his gut, his arms, his spine. That kind of intimacy and spontaneity was completely foreign to him.

She did a little skip step to the left, so he headed right. Strange, he hadn't thought of his bed as anything other than an instrument for sleep in such a long, long time, but as soon as his weight settled on the mattress and he felt her shift beneath the covers, his body responded, getting all hard and ready, recalling the memory of having a soft, warm female in his arms. The part his instincts omitted was the willing aspect. And he doubted Grace would be that.

He rolled to face the outside edge, and she did the same, but even the king-size bed didn't put enough distance between them. He could feel the heat radiating off her body onto his back.

Grace wiggled and moved behind him, tossing and turning. Hours passed as he listened to her even breathing while she slept, then fits of dreams had her thrashing about. The mattress telegraphed her every move. The urge to hold her and calm her kept him awake, along with the other things he longed to do… He forced those instinctive cravings from his mind.

Then she screamed. He rolled toward her, just enough to see the terror on her sleeping face. Even in the darkness, his exceptional vision allowed him to make out her open mouth and arm hiding her eyes. When she scooted over to him and nuzzled into his side, he let her. And he accepted her into his arms to comfort her. He stroked her silky hair. "It's okay," he whispered. "I've got you. You're safe."

She pressed her cheek into his chest and sighed sweetly. For the rest of the night, she didn't budge and peacefully slept. He couldn't close his eyes as he continued to stare into the darkness.

11

When Grace opened her eyes in the morning, rays of sunlight flooded the room. What time was it?

The enormous male chest beneath her head rose and fell, making her acutely aware of what had transpired last evening. *Ian.* He'd been kind, allowing her to stay when she'd been so frightened. And she'd slept in his bed all night... A series of yearnings surfaced of their own accord, and she groaned inwardly. Nonetheless, she felt totally content, warm, safe, rested, wrapped in an emotion she hadn't experienced in a frigging long time. What was with that?

She pushed to a sitting position and glanced down at him. The bubble of serenity popped. "Morning," she said, then rolled away from him and hopped off the bed.

"If you say so," he replied as he finger-combed his hair.

"Gee, someone's a little grumpy," she said, teasing. "How's your shoulder?"

"Fine." He swung his legs over his side and stood.

Her gaze skimmed appreciatively over his fine muscles and planes, wondering about his honesty—he didn't even test the shoulder or anything. Her perusal halted on the bulge in his pajama pants, then slid up to meet his eyes. She tensed.

"I can change the dressing for you," she offered.

"Thanks. Not necessary."

"Okay." She crossed the room, eyeing the crumpled bed they'd gotten out of. "I think I'm brave enough to handle the guest room in daylight."

He nodded. "Come back if you need to." His voice was softer now.

"I will." In a secret place in her mind, she thought of him as they'd been upon waking. A swirl of desire curled through her tummy.

Maybe she should play the wimpy girl card and return ASAP. What would he be doing then? With a purr low in her throat, she turned into the hall and headed away from the hunky shape-shifter.

In the guest bath once again, it was difficult not to think of last night, not to remember Death attacking her or Ian's heroic actions against the beast, not to think of Skylar, that she was truly gone. Grace kept looking over her shoulder.

Even though she had a hard time focusing, she managed her morning ablutions of face, teeth, and hair. Her clothes were spot free and hanging on a hook. Goodness, the staff was quick. She dressed quickly, not wanting to spend any more time in this contaminated space, and she headed downstairs.

Ian trudged through the house checking every fireplace flue. The suspicious culprit showed in the smoking lounge as he'd suspected. He drew it shut with a forceful tug.

Next he found Bernard. "Death got in here last evening. In. My. Home." To say he was furious was an understatement.

"How?"

"An open flue." Ian fisted his hands, then released them. "Get the maintenance team in here this morning and have every fireplace sealed. Have them check the locks on the doors and windows while they're at it. This reaper is too bold. He *will not* enter my home ever again."

"I'll get right on it, sir."

"Bernard." When his assistant turned, Ian continued. "Death killed Mademoiselle Wenger's friend, Skylar. The Divine Tree has taken her in for safekeeping."

"Mon Dieu." He made the sign of the cross over his chest. "That's horrible."

"Mademoiselle Wenger is in shock and quite distressed, as expected. Be warned."

With a nod, Bernard turned toward the kitchen. "Poor girl."

"Yes. And there's been another delay in Venn's arrival."

So many problems.

Ian charged out the door and changed into his bear form. This evil called for regular scouting trips, beginning now.

She wasn't hungry until she entered the kitchen where Bernard had a delicious breakfast spread arranged on the table. French bread, pastries, yogurt, cheeses, and fruit all caused her stomach to churn in anticipation.

Bernard greeted her with an infectious smile. "Bonjour."

Grace returned the greeting, with far less enthusiasm and made a beeline for the croissants. She selected a *pain au chocolate* and some fruit and sat by the window at a small table. The sun bathed the vineyard in a golden glow, and it looked so peaceful. Only Grace knew better. She closed her eyes and sunk her teeth into the chocolate-filled delight, the rich, creamy flavor washing over her tongue.

When she opened them, Ian was standing beside the table. He'd been soundless in his approach, and she jumped when she saw him.

"I didn't mean to startle you." He pulled out the seat across from her and sat.

She licked her lips. "These are to die for."

They stared at each other. She regretted her choice of words as Skylar immediately came to mind. Was he thinking the same thing? Or was such an outrageous occurrence normal within his world?

She swallowed. "I want to see her."

He hesitated. Would he deny her? He'd never actually admitted that he could take her there. But she could hope.

"Please," she added.

"You don't hold things back, do you? Always straight to the point." His eyes did a look-into-your-soul thing.

"Why should I?"

He shrugged. "Most people censor their words or concoct some sort of manipulated plan of attack. You don't." A hint of a smile lifted one side of his mouth in a sexy grin. "It's…refreshing."

She angled her head. "I'm glad you think so. Now, can we go see her after breakfast?"

All this talk about her personality made her uncomfortable. She took another bite of her pastry, even larger than the last. His eyes seemed to watch her every move. Feeling the tiniest bit nervous, she dabbed at her mouth with a napkin. "Aren't you going to eat?"

"In a minute."

She raised an eyebrow at him. "Come on. Eat something so we can be on our way."

"You Americans… Always in a rush."

"Well there are things we need to figure out."

"Nothing is going to change in the next thirty minutes."

"Thirty minutes? Is that how long it takes you to eat breakfast?" Her voice pitched higher. "I usually have a granola bar as I go out the door."

"Patience, my dear. Patience."

She rolled her eyes and stuffed the last bite of croissant into her mouth. His lack of urgency bugged the hell out of her. As she chewed, she refrained from saying something she might regret. And if he wanted to be a lazy butt about leaving, then she might as well have another pastry.

She walked beside him to the food table, noting the loose swing of his arms and taut play of his pecs. Geez, he made a button-down shirt look athletic and striking at the same time. His shoulder didn't seem to be giving him any trouble, either. He reached for a plate with his injured arm without a hint of difficulty. That was a good sign.

She ate quickly, he slowly. "I put your equipment in a storage room," he said. "The bad news is…something broke when I dropped it last night."

"Dropped it?" Dollar signs floated in front of her eyes.

"Your scream last night provoked immediate action. My arms were loaded, and I rectified the situation."

"Oh… Well I guess I forgive you, then."

He drained the last of his coffee. "I thought I would drive you to check out of the guesthouse and get your things to bring over here."

"What about Skylar? I'd like to see her. To have closure. You understand, right?"

"I'm not sure that's possible."

She wagged her finger at him. "I'll keep asking."

"I know," he said, standing. "You're quite persistent, you know."

"So I've been told." And he had no idea. Once she latched on to something, she was like mortar to brick.

As Ian pulled the truck into the guesthouse's parking lot, Grace contemplated the step she was about to take. How much did she really know about Ian Hearst? People did things to save their own butts all the time. Was that what Ian intended now with getting her to stay at his place? It taxed her, drained her energy to think these things through because she'd found people didn't really do things for the good of others.

She dragged her feet with indecision as she went inside. Ian walked beside her, offering to help her gather Skylar's belongings, as well. She was thankful for that at least, even if she was still skeptical of him. This was not about her, she reminded herself. It was about Skylar, and she owed it to her friend and employee to bring her home. After all, Skylar didn't have anyone else to rally for her.

With that thought thrumming in her head, she decided accepting Ian's offer to stay at his place was the only way to get to the bottom of whatever happened. Yet at the same time she had no desire to encounter Death again. She sighed aloud.

Grace walked up to the counter to speak with the owner. "Good morning," she started. "Your winery is absolutely lovely, but I need to check out early. My friend has taken ill." She hated to lie, but she supposed it wasn't any of his business anyway.

The man glanced from her to Ian, a questioning look flickered in his eyes, and then he looked back at her. "I'm so sorry to see you leave." She wondered what he thought about Ian being with her.

She shrugged it off. It didn't matter.

"Everything okay?" Ian asked.

"Yes. This is just kinda hard."

He searched her eyes, sincere, understanding. "You're doing great. Trust me, you'll get through this."

Her mood lightened a fraction, even though she wasn't keen about relying on him. "Thanks."

Grace must have zoned out or something as Ian drove because before she knew it they were back at his chateau. "After we put these in my room, I'd like to put all my equipment there also."

"Your things are safe at the winery. We'll get them later," he said, all calm and cool.

Really? She wondered what he was hiding. "I can go with you and help get it."

"There is no hurry. It's not going anywhere."

The guest room had a large, nearly empty closet, and they deposited the suitcases and bags there.

"I need my equipment." She placed her hands on her hips. "How badly did you break it?"

He growled under his breath. "It records things, right? I don't think you should be watching it yet."

She glared at him. "That's for me to decide."

"I'll get your things after lunch." He exited, leaving her all alone.

She swallowed nervously, then dove onto the bed, executing a spiral rotation of her body so that she landed on her back. She flung her arms over her head and stared at the ceiling. It was high and framed with an ornate cornice.

In the daylight the room wasn't so bad. She only felt a little creepy. Still, if the reaper got in here once, he could get in again.

Her gaze slid to the bathroom where Death had come upon her. Uncertainty warred against determination as she considered what to do next. When she got her equipment, she planned to examine the tapes and data in order to confirm what her own eyes had seen. A magical tree, two shape-shifters, a reaper, a scythe, and a deadly action.

Oh man, she'd struck the mother lode this time. The cliché *Be careful what you wish for* came to mind.

Awhile later, Ian traipsed into the sitting room of the guest suite with his arms full. Grace rolled off the bed to join him as he deposited her stuff onto the coffee table.

"Here you go," he said.

She trotted over for a quick perusal of her not-so-neatly stacked gear. A few pieces seemed scraped up, but otherwise everything appeared in order. She lifted the video recorder and popped the disk door open. It was empty. "Where's the disk?"

A defensive scowl brought his brows together. "I kept it. I'd like to watch it together."

Her ire rose. "That's not for you to decide. It's my property."

"Used on *my* property. Without permission."

She stepped closer to him, holding out her palm. "Hand it over."

He frowned. "I never said you couldn't have it. Just not now."

She rumbled her frustration at him.

"We'll watch it together. Later," he assured her.

Ugh, the controlling beast. He had her, though. She was in his house, on his property, playing under his rules. And if she wanted the answers to her questions, then she'd have to work with that.

But for an antsy, fly-by-the-seat-of-your-pants gal like her that equaled sheer agony.

He must have sensed her tension because he placed his large, strong hands on her shoulders and massaged her tight muscles. "Relax. How about a tour of the winery?"

Relax? Impossible. But his hands felt so good, she

nearly melted into him. No, she should protest his controlling manner. Instead, her shoulders rolled forward. She needed to show him she wasn't a wimp. Oh, but her chin dropped to rest against her chest. "Mmm."

"We'll have lunch and discuss our options dealing with the reaper."

Finally, she stepped from beneath his magical fingers. "Okay. But, after that you are going to take me to see Skylar, and then we will go over my tapes," she proclaimed, ticking her terms off on her fingers for emphasis. She came up close to him, nose to chest, tilting her head back to meet his eyes. "I won't be put off."

"Of course not. All in good order."

Although she was far from happy with him at the moment, his touch and calm response warmed a sweet spot inside her. She closed her hands into fists, not because of anger, but to stop from testing the feel of his lips with her thumb and examining the delicious cleft of his chin.

He eased his palm to her back between her shoulder blades and guided her out the door.

12

Lunch had been a yummy three course meal—exquisite French cuisine consisting of more fabulous bread, butter-roasted flounder with grain mustard beurre blanc in brown butter sage sauce with toasted almonds, sautéed Brussels sprouts, and potato allumettes, and then a raspberry poached pear and a chocolate almond tarte for dessert. Once again Grace was reminded that the French were serious about their food. Grace was so full, she considered returning to her room in order to change into a pair of jeans that weren't quite as snug, ones that didn't reveal her every imperfection.

Instead, she decided to walk, demand that her body reengage despite her loss. But all her energy and life had been sucked out of her. "Can we take a walk?" she asked, trying to muster some enthusiasm.

He frowned. "Yes. Give me a second to check on some things first."

Grace wondered at his distracted tone as she nodded.

She felt a keen awareness of being alone as soon as he left the room.

A few minutes later, he returned to the kitchen. "Okay. We can go now." He motioned for her to proceed out the door, and she sensed his eyes follow her. Mixed feelings ran through her, a combination of unease and excitement, making her aware of his maleness and his commanding presence. Wait, was that a gun tucked in the back of his pants? Is that what he left the room for? Great, she was attracted to a gun-toting shape-shifter.

Placing his hand on the small of her back, he guided her along a stone path to the winery. The day revealed a combination of mellow sunshine and old-world charm. It was deceiving, though, for it made her feel as if everything were fine when she definitely knew otherwise.

She noticed Ian glancing about. "Is he out here?" she asked, feeling certain he was looking for Death.

"Probably. But I don't feel him now."

"Do you think he'd get me if I were alone?"

"Most likely. That's what he does…waits around and strikes the vulnerable, easy target. Usually he goes after someone who is already sick or weak in some way."

She stopped, tension amplifying through her, and stared at him. "And he takes their souls? To Hell like in stories?"

"Yes. A reaper has a certain number of souls he must capture in order to get perks. Kind of like a sales-commission plan where the employee wins a Mediterranean cruise if he's the top sales person. Plus, when he reaches a particular high figure, there are additional perks."

"Like what?"

"I'm not sure. Maybe special compensation outside of hell. Whatever it is, it's not enough because Death is determined to escape his contract."

She shivered and started walking again. "Is that the

winery over there with the logo on it?" She motioned toward the nearest building.

He nodded and led her inside the winery. It was made up of vast, open rooms, each with an arched vaulted ceiling supported by pillars. Each pillar had a sconce shell for indirect lighting, which produced adequate light but still left much of the room in shadows. Oak barrels filled every available space, stacked in rows and nearly touching the ceiling in many places.

Ian led her to a terrace of sorts, bordered by a wrought iron railing. It, in turn, progressed to a staircase that descended to the cellar floor. The entire place revealed an ancient, man-made cavern with distinctly modern touches. It possessed a beauty all its own.

"This is the wine master's domain. I meet with my staff every Saturday, and when the season ramps up in a couple of weeks, then I'll be here every day," he said with pride in his voice.

"You enjoy the business of growing grapes," she said.

He leaned a hip on the railing and offered her a heart-stopping smile. "The land and fruit have been my saving grace. If not for them, my service as Guardian would have become burdensome." He shifted position, bracing his hands on the railing now. "Not that I don't accept my duty to the Divine Tree and all that comes with it. But the vines have been my family. I have plants, not many, but a few, that date back to just after I arrived in 1121."

She felt her eyes grow round with wonder and surprise. Holy shit…that was a long time. "You've been here since then?"

"I have." He stepped back, closed his eyes, and inhaled deeply through his nose. "And I've witnessed countless generations come and go on this land. Wars, and industry, and electronics, and people… Times change."

In that instant, she again saw him as a very old soul. Not necessarily in a bad or negative way, but in an extremely complex way, like the wines he produced. The men she'd known—not to mention dated—had been shallow. Always worried about football games, or Indy car races, or the stock market, or drinking games. She realized how much more Ian Hearst hinted at being.

"Come," he said, interrupting her thoughts. Then he traveled down another barrel-lined corridor. Awed by what he'd just shared with her, she most likely would have followed him into the desert without a drop of water.

The room he entered was a gorgeous wine cellar with a small, quaint, marble bar table positioned near an arched display where a single bottle of wine was positioned in a beam of light.

"Have a seat," Ian said. "I'll be right back."

He disappeared between rows of wine, and as soon as he moved from within her sight, an unreasonable sense of panic pinched her chest.

Breathe, silly girl, breathe.

He returned a few minutes later with a bottle in hand, which he deposited carefully on the table in front of her while he got two glasses from a tray on a nearby rack.

Grace lifted the bottle and read, *"1837."* She gently set the bottle back on the table. "From your winery?"

He nodded.

"OMG, that's one hundred and seventy-nine years old." She swallowed hard. "This was made the year Queen Victoria began her reign. That's…that's absurd."

"One of the perks of being immortal."

"The history you must have witnessed and experienced firsthand. I can't imagine. And here I revel in the past stories of ghosts."

She winced as he opened the bottle. "I have more. This isn't the last one," he explained.

With a nod, she tried to relax. "I've heard of people coming across old wines in ship wrecks and such."

He chuckled, a deep rumble of sound. It was a pleasant

tone her body reacted to, and she leaned closer to him. "The bottom of the sea is one of the best places to keep wine. It's cool, dark, and pressurized so air doesn't get in the bottle."

He moved with slow, deliberate movements, tantalizing in their effect. *Restless* couldn't begin to describe her right now, and as he progressed, the feeling intensified. She folded her hands and set them on the table, calling on every ounce of strength as she fortified herself against his charm.

Resist, resist, resist.

For as much as she tried to control a yearning she was shocked to discover existed in the first place, watching his hands and the minute play of pleasurable emotions over his features made her abdomen tighten and a flush washed over her from her cheeks into her chest. She shifted in her seat.

No, not him. Don't fall for him.

He waved the cork beneath his nose, inhaling the fragrance. His mouth curved into a smile.

And what a charming smile it was. She wished he smiled more often, such straight teeth and a hint of a dimple.

A brow lifted, and his eyes dilated, his silver irises turning a deep grayish blue.

Had she been staring? He looked so…intense. She glanced away, then back. For a moment, she bit her lip and then crossed her legs, trying to stifle the sudden rush of warmth.

"Mmm, exquisite," he murmured. The sensual way he said it made her feel as if he wasn't only speaking about the wine.

He poured two glasses and set one in front of her. She watched him carefully, replicating his etiquette down to the swirl of the goblet and swish of the wine over her tongue. "Wow," she said softly. "Even better than I expected. A lot sweeter, too."

"We used more sugar back then. Today we rely more heavily on the mature, quality grapes. Many wineries use a blend of different varieties of grapes together. We use the same single varietal we've always used."

The cellar grew extremely quiet as they sipped their wine and peered at each other over the rim of their glasses, wrapped up in their own thoughts.

Grace swished the final quarter-size puddle of red around in her glass, watching the swirl. "So is it true that your wine has medicinal properties as the townsfolk claim?" she asked.

He raised one muscular shoulder.

She suddenly wished he would nix the shirt so she could have an unobstructed view of his powerful physique.

"Apparently it does have a measure of healing properties. I'm not certain why, but I suspect it has something to do with the proximity of the Divine Tree."

She brought the glass to her lips and drank the last swallow, hoping it was strong enough to shrink her tumor.

Grace would never make a good poker player, Ian thought, observing the kaleidoscope of emotions playing over her beautiful face. Even with the stillness in the room, her reaction to the chatter within her brain was revealed as she nibbled her lip, or wrinkled her nose, or showed her dimples. Her face was an ocean of emotion. And her guileless enthusiasm appealed to him.

He raised the wine bottle. "Would you care for another?"

She pursed her sweet lips. "No, thank you. Maybe later."

Distractedly, he wondered if she would choose to sleep in the guest room tonight. He had to admit that he liked sharing his bed with her. Another night like the last wouldn't be too bad. In fact, it had been nice to wake with her snuggled into him.

He finished the last of his wine, too hastily for what it deserved, but he discovered she made him feel impatient, edgy, and something else—sexually charged, aware.

From the entrance of the cellar, the sound of his staff could be heard as they returned from their midday meal. He stood slowly, not at all looking forward to fulfilling his promise. "I'll take you to see Skylar now."

She hopped right off the stool with none of the hesitation he was feeling. Perhaps it was because he knew the whole story, whereas she was still in denial. He sighed to himself. Sometimes life sucked, as the youth said today.

He carried the half-drunk bottle with him as they left the cellar and placed it on his foreman's desk with a note to have it delivered to the château.

He paused when it came time to take her to the tree. The best way would be through the tunnel, but he'd never taken anyone there before. What would happen if he did? Would the tree allow her entrance? Belatedly, he realized he shouldn't have promised to let her see Skylar. Entrance into the Divine Tree alone might be impossible.

He swiped his hand along his jawline.

"What's wrong?" she asked.

"There are some things I hadn't taken into consideration."

"Such as?"

"The oak may not allow you entrance."

"There's only one way to find out," she said matter-of-factly.

"I'm aware of that. It's just… I've never taken anyone there before."

"Never?"

"There hasn't been a need to."

She shrugged and stepped closer to him. "No time like the present."

He didn't understand her easy acceptance and quick manner of turning things around.

When he remained rooted in place, she slipped her arm into the crook of his, tugging gently. "Which way do we go?"

"You'll have to close your eyes," he said.

"Huh?"

"I don't have a blindfold, and it's probably not a good idea for you to know your way around."

"That's ridiculous. I'm not here to steal your secrets or anything," she said, wincing inwardly at the lie. At least it wasn't for any other reason except for her own healing. Did that make her a bad person?

Ian led her into a new room, a cross between an office and a private tasting room. "Close your eyes," he commanded.

She gave him a long, hard look before she complied, making a huge show of the ordeal as she squeezed her eyes shut and crossed her arms over her chest. "Are you going to tie my hands, too?"

"No. I think you'll be a good girl."

She opened one eye, saying, "You don't know me very well, then."

For a few seconds, Ian's imagination ran wild with the images she evoked—her hands tied above her head, blindfolded, and trusting him. A low growl formed in his throat, and he swallowed hard to bury the sound. Why did this woman arouse his interest in every way possible?

He placed his hand at her back and guided her forward. He tapped the control to the hidden stairwell as they went. "There will be fifteen steps down," he said, approaching the landing.

"Hmm, some sort of mechanical door. Very cool."

"You're too observant for your own good."

The passageway closed behind them, and he quickly steered her onward so as to disorient her as best he could.

They had traveled past the connecting tunnel hallways when she stopped and asked anxiously, "Can I please open my eyes?"

"Fine."

She did so on a heavy sigh, then blinked rapidly several times as her vision adjusted. As they moved forward, lights came on. "Motion sensor lighting?"

"Yes."

"Wow. More high-tech than I expected."

"I've kept up with the technology," he said.

"I guess so." Her voice was tinged with a hint of awe. She glanced up and down the corridor. "Light sensors, maybe video cameras."

He began walking, expecting her to follow, which she did. "I suppose you're familiar with a certain amount of tech equipment given the...*business* you're in."

"You don't have to say it so sarcastically. It's a perfectly legitimate occupation, albeit somewhat unusual." She caught up to walk beside him. "I mean, you're one to talk. You're immortal, for heaven's sake."

"No other human is aware of that."

"Really?"

"Just you."

Then she grabbed hold of his bicep, halting him. "Wait a minute. You said no human. That sounds like there are others, perhaps nonhumans, who are privy to more than I am. Are there more immortals? Not Guardians, but *others*? Like Death?"

Ian shrugged. He removed her hand from his arm and placed it within his own larger hand, cupping his fingers around hers. "Come. The Divine Tree's entrance is mere feet away."

They took several more steps, and dim lights illuminated the entrance. She inhaled sharply. "Oh my. It's beautiful."

Her tone pleased him.

Ian began the anointing ritual, holding his wrist beneath the root, allowing the sap to drip onto the tree tattoo there, and reciting his vow. "My strength and loyalty are yours."

Guardian, what are your intentions? Custos asked.

The words rustled in his head, unspoken.

Shock coursed through him. In all the time he'd served as Guardian, the oak had never posed such a question. Ian straightened his spine. *I have Grace, Skylar's friend with me. She wants to see the body.*

Impossible. The woman is in my protection, the tree replied.

May I bring Grace in and allow her to see for herself? Ian didn't dare turn and look into Grace's eyes. He could feel the anxiety emanating from her.

A long silence ensued before the Divine Tree responded. *No, that won't work at all.*

Grace clutched his upper arm. "Please," she whispered.

Ian snapped his head around. Had she heard the conversation? Her heavy eyelids and downturn lips revealed that she had. But how was that possible?

Her soft voice interrupted his thoughts. "I'd be forever grateful. She was my friend. It's my fault she died."

I'm sorry, the tree intoned. *I have succumbed to far too much influence of late.*

Ian knew better than to push the issue. He turned to Grace. "Remember, I told you I wasn't sure we could enter."

Her shoulders slumped. Then she straightened again. "Perhaps you could bring her out here. I don't need to go inside the tree. I just want to see her. To have closure."

He shook his head. "No. She is under Custos's protection. As long as she stays inside, she remains the same, preserved, as you will. And her soul is also sheltered."

She did that thing of hers, gathering her hair and sweeping it over her shoulder. "Then I will wait here until the oak lets me in."

He placed his hand behind her shoulder with the intention of directing her back down the tunnel.

She jerked, rotating away from his touch, assuming a defiant stance. "I *will* see her."

He nodded. "Just not today."

"Argh. This is so frustrating," she ground out, balling her hands into fists.

He watched the subtle change in her posture, the slightest hint of her muscles relaxing as she succumbed to the idea that she wasn't getting what she wanted, and her feet shuffled backward the slightest inch.

"We can try again tomorrow," she said with determination, looking him square in the eyes.

"Yes."

Her long, thick lashes swept down, then up. She had lovely eyes. Even in the dull light of the tunnel they were like looking into the sun-kissed ocean near his home in Scotland eons past. Even with the sadness in them now, they were extraordinary. He leaned into her. This time, he stroked her hair from the crown of her head to the shoulder where she'd swept it. He wasn't quite certain why he didn't flat-out send her home.

"Yes," he repeated. "I'll bring you back tomorrow, and the next day. We can keep trying, if that's what you want to do."

"Fair warning, I don't give up easily."

"Duly noted." He escorted her back the way they'd come until they arrived at the fork.

"Are we returning to the winery?"

"No, to the château."

"Darn. I'd like some more of that delicious wine."

"I had it delivered to my home, so it should be there awaiting us," he said. "We'll need to take a different tunnel, though. Close your eyes again."

She sighed. "Is this really necessary?"

"Just do it."

When her eyes slid shut, he took hold of her hand. For a second, he stepped close to her. So close the length of their bodies almost touched. The titillating thought had him holding his breath as he considered testing the theory. His skin fired alive with anticipation. If he sucked in a little more air, her soft breasts would press against him and he'd feel her heart beat.

"Well?" she asked, interrupting his thoughts.

"I was allowing you to get your bearings," he lied, stepping to the side and leading her onward. He sighed. It was for the best, and he knew it.

Grace tried to control her racing heart. The warmth of his fingers eased over her senses, intimate and sensuous. Her foolish brain was making more of this than it actually was, she told herself. He didn't really even know her. He merely did it to guide her through the darkness. And while she knew this was the case, at the same time, something inside her wanted it to be more.

She breathed air into her lungs and let it out slowly, hoping he didn't sense the underlying feelings she herself couldn't comprehend.

Her mind wandered as she walked along beside him, sometimes bumping against his shoulder when her gait grew unsteady. What was the extent of his talents? They hadn't talked much about all the details surrounding his life. She would get to that. She knew he was a shape-shifter, able to transform into a bear and eagle, that he was immortal, served the tree, and had enemies. As if that wasn't more than enough to take in right there.

No, what she felt wasn't attraction at all, but anxiety over the events of the past twenty-four hours. Who wouldn't be mixed up after their friend died, killed by a reaper?

She shivered, confused and unsure of what to do about Skylar. Could she take her home? Were there paranormal consequences with such a death? She wondered if there were any resources available to her online regarding this sort of thing. Or perhaps a paranormal acquaintance could help her.

"Are you okay?" he asked.

"Yes. I'm just overwhelmed by it all." Plus the blindly-following-him act was beginning to wear her nerves even thinner. In a show of defiance, she planted her feet and stopped walking. His movements were so seamless and graceful, he managed to stop without so much as causing her arm to yank.

She opened her eyes and stared at him boldly. "That's it. I'm not closing my eyes again."

He released her hand and then crossed his arms over his chest. "Is this how you get all of your paranormal suspects to cooperate?"

Her brows came together so hard, the frown brought on an instant headache. "What are you talking about?"

"You're used to dealing with ghosts and apparitions, right? And you're accustomed to doing so on their turf?"

She put her hands on hips. "Well, of course. And I've broken about every rule in this case."

"There are rules for ghostbusting?"

"Ghost *hunting*," she corrected. The tunnel seemed to close in around her. She swallowed. "Rule number one, don't go it alone."

He gave her a skeptical glance. "You're not alone. I'm here."

"I *had* Skylar. Now look where I'm at." Her posture wilted as she let her hands fall.

He placed his palms on her upper arms and rubbed up and down. "Maybe you should cut your losses and go home."

She shook her head vehemently. "It's too late for that."

"Why? Surely there are investigations that don't reveal an outcome."

"True. But that's not the case here. There is plenty of paranormal activity going on." She moved out of his consoling grasp and progressed again along the passageway, figuring he'd direct her what way to go. "And I'm not leaving until I have what I came for."

"A story for your show," he snarled.

"I haven't decided what I'm going to do with the info yet. The world may not be ready for this kind of experience." It was a judgment call she'd have to think about.

"You realize I can't allow you to go public with this, right?"

She stopped and whirled around to face him. Again, he was quick to react as he halted. "Is that a threat?"

"Take it as you see fit."

"Because I might ruin your reclusive lifestyle?"

"No, because I cannot allow attention to be brought upon the Divine Tree."

Grace went back to walking. She didn't know if she wanted the oak discovered by the outside world, either. All she knew was that, if possible, she needed the same kind of healing Maely had received. In the recesses of her thoughts, she worried if that made her akin to Death in that she wanted to use the tree for her own purposes.

"Go left," he said when she came to a fork in the path. She followed his instructions, finding a steep set of stairs. At the top, he reached over her shoulder and opened the door. She blinked as she stepped into the bright light of Ian's bedroom suite.

Once inside, her gaze landed on the king-size bed, all remade to perfection with the silk pillows arranged just so, leaving no evidence that she and Ian had slept there last night. But the zing of excitement that rushed through her body told her how much she enjoyed having him close and just how much she'd liked feeling safe and protected by him.

Ian shut the door behind them, and she glanced back to the seamless wall. At least it appeared that way. If she hadn't just come through there she would have never suspected the hidden door.

"Convenient," she said.

"That was the plan."

She strolled into the sitting room, as did Ian. "More wine?" he asked as he made his way to where the glasses and bottle sat on an antique table. His staff was extremely efficient.

"No. Thanks." She progressed to French doors that led onto a balcony where she looked out over the vineyard. She had much to think about.

He silently poured himself a glass of brandy. "I have work to do in the vineyard this afternoon."

She gave a nod. "Okay." She could use some time to herself. Maybe she'd even get in a little online investigation on reapers. Even though the day hadn't unfolded exactly as she'd hoped, she tried to stay positive. Perhaps there would even be another opportunity to approach the magical oak and convince it to help her.

13

Ian escorted Grace to her room and then headed for the back door. He burst outside, expelling his pent-up energy by changing into his eagle and soaring high, circling the Divine Tree like a warrior hunting his target.

His primary duty was to the tree. He needed to let Death know he was up against his ultimate opponent. He would not be weakened by a woman, the death of a human, or any other circumstance. He was a Guardian first and foremost.

With his wings stretched wide, he glided the direction he'd last seen the reaper. The thing about the executioner, slayer, and destroyer—as he was known—was he hung in wait. And was damned good at it.

Eyeing the ground and trees and vines, Ian crisscrossed over the land. Nothing. He was ready to turn for home when he spied the reaper coming from among the dying vines. He was in human form, but Ian's sight was keen. He swooped down and attacked. It didn't matter where he clutched and ripped at the evil creature, Ian would tear away the flesh Death had stolen in order to make his fake human body. Ian first went for the shoulders; on his second dive, he aimed for the arms.

Death thrashed his limbs like a living scarecrow. Then he changed into his vulture form. They flew around each other, taking shots, ripping flesh and feathers. When Death had enough, he winged away.

This is what he needed to do, Ian thought. *Keep pressing Death. Keep beating him down until he decided it wasn't worth the fight.*

The reaper searched out easy prey—the dead and dying. Ian didn't think he would battle for long. He wasn't used to fighting his opponents very hard; it wasn't his style. But how much could desperation change a being? That was the mode the evil beings would take on as they moved toward the Atonement. The evil beasts would grow desperate in their attempt to turn the tables and change their plight somehow. They had nothing to lose.

It was either grow the malevolent Dark Realm to take over the world or be crushed into nonexistence when the Atonement came.

Ian sat at his computer and set aside his earlier concerns for his vines and messaged his brother Venn. Something sinister was brewing, and he needed to give Venn a heads-up before he arrived. What if there was a bigger picture he was missing entirely? Venn had recently thwarted, Io. Could there be a connection between Io and Death? A link in the Dark Realm? The Dark Realm banning together?

He also messaged the other nine Guardian brothers, letting them know about Death and what had transpired with his Divine Tree. He called for a Guardian Congress— a conclave where they met through a connection of their trees—while Venn was here. It was imperative to unify in their efforts throughout the Thousand Days before AOA. To imagine the Dark Realm gaining power... It was unthinkable.

Ian's phone chimed, letting him know it was time to meet Grace. He logged off the computer and left the room. His step picked up as he entered the kitchen at their usual gathering place. She was finishing a cup of tea that had some kind of minty aroma. "Rested?"

"Mmm... Yeah," she said with a bob of her head as she stood.

"The horses should be ready for us." He led the way out, holding the door for her. "We'll take the truck there."

Five minutes later, they reached the stables where his manager already had the horses in hand, waiting for their arrival. Grace sauntered up to the mare, patting her withers and rubbing her nose, as though she'd been doing it her whole life.

"Can you give me a boost?" she asked Ian.

He moved to her side, placed his hands on her slim waist, and lifted her effortlessly onto the horse.

"My gosh, you're strong."

Without explanation, he mounted his gelding. The horse went into somewhat of a fit, tossing his head and stomping in a circle. "Easy there," Ian ordered. The animal instantly responded to his voice with a snort and calmed.

Grace seemed to sit well in the saddle—her weight tilted forward, the reins held in a firm yet responsive grip. "What's her name?"

"Intégrité," Ian responded. "And this is Fardeau."

"Fardeau? As in *responsibility*?"

He nodded once, impressed she knew the translation.

"Interesting," she dragged out the single word.

He chuckled to himself. He'd named them after things that mattered to him. With a kick, he coaxed the gelding into a gallop. When he turned his head to check on Grace, he was pleased to find she was keeping up. And she had the biggest, broadest smile on her face. It was infectious. He grinned back.

The lightness on his shoulders and stirring in his chest caused his smile to widen. What sort of feeling was this? He tried to identify it, not knowing when he'd felt it last.

Setting an easy pace, he led them through row after row of vines, beginning on the outer perimeter and working their way inward. The sound of the hoof beats, the feel of the cool breeze on his face, and the taste of contentment made him hungry for more. He could have ridden on and on and on. But regrettably, after they'd threaded many times in and around rows of vines heavy with plump, red grapes, they reached the Divine Tree in the center of the field. The late-afternoon sun slipped behind and then peeked out of lazy orange clouds.

He dismounted and helped Grace down. As her feet touched the ground, she leaned toward him, tossing her arms around his neck and squeezing. "That was remarkable. So much fun! Your vineyard is gorgeous. I could stay here forever."

For a long moment, he was rooted in place, speechless. Her soft breasts pressed against his chest, her breath whispered over his cheek, her heartbeat escalated and fluttered with a double beat. A primal, long-suppressed part of him took over, and he moved in closer, pressing his lips to hers in a swift, rough, hungry kiss.

To his immense surprise, she answered his fervor with equal enthusiasm as she returned the kiss. He drew back. They both exhaled heavy breaths.

Awkwardness rushed between them. He wasn't about to apologize—it had felt so right somehow—but he moved silently away and let her have her space.

"I can't remember when I enjoyed such an invigorating ride," she said. Then her lashes lowered slowly before popping back open, two windows into her soul. No guile there, just effervescent joy. "And the kiss wasn't bad, either."

With an unsettled growl, not quite believing he'd actually kissed the spirited woman, he went to deal with the horses' tethers. Near the vines, there was a stake with a loop he'd installed for that very purpose, and he tied the lines.

"It's cool the way the tree is in the center of the vineyard," she said, effortlessly changing the subject.

Which was fine with him. They both had to know the kiss was a mistake—one that would be hauntingly appealing every time he relived it. He put more distance between them as he traveled along the vines, checking the fruit. "The Divine Tree was here first. Everything else was built around it."

She strolled to the tree, swept her fingers over it, wrapped her arms around the enormous trunk as much as they would go and then rested her cheek against the rough bark. "What do you call it again? Custos?"

"Yes, it means *custodian* or *guard*."

"It's beautiful."

"Yes." His gaze canvassed the area. He could sense Death. Not close but watching. "The vines I need to check are down this way. I think you should walk with me."

Grace stepped away from the oak. Her mellow mood vanished, and her scent changed to one of alertness. "The reaper's near, isn't he?"

"It's just a precaution," he assured her.

In a few rapid steps, she sidled up beside him. "Can I eat some?" She pointed to the fruit-laden vines.

"Sure." He cut the ripest bunch free. "They're a little tart right now, but in a week or so they'll be perfect."

He handed her the grapes, which filled her delicate hand to overflowing. She pulled one free and popped it between her lips and chewed. She squeezed one eye closed with the first bite. "Sour, but juicy."

She ate a couple more, then offered him one, holding it

between her fingers right in front of his mouth. He hesitated, searching her eyes, where he found delight and mischief.

"Come on. You know you want it," she said in a singsong voice.

Oh God. He groaned inwardly, admitting it wasn't the fruit that he wanted. He snapped his mouth open, inching forward at the same time, and captured the grape along with her fingers down to the first digit. He allowed his tongue to flicker over her skin as he pulled back and savored her enjoyable taste.

"Good, huh?"

He smiled, amused, and shrugged. "Nothing new. I taste-test the grapes every day."

She pushed her bottom lip forward dramatically. "Well, it's new to me. Don't spoil my fun."

"Wouldn't dream of it," he said with a chuckle. "Let's go this way." He led her in the direction of where he'd removed the sick vines. He was totally aware of the way she matched his stride, totally consumed with her easy laughter, totally enchanted with her honesty and candor.

But at the same time, the voice in his head warned, *Stay removed. Don't get too attached. There is no long-term future with people in the human world.*

Today was not the day to heed that voice, though. She had affected him with her positive approach to life. "Tell me about yourself—your childhood, your life in the States."

"I grew up not far from Disney World." She ate between sentences. "As a kid, I was pretty normal. However, my younger brother wouldn't agree, I'm sure. I took dance classes, sang in the high school chorus, participated in drama and gardening clubs, and did pretty well in school."

"No paranormal inclinations?"

"Nope. That came later." Her voice became a little heavier.

"What happened?"

She lifted her shoulders to her ears, then let them fall. "My parents got divorced. I didn't take it well and went into a funk. I mean, one day my mom simply claimed she didn't love my dad and hadn't for a long time. She stuck with him until my brother and I were out of high school and then she struck out on her own. It wasn't a bad thing, I guess, just...different after that."

"Many people get divorced today."

She stopped walking. "I know, but...that's not it. She lived a lie. Don't you see? All those years of Disney outings, trips to our beach condo, Caribbean cruises, all the Christmases and Thanksgivings and family events when she seemed happy and we were all cheerful... The big happy family was all fake."

"I'm...sorry." He tried to think of his celebrations over the years. Sadly, they were few and far between. Definitely nothing special. But that wasn't his purpose, was it? "When did your paranormal interest start?"

They resumed their stroll. "After the divorce, while I was in college." The final grape went into her mouth. "I changed my drama major to broadcast journalism with a minor in psychology. One of the assignments covered paranormal activity, and I was hooked. The feeling I had during that first experience when I was in college... Wow. I can't explain the connection. It was powerful, that's all I can tell you."

Ian watched her face light up as she came to the end of her explanation. The tug on his heart caused him to pause. He'd never met anyone like her.

When the area of vines he sought came into view, he couldn't believe his eyes. And not in a good way. Decay seemed to be running rampant. He quickened his steps, taking on a more determined gait.

Holy shit.

"What is it? What's the matter?" Grace asked, seeming to pick up on his alarm.

He had reached the vacant spot. "I removed eight dying vines from here the other day. I was transporting them to town for examination when I met you along the road."

Her eyes followed where his landed. "Oh my!"

A dozen more vines were half covered with black, drooping leaves. He tipped his head forward and thrust both hands into his hair, hard. "Christ, this is turning into an epidemic."

She inched forward, grabbing hold of a leaf. "It's limp, not crisp and dried."

"Don't touch it," he snapped. "You could spread the disease." The next words hurt to speak aloud, even to think. "I'll have to take more drastic measures and remove even more plants."

She peered up and down the row. "Really?" A sad breath of air pushed from her lungs. "The thought makes me ill."

"Me too. We need to go. There has to be something I can do to stop this. I just need to figure out what that is." He turned briskly and marched back to their horses. This time he didn't even try to converse with Custos. He wasn't feeling very chummy with the oak right now anyway. They mounted and began to ride toward the stables when the sky opened, spilling a light rain over them.

Had it not been for his dilemma with the vines, the situation might have been pleasant. Grace's blouse clung to her in all the right places. She didn't even seem to mind being wet. The sight of her stirred his desire despite his concern for his vineyard.

Shit. Shit. Shit.

Death soared to the chimney where he'd gotten into the château the night before, but now the flue was sealed shut.

Exasperation nipped at him. Optimistic that the Guardian hadn't thought to lock them all, he checked every one. Not a crack to squeeze through among them.

He flew directly to the balcony of Grace's room, instead, where he hid behind a gigantic clay pot filled with pink flowers. *Sissy pink. Why not blood red?* he thought as he tucked in his vulture wings, going for inconspicuous. Too bad he couldn't get inside this way.

He peeked out around the container and between the pieces of the decorative wrought iron railing. He watched Grace stretch out on the bed. She was a beautiful piece of work. Then a furious howl sounded behind him. Ian. He glanced over his shoulder. From this vantage point, he had an almost impeccable view of the vineyard. And of Ian ripping up his beloved vines. Overkill, in Death's opinion. The Guardian was uprooting two rows of plants on either side of the damage, probably fifty vines total.

The reaper tsked. It wouldn't do the guy any good because one touch of Death's foul hand would produce the same result.

It was oh-so-much fun to torture the Guardian.

Enough about Romeo. He turned his attention to inside the room, where he sensed Grace was in bed. The mattress creaked and groaned as she tossed and turned.

Poor baby can't get comfortable.

Through a crack in the French door, he blew hot air into the room.

That ought to make it worse. He cackled at his own nastiness.

Sadly, he couldn't merely pounce through a locked door. Wouldn't that make things so much easier? But there were other ways to get the job done. His mind was a powerful weapon with the capability of willing people to do things. Sometimes it worked; sometimes it didn't.

The way he *could* get around was similar to floating like a ghost, and his depraved essence entered through the same crack that he'd forced the hot air through. Although his physical body remained outside—as much as a reaper could be corporeal—there were things he could do in this spectral form. He paused at the bed, looking over the charming package she presented. She wore a T-shirt with a kitten on it. *Aw, how sweet.* The sheets were a tangled mess from her thrashing, and a leg was hanging out, a long length of thigh exposed all the way up to her white panties. It was a damned shame he couldn't experience more carnal pleasures.

He squashed such thoughts as he leaned over, placing his hand on her head. *Dear, sweet Grace.* Soon she would be his next victim.

The human body presented many challenges and opportunities for a guy in his line of work. It only took a few seconds to explore her brain and hit on what he'd sensed earlier: beautiful Grace had a tumor. He produced a wave of destructive energy then gave it a nudge, sending it into her head. The same way fertilizer boosts plant growth, this should give the tumor a burst of growth.

As much as it would please him to hang around, that would be pushing his luck. So he floated back out the way he'd come.

From below, a door clicked open and shut.

Perfect timing. Ian was fond of this woman. Death wondered how far he could push him. Io had indicated a Guardian's love could be used against the tree, that the Guardian would abandon his duties for his mate.

Something to consider. Something to use. Because love could be a double-edged sword.

Grace came awake with a start, overcome by some kind of creepy sensation, as if there was someone in the room. She raised her head and glanced around. Nothing. But the room was deeply shadowed, with only the moon in its third quarter shining through the balcony doors. She threw off the sheets and launched herself at the light switch.

As she glanced around the room, her breaths came rapidly. All around her was emptiness. Stillness. Silence, except for her heartbeat pounding in her ears. She swallowed.

This is ridiculous. I'm a freaking ghost hunter afraid in my own bedroom.

Her gaze shot to the balcony doors. Was someone out there maybe? She donned her robe, tiptoed closer, and peered out.

Not a thing in sight.

She released a whoosh of air from her lungs. Even so, there was no way she would stay in here. She couldn't believe she'd actually fallen asleep in the first place. Tomorrow she'd ask Ian if she could have a different room—one without a balcony.

In the meantime, perhaps a snack from the kitchen would help. Still shaken, she cautiously opened the door and slipped into the hall, hoping to make it downstairs without waking anyone. Or maybe they weren't sleeping yet. She didn't know.

Down the hallway, she noticed light coming from beneath Ian's bedroom door. She sucked her bottom lip into her mouth. Last night she'd felt safe and secure. She wondered if it would be too much of an imposition to ask to sleep there again.

Her feet began moving in that direction before she'd even made a conscious decision, but the idea of grabbing a snack vanished from her mind, replaced by the thought of Ian by her side. She walked slowly, giving herself the option to change her mind.

She hesitated when she reached his bedroom door. Then with a soft rap, she entered. "Ian?"

When he didn't answer, she inched into the sitting

room. He wasn't there, so she progressed to the bedroom. The light shown on the nightstand. A flash of memory took her back to her childhood, when she used to sneak into her parents' room and stand beside their bed until one of them woke and noticed she was there—usually with a resounding flinch. Strange, she hadn't thought of something like that in a long time.

"Ian," she said again, a bit louder this time.

Guardedly entering his room, she found it empty, too. But the sound of the shower running let her know where he was. She hesitated, then shed her robe and climbed up on the bed. Snuggling beneath the covers, she hugged the edge she'd slept on the night before. Slowly, listening to the sounds of the shower in the bath, she closed her eyes. Just for a minute.

14

Ian could feel Grace's presence in his bedroom before he'd even entered. Her scent had become so beguiling, the bear and eagle within him picked up on it immediately upon exiting the shower. His emotions warred with his head. Perhaps he should sleep somewhere else tonight.

He stepped into a pair of boxers before entering the room. The last thing she needed was for him to greet her naked and with a hard-on. Just the notion of her in his bed did that to him. He sighed, and she opened her eyes.

"I hope you don't mind," she said, blushing. "I woke up and had these weird vibes. I really don't like that room. Maybe tomorrow I can try a different one?"

"That's fine." He skirted the bed, turned off the light, and slipped beneath the covers. "We'll address the issue in the morning."

"Thank you," she whispered.

"Not a problem," he said quietly, using as much control as he could muster. He draped one arm over his head and stared at the ceiling. Despite the blackness filling the room, he observed a moth as it fluttered into a spider web.

The mattress pitched as she changed positions. He could sense her fighting against rolling toward him, and he resisted in a similar fashion. Tensing, trying to remain very still, he tried to clear his mind, to imagine being someplace else, anywhere but lying next to this female with her delectable breasts, fine womanly curves, and sweet floral scent he found difficult to resist.

Asia, he thought in way of distraction. His brother Aidan had a Divine Tree on some remote island in Japan. He would be awake about now, a good time to Facetime him. Aidan was his closest brother in age and always had a different take on things. He could use that. Yes, he should confer with him about Death, and then again with Venn when he finally arrived.

She flopped to her side, facing him, judging by the breath of air whisking faintly over his cheek.

He inhaled slowly through his nose and closed his eyes. *Sleep.*

"How did you become a Guardian?" she inquired softly.

His lips thinned in the darkness. She was the only person he'd *ever* spoken to about his life and duty. Then again, this was the first time he'd met someone who understood there were paranormal creatures and individuals outside the human race.

He took so long caught in his thoughts, she broke in, saying, "Come on. I shared my childhood with you. It's your turn."

"You're the one person I shouldn't tell, Miss TV Show Personality. Honestly, I can't risk you turning it into a program."

"I've given up on that in this case," she told him. "No one would believe it anyway. It's too far beyond the norm for the average person." She reached over and rested her hand on his arm. "I don't report on everything I find. Some things are only for me."

He rolled toward her, taking her hand in his. "My job is to protect the tree. If the world were to discover it, who knows what chaos would ensue?"

"What do you mean? What could happen?"

"The trees of life know everything from the beginning of time. And with this knowledge comes great power," he said.

"How much are the Guardians privy to?"

"We aren't permitted to use any knowledge gained from the Divine Tree."

"But you do know things?"

He surprised himself by pressing his lips to the back of her hand, seeking to guide her away from the topic of the tree. She was a far more intriguing subject, curled up so close to him. "No more about Custos. Let's change the subject." He brushed his fingers along her temple and into her hair. "In fact, let's not talk at all."

He struggled to control his desire as her aroused scent poured over him. A connection was happening between them that he didn't quite understand and knew he couldn't trust. If he were a mortal man, he'd be making love to her right now; if she were an immortal woman, then they'd have a chance at a life together. But as it was, there were few tomorrows for them. And that separation and loss was too much to endure.

No, he didn't need someone else to fulfill his life. He'd been doing just fine on his own for hundreds of years.

"But…"

"Go to sleep," he insisted in a hoarse whisper.

She clutched his hand in hers and wound it inward so that

his knuckles rested against her chest. Her heart thrummed over his pulse point, and in her mind, there was a commingling of sorts. She absorbed his essence and strength and resolve. For tonight, she tried to make that enough.

"Mmm," she purred on an exhale. She was a person of quick decisions. However, ever since she'd stepped foot on Chêne Sacré those choices had gotten her into trouble. What did it matter anyway if he didn't confide in her? People often didn't do what they said they would.

A sharp pinch of pain pierced her head. She squeezed her eyes tighter, then opened them. Geez, that hurt. As the agony eased, a throbbing headache set in. She thought of getting up to fetch some meds, but they'd only gotten settled and she didn't want to disturb Ian.

He moved. "What's wrong?"

"I have a headache."

He immediately got up. "What's your preference in meds?"

"That's okay. I can wait until morning."

"No. I don't mind getting it for you."

"I have something for migraines in my bathroom." She pushed up in the bed, attempting to rise, and swayed, feeling woozy.

"Stay put. I'll be right back."

She eased her head back onto the pillow, careful to avoid any jarring motions. Her stomach roiled. Inhaling a good whiff of air, she breathed deeply, trying to relax and incorporate some of the yoga practices she'd been studying, stretching her shoulders back and opening her neck and spine to allow better blood flow.

In her heart, she knew it was the tumor, though. Time was running out.

Ian walked briskly into the room, heading straight for the bathroom and returning with a glass of water. He turned on the lights, and she moaned.

"Here you go." He held out the pill bottle and drink.

With difficulty, she rose again, took the meds, and handed everything back to him.

"Do you get these often?" he asked, stress in his voice.

She rubbed her temples and nodded. "They seem to come in sets."

He gently replaced her hands with his and massaged. "Do you need me to take you to the doctor?"

"No. The pain meds will kick in. But thanks," she said. "I guess you don't get sick, huh?"

"Not in thousands of years."

"Lucky." His ministrations helped, and her relax.

He must have noticed the change, for he stopped, saying, "Maybe lie down and try to sleep again."

Too exhausted to resist, she complied. This time he coaxed her into the middle of the bed while he perched on the edge. She curled away from him. Over her shoulder, she noticed that he leaned forward onto his elbow. When his fingers rubbed her neck in firm, slow circles, she sighed. The ache had diminished.

His thoughtfulness went beyond what she'd expected from him, making her heart smile and warm.

15

Ian awoke curled around Grace. She was cocooned in his arms with her back pressed to his chest, her ass snuggled against his groin. In her sleep, she ground her hips backward, pushing on his erection. He could have died at the pleasure that shot through him, and it took everything he had not to press into her. With a groan, he inched away, rolled onto his back, and tugged the covers up.

Day had broken on the horizon, but he was loath to rise. He breathed in her floral scent, and savored the warmth radiating from her perfect body. She was the one sparkling thing about yesterday. He couldn't explain it, but between Custos denying them entrance and the problem he was having with the ill vines, *and* Death hanging around, nothing seemed quite as bad as maybe it should with Grace here. *Except for Skylar,* he amended. The young woman presented a sad dilemma.

He scrubbed his palm down his face. Yeah, he had to get up.

Slipping quietly from the bed, he headed to the bathroom and adjoining closet to dress. Venn was due to arrive today—a fortunate event he couldn't quite believe. They had a lot to catch up on since they'd parted Scotland so many years ago. And Venn had hinted at dire things occurring leading up to the Age of Atonement.

In the bedroom, he heard Grace yawn and stretch, and then the rustle of sheets. Her bare feet padded softly across the floor as she approached. He stepped out of the large walk-in closet fully dressed.

She looked adorable with sleep-mussed hair framing her gorgeous eyes. "Good morning," he said. "How's the headache?"

"Much better, thanks."

She approached him, wrapped her arms about his ribs, and squeezed. She rested her chin on his chest. "I appreciate the TLC you gave me last night."

He stroked her hair with one hand as the other arm hugged her in return, allowing his palm to smooth against her spine, cradling her. "I didn't like seeing you ill."

She didn't say anything but lifted her head and gazed into his eyes. A powerful wave of desire crashed through him. He tipped his head down and kissed her, tasting her lips and dipping his tongue inside her sweet mouth until he found hers. She kissed him back, thrusting her tongue to meet his as she groaned deep in her throat.

Heat coursed through him, feelings he had suppressed and told himself he didn't want or need. Feelings that were a reminder of life, not just existence.

When the kiss ended, she whispered, "I can't thank you enough. You've been so kind and helpful, fetching me medicine…but don't think for a minute I'm going to let up about the tree."

She stepped back. An emptiness hit him hard in the gut. He didn't know if they would ever come to terms with that.

"Do you feel like eating?" he asked, trying to change the subject.

"Yes. I'm starved."

He was, too, but food wasn't what was truly on his mind. He'd been fighting his attraction to her from the beginning, knowing there was no way for a long-term relationship. But what about a short interlude, a fling? She'd be returning to the States; there would be no expectations of something permanent.

"I'll bring something up here for you. Take your time. And by the way, my brother is arriving today."

She inhaled a surprised breath, then gently said, "I'd like to hear more about your family."

"I'm afraid you're soon going to hear more than you expected."

As soon as he'd left the room, she realized she needed to get her things. She headed down the hall and stepped into the guest room. A shiver ran through her as it reminded her of the sensations she got when on a job that was haunted by evil ghosts. She paused, glancing around. The place was super old. Maybe it could have possessed imprints or spirits.

This time, instead of merely picking out an outfit, she grabbed her entire suitcase and wheeled it back to the shelter of Ian's room. She sighed. *Much better.*

She opened the suitcase on the bed and selected a pair of jeans and a light-blue T-shirt. Back in his bedroom, freshly showered and only half-dressed, the sound of a door closing downstairs caught her attention. Ian?

Her top slid over her skin, getting caught on the parts of her flesh that weren't quite dry. She plucked it free. The changing-in-his-room routine made her a tad uncomfortable. She wrestled with relishing the intimacy and knowing he was a man she shouldn't get involved with. He was immortal, for heaven's sake. But then again, what did that matter to a woman who was dying?

"Breakfast," he announced from outside the bedroom door. The sound of his rich voice caused her heart to patter faster.

"I'll be right there." She ran a comb through her wet hair and wrapped it in a towel, turban-style.

When she came out into the sitting room, the balcony doors were flung open wide and he'd arranged a spread of food on a small wrought iron table—quiche, fruit, cheese, croissants, and coffee.

"It's so beautiful out here. I feel silly with my hair all wrapped up."

He glanced over his shoulder as she approached, his brow lifting roguishly, a sexy smile on his face. "You couldn't possibly look anything but fabulous."

A flush of warmth rushed into her cheeks, matched by a swirl in her tummy. "Thanks."

Stop reacting to him, she counseled herself.

The spectacular view of the vineyard captured her attention as they ate—a welcome distraction from Ian's alluring silver eyes and handsome face. She'd eaten the last bite of fruit, when a posh sports car pulled into the drive.

She angled toward the railing for a better look. "Nice."

"I gather that would be my brother and his wife."

"He's married? But if he's immortal, too, then—"

"Evidently he managed somehow." He stood and waited for her to do the same. Together, they went downstairs to greet the guests. Ian jogged down the stairs as a boyish excitement seemed to come over him. She almost had to run to keep up.

Her mind raced with every step, wondering about the woman who had wed a Divine Tree Guardian. How was that possible? Did that mean she was immortal, too?

Ian threw the massive doors open as if they were

toothpicks instead of weighty, solid panels of wood. He strode onto the portico. When the brothers locked eyes, she could feel an electrifying energy explode around them. They simultaneously broke into a full sprint toward each other, leaving the women on the sidelines. The brothers leaped forward to embrace, slamming chests and wrapping arms in a fierce bear hug. Ian lifted Venn off his feet. They wrestled and punched biceps. They clasped each other around the back of the neck and pressed their foreheads together. They growled and tumbled to the ground, and for several stuttering heartbeats Grace swore she witnessed a bear and a wolf wrestling instead of two brawny men. She deliberately blinked to clear her vision, but the picture remained the same until, with a seamless transition, they stood facing each other in human form again, both breathing hard.

Grace chewed her lip. Shoulder to shoulder, the two began strolling in sync toward her—or more correctly, the front of the château. Like many brothers, they had striking similarities. Both had tall, broad shoulders and firm jaws, though Ian alone had that enticing dimple in his chin. When they were close enough, she realized they shared the same large, deep-set eyes in different colors. Venn's were a reddish gold compared to Ian's silver.

Venn glanced at his wife and held out his hand. She stepped up and accepted it. The look that passed between them was one of an unmistakable connection laced with passion, adoration, and devotion.

Despite the pep talk she'd given herself earlier—all that "keep your distance" dialogue—she couldn't suppress a hint of jealousy at what she saw in their eyes. Would she ever know such love?

Ian felt conflicted as they approached the château. While

he was overjoyed to see his brother, he wondered at the real reason Venn was in France. And why now? Plus, setting his attraction aside for Grace—not an easy task— he contemplated her position in all of this. Should he trust her? Because by Satan's horns, she had landed smack in the middle of a rabbit hole.

He cracked his knuckles, then tried to push the questions out of his head when they reached his home. He introduced Venn and Emma to Grace, and then to Bernard who exited to assist their guests.

"I'll see to your luggage, if that's agreeable," Bernard said to Venn.

"Thank you," he replied.

Ian followed his brother's speculative glances toward Grace. "Grace is here as a paranormal investigator," Ian explained.

"Really?" Emma asked.

A judgmental glance was passed around.

Venn slung a protective arm about Emma's shoulders. He paused on the top step, taking in the vineyard and grounds. He gave a low whistle. "You've done well, brother."

"I've had many ups and downs over the years."

"Haven't we all?" Emma said in a level tone.

The four went inside and into the main sitting room. Ian opened a bottle of wine and served them. "From 1898…a very good year."

Venn accepted a glass, and they toasted. "To face-to-face visits. May there be many more."

They chinked glasses. "I'm shocked there's even this one," Ian said. "Please, make yourself at home." He motioned to the furniture.

Venn and Emma took the loveseat, Ian and Grace the two chairs across from them.

"Did you find what you were looking for in Paris?" Ian asked.

Venn took another long gulp of wine. "Yes, I think so. From the people we spoke with—"

"Interrogated," Emma corrected.

"It seems Io was behind the burning of Emma's apartment, as we thought," Venn went on.

"Thank God my roommate wasn't home." Emma drained her goblet and then set it on a side table.

"Oh my," Grace exclaimed. "How horrible. Who is Io?"

Emma pressed her lips into a thin line. "A wicked demon who almost killed Venn and his Divine Tree."

Ian tensed. "It's a good thing you overcame his plan."

Venn shrugged. "It was touch and go for a while. If it weren't for Emma, I wouldn't be here."

"Yes, you would," she proclaimed. They shared a secret look. She wrapped both hands about his arm and held on tight.

Ian didn't believe he'd ever have a woman cling to him like that. He rose and refilled Emma's empty glass. She smiled and nodded her thanks.

Emma turned her attention to Grace. "How long have you known Ian?"

"Only a few days."

The look Grace gave him, full of trust and admiration, made his heart squeeze.

Ian glanced between Grace and his brother. "I have a conflict going on right now in my own backyard. A reaper is wreaking havoc."

Venn straightened. "I'm not surprised. Since we've entered the Thousand Days before the Age of Atonement. Every evil creature out there will be looking for an advantage, some way to escape their punishment. I'll do what I can to help."

Ian rubbed his jaw and shot to his feet. "So that's it, then, after all. The reason behind the shift I've felt and the dissonance surrounding the tree?"

"Yes. And according to Seth, it's up to us to stand firm and not allow the Dark Realm to glean what they need from the Divine Trees," Venn said.

Ian heaved a large sigh and began to pace. It seemed his brother's visit had been motivated by more than he'd realized. He paused and peered at Grace. "Do you mind keeping Emma company while Venn and I consult?"

"Sure. It will be great to have another female to chat with." The women look at each other and smiled.

"Yes," Emma said with a smirk. "I'm sure we have much to discuss, as well."

16

Grace wasn't too sure about this newfound hospitality position that had been thrust upon her. On one hand, it was nice that Ian regarded her highly enough to entertain his sister-in-law in his stead. On the other, she was so overwhelmed by the events of the past two days, it amazed her that she could even put two words together intelligently.

Ian led Venn into the study, leaving the women alone.

"I'm not a very good hostess," Grace admitted, trying to sound enthusiastic.

"That's not really your role, is it?"

"No." She searched Emma's eyes and let out an awkward chuckle. "I manage to land myself in the craziest situations."

"What exactly does a paranormal investigator do?"

"I'm primarily a ghost hunter."

"Oh," Emma raised a brow with a slight chuckle. "I need to introduce you to my grandmother some time."

"I'm down with all the phantasm stuff: ghosts, spirits, specters, apparitions, ghouls, orbs, and such. But these

Divine Trees and shape-shifting Guardians? Wow! Way over the top."

"Yeah, I know what you mean."

Grace poured herself another glass of wine. If this vineyard produced medicinal libations as the town alleged, then she sorely needed it, especially considering the headache she'd had last night. "Would you like some more?"

"No, thank you."

"You sound like you're from the South. I don't think Ian ever said where his brother lived."

"Georgia," Emma said with a smile.

"I'm from Orlando. We're almost neighbors."

"Then we have something else in common."

Grace tilted her head, confused. *What was the first thing they had in common?*

"What's that?" she asked.

Emma met Grace's gaze. "We both love a Guardian."

"Oh no." Grace shook her head. "Ian and I don't have that sort of relationship."

"Hmm. The way he looks at you says otherwise."

"You must be mistaken." She tucked her legs beneath her. "Besides…" She leaned toward Emma, glancing around to make sure no one else was within hearing. "I mean, I'm human, not immortal."

"So am I."

Grace flung her hair over her shoulder as she let the shocking news sink in. A tiny flash of foolish hope took root, but she refused to nourish it. She cleared her throat and stood. "Would you like to freshen up? I can show you to your room."

Emma looked at her for a moment, as if assessing her before responding. "Yes, that would be lovely."

"The Age of Atonement?" Ian asked as soon as the

women were out of earshot. "Tell me more of what's actually happening."

"I knew I'd see you soon so I thought it best to discuss the situation in person."

"Yes, but how bad is it?"

Venn grimaced. "Think back over history. Add up every bad event and multiply it tenfold."

"Shit. I didn't make the connection. Had I realized, I would have considered Death's visit in a different light."

"How so?"

Ian rubbed the stubble on his chin. "In the past, this reaper has never hung around for more than a few hours. He's the hit and run sort. As soon as he stuck around, I should have known something was up. Perhaps I should have come down harder on Grace right from the start and chased her off. Maybe her partner would still be alive now."

"I bet two Guardians could run him off."

"Worth a try."

Ian sensed the pent-up energy emanating from Venn. "Been a long while since you've had a good run, I take it?"

"Feels like ages ago. And that damn plane ride." He shook his head. "I don't like relying on those machines. Flying over the earth like that… It was far different than soaring over the treetops as a hawk."

"Shall we?" Ian transformed into his bear form, taking the lead. Venn changed into his wolf, and with both of them on all fours, his brother came almost even with his shoulder. Breaking into a run, he darted into the vineyard, Venn at his side. The breeze on his face felt great. His brother's long strides matching his heavier tread seemed right. And for a moment he was transported to a long ago day when they'd raced across the moors of Scotland. Long ago, indeed.

They covered the property in a shell pattern, circling the outskirts and working toward the center where the oak stood. As they came upon the Divine Tree, Ian changed into eagle form, Venn into his hawk. They split, approaching from opposite sides, and Ian was reminded of an air show where the planes coordinated rolls just after they'd crossed paths. In perfect sync, Ian and Venn rolled and came around, effortlessly finding the vulture and dive-bombing him. But Death was no easy target. He jumped from his perch and escaped their attack.

The brothers banked tightly and came down on Death again. Three sets of wings clashed, flapped, and tore at one another in a tumbling mix of feathers and shrieks.

All at once, the vulture peeled away and flew out of sight.

Ian and Venn landed near the Divine Tree and changed into their human form, both oozing blood from their battle wounds. "Ha! That was the greatest challenge I've had in ages," Ian said.

"Reminiscent of what I just went through with Io."

Ian stared in the direction Death went. "He'll be back." Moving to a specific spot in the oak beneath a thick branch, he entered the tree through the porthole. Venn followed.

Inside, they paused to allow their wounds to heal. Venn's were far worse than Ian's, with his flesh flayed open and the gash covered in blood. Venn shrugged. "Guess I haven't recovered fully yet from my near-death experience."

"That's something I haven't thought about in a long time…"

Venn's brow furrowed. "What do you mean?"

"Dying."

"Oh, right." Venn chuckled with a frown. "As immortals, we seem to forget about that."

"What was it like?" Ian asked.

"I'd only met Emma so the thought of losing her… I could equate it to being drawn and quartered."

"Now there's a term I haven't heard in forever, either!"

Ian nodded at his brother's injuries. "Do we need to get you patched up?"

"It'll heal. Just a lot slower than yours."

Ian's wounds were already closed, actually. He started to say something, then clammed up. Witnessing his brother's pain and vulnerability tugged at him. His chest tightened, and he cracked his knuckles.

Slowly, yet far more quickly than they had been a few moments ago, Venn's cuts sealed together.

"Thank you, Custos," Venn murmured.

Ian scanned the work of the oak. From the beginning, Guardians had been able to heal rapidly. But here Custos had managed to speed up the process. Good deal.

"Come," Ian said. "Our other current problem is down below."

He led the way deep into the catacomb in the root structure, moving through passages of smooth, golden wood. He halted where Grace's assistant was sprawled over the polished floor.

"This is Skylar. She's here because of Death. And Custos took her within to protect her soul."

"She looks peaceful. Like a goth Sleeping Beauty."

"If only it were that simple." Ian sighed. "But at least as long as she's with Custos, we have options. As long as her soul remains close by with her, maybe she could even be revived. I don't know. I mean, that's the reason we have Euler here, right?"

"Exactly."

Ian swallowed, not wanting to tell his brother what Death's next move was, not wanting it to be true. "I'm afraid Death has his sights on Grace."

"Then we shouldn't have left her."

"The house should be safe. The reaper entered through the chimney once, but I had that problem fixed."

"It's never safe where the Dark Realm is involved," Venn said, shaking his head.

"Which is why I think we should arrange a Guardian Congress via the Divine Trees," Ian said. "Have Custos send a call out to the brothers. Give a time for all of us to converse on the threat posed by the Dark Realm. Then we can prepare and be ready and fight."

Venn thumped him on the back. "How can my baby brother be so smart? I agree. We need to unite."

Ian nodded. "Custos, can you reach out to the other trees and brothers and arrange a meeting?"

I can. But be warned: such a gathering draws upon enormous energy. There will be vulnerability and weakness following the meeting. Would that not give Death the opening he's searching for?

"Perhaps," Ian admitted. "But it's a necessary risk."

The rattle of the wind echoed down into the bowels of the tree. *When should I arrange the meeting?*

"Let's gather tomorrow at dawn, our time." Ian stared at Venn, who tipped his head in agreement.

Very well, Custos moaned.

"This way." Ian guided them through the tunnels.

"Feels like home," Venn muttered nostalgically with a soft chuckle.

Grace headed into the huge hall framed by dual staircases. She was about to take Emma upstairs when something stopped her. A strange apprehension made her look down the corridor to the far end.

"What is it?" Emma inquired.

Grace reached for her hair, then paused, letting her hand fall to the balustrade. "I don't know. I felt something… A ghost, perhaps."

"Hmm."

"Does that shock you?"

"Not in the least." Emma's eyes met hers. "I'm

reincarnated with a touch of weirdness. I can heat metal with my bare hands." She showed Grace her palms.

"They look normal to me."

Emma walked over and grabbed hold of a door knob. Around twenty seconds later, she released it and the thing glowed red.

"Wow! Awesome!" Grace paused for a moment, hoping she'd just gained a friend who wouldn't think her occupation was totally weird. "You know, I haven't checked out a particular area of the house yet that I've been getting weird vibes from. Interested in doing a little hunting with me?" As she heard excitement enter her voice, she realized her curiosity had been stifled by recent events.

"Sure."

They stepped off the lower treads and proceeded down a main hallway. Perhaps it was because Emma had trusted her with what must be personal information, but Grace found she liked Ian's sister-in-law. Plus, she enjoyed having company. A pang of sadness nabbed her again at the loss of Skylar.

The room at the end of the wide corridor appeared to be an American-style family room or entertainment center. Beyond the French doors, she could make out a swimming pool and garden. "Nope. The weird vibrations aren't coming from in here."

"Maybe another room along the way," Emma said brightly.

Simultaneously, they turned around and retraced their steps until Grace came to a set of large double doors. "This is Ian's study. I've haven't been in here."

"Well? What are we waiting for?"

"Yeah, I guess we should check inside."

Shoulder to shoulder with Emma, Grace grabbed the cut glass doorknob and turned it. They quietly snuck inside and glanced about.

Their eyes met, Emma's holding that same *well?* expression.

Then a cool rush of air breezed over Grace. "Yes. A ghost, I think."

Emma gave an excited smile. They moved a few steps farther into the room to stand near the enormous desk. Then the panel on the wall folded to the left and out strolled Ian and Venn.

"I didn't expect to find you ladies, here," Ian said, a rumbling in his deep voice.

Venn hurried over to Emma, took her in his arms, and hugged her fiercely, topping the embrace with a passionate kiss.

Grace swallowed hard as her eyes skipped to Ian.

Emma held her husband at arm's length, her gaze roaming over him, where obvious remnants of nearly healed wounds showed on his arms, neck, and jaw. "What happened?"

"It seems we're not the only ones having trouble with evil forces," Venn explained. "A reaper called Death is wreaking havoc here. I think this is only the beginning as those from the Dark Realm grapple to save their asses before the Atonement arrives."

Venn drew Emma into another embrace and kissed her once more, hard and full of fervor and hunger.

Grace moved closer to Ian, and he surprised her by slipping an arm around her back and pulling her close. She sighed, unsure which emotion to give in to: desire, anxiety, or fear. "Is Death ever going to leave?"

Ian squeezed her more tightly to him. "Only when he's convinced he won't get what he wants."

"Or if he *does* get it," Venn added.

"That's not going to happen," Ian said. "He wants to be human again. Either that, or he wants Grace." He passed a possessive look over her.

Grace's lips parted and her breath caught as warmth

spread down to her toes. He would protect her. She felt it as if he'd stated as much.

Her body responded with a mind of its own, and she couldn't help wonder what it would feel like to have Ian kiss her as if she were his last meal.

17

Long-suppressed desire surfaced and whipped into a frenzy within Ian. He had told himself that he wasn't capable of loving the way mortal men did. Now, witnessing his brother so happy and in love… Well, it made him wonder. Was there someone for him, too?

The urge to protect and love Grace raged through him like a wild stream in spring, the current stronger than anything he'd ever felt in his immortal life.

Custos interrupted with a murmur. *I have spoken with the brothers. The Congress will be at sunrise.*

I'll be there, Ian replied, stifling his annoyance at the oak's awful timing. He finger combed Grace's hair at her temple, thinking. Even with his duties to the Divine Tree, it was important to him to protect her, too.

She looked at him with her big midnight eyes, and his beast pawed and clawed to come out and play. That, plus the scent of sexual arousal that was wafting through the château. His brother's and his mate's for sure, but also another's—Grace's.

She probably wasn't even aware of it, but with his increased senses, the effect of her natural, sweet scent was driving him wild. He needed to put distance between them, go for a run or something.

After they'd had dinner and he'd shown Venn and Emma to their room, he and Grace paused in the hall outside his room. "Bernard prepared another room for you if you'd like to move in there."

"You don't want me to sleep with you?" she asked, her voice somewhat small, maybe even hurt.

"That's not it. I just wanted to give you options." And also offer himself an out. As keyed up as he was this evening, he'd need to spend the entire night in a cold shower.

She inched closer to him, the slow exhale of her breath fanning his neck.

Unable to resist her, he stepped nearer, threading a hand into her hair. "I'm crazy attracted to you," he started, "but you'll be leaving soon."

"If you're trying to push me away, don't. *Not* doing something is the greatest regret." She clutched the front of his shirt and drew him down to her, their lips mere inches apart.

His heart hammered in his chest. What she wanted was clear, and he definitely wanted the same. He closed the tiny space separating them and pressed his lips to hers in a languid, exploring kiss.

Oh God, her lips were incredibly soft and tasted of the sweetest wine he'd ever tasted. He pulled back, his mouth still brushing hers. "Realize that I won't be able to stop myself if you're in my bed tonight."

She gave him a sexy smirk. "I know. I like living on the wild side."

He yanked her against the length of his entire body.

"Oh? I hadn't noticed," he teased with a chuckle.

Somewhere in his mind, he thought he'd be able to stop if he really needed to. But damn, it would probably kill him. Not at all sure this was the right course, Ian opened the door and led Grace into the room and to the bed. There was no sense pretending anymore—they both felt the sexual chemistry firing between them.

She grabbed hold of his hand, tugging him onto the bed. The desire for a connection with her screamed through him. *Touch. Share. Join.*

He dropped one knee onto the bed, allowing her to fall back. Cupping her cheek and searching her expressive eyes, he kissed her again, taking a thorough sampling of her mouth. He inhaled her floral scent and reveled in the excited thrust of her tongue as it met his.

Sensing she needed a moment to catch her breath, he drew back and stared at her. There wasn't an ounce of shy and coy in Grace Wenger. He'd known that from the first moment he'd met her along the roadside when her car had been stuck. Once again her features revealed exactly what she was thinking, and her eyes flared with desire.

She tugged at his clothes and then at her own blouse, stripping it off in hurried, frantic movements, as if she were afraid the moment would disappear. He mimicked her actions, removing his shirt as she did hers, followed by his trousers. He was amazed at how effortlessly she unfastened her bra, freeing her breasts to his greedy gaze. Her nipples were the palest rosy pink and jutted into delicious peaks. His gaze followed the curves of hips until his eyes caught on the black lace of her panties.

He swallowed a lump in his throat. Good heavens, it had been so long since he'd been with a woman.

His sex jerked as she slipped the lace down her long legs and cast them to the floor. She moistened her lips as she noticed his fullness.

"You are absolutely stunning," he whispered, still

afraid she'd change her mind and dash beneath the covers.

Her gaze raked over him. "And you're so strong, and…big." She paused, then asked with a shyness he'd never seen in her before, "Do we need to use protection?"

He furrowed his brow in confusion before he realized what she was asking. A condom. Humans used them to guard against disease and pregnancy. "No. Immortals don't have to deal with any of those issues."

She raised one arm up to him. "Mmm, then show me some magic, my immortal Guardian."

With the utmost of care, he lowered himself onto her, pressing the length of his body against hers, savoring the soft, giving push of her breasts against his chest, the flat hollow of her stomach against his skin, the warmth of her welcoming folds against his rigid cock, and the curve of her thigh as she wrapped a leg around one of his.

Ahh, her body felt perfect, absolutely perfect. He forced himself to lie still and memorize every inch of her, because this was too good to be true. And too good to last.

Grace clutched Ian's shoulders, and everything else faded from her mind. At this moment, he was the only person on Earth. She splayed her palms across his powerful physique, traced along his collarbone, then slid down his bulging biceps and back up again to cradle his face.

Such a beautiful, beautiful man.

He tipped his head down, capturing her lips in a long, slow, sultry kiss. His tongue dipped inside her mouth and danced with hers. Little pings rushed through her body like beams of light, shining on all the best parts, awakening and delighting her nerves in a rush of sensation. Her breasts nudged against him firmly, her hips grinding against his.

She moaned at the promised pleasure, and at the sound in her throat, he thrust his tongue deeper, as if trying to fan her whimper into something more. She slid her hands along his torso and around his waist, and she grasped him harder, melding her body to his.

Closer. She needed him even closer.

He drew back from the kiss and shifted slightly so his weight rested on his side as he propped himself on an elbow to gaze at her. Oh, those gorgeous silver eyes. They met hers, and she melted a little more at the hot desire she saw in them.

His body still embraced hers, his ribs grazing hers with each breath, the fine brush of his body hair over her skin exciting her. He brushed a hand over her tummy until he found a breast to knead and savor.

"You're so beautiful," he whispered in a husky voice.

All she could do was groan and arch into his touch.

Then he slid his hand to the vee between her legs. She didn't close her eyes, just watched him watching her. He slid his fingers to her most secret spot and stroked the length of his finger over her swollen bud in long and slow glides. She grew slick and excited under his touch, and she rocked her hips to the rhythm he'd set. When she whimpered again, he eased two fingers into her beckoning channel, unhurriedly, deliberately, drawing out every sensation and response from her body along the way. It took mere strokes to send her crashing over that peak into the ecstasy of quivering pulsations and throbbing vibrations as her muscles convulsed with pleasure.

"I…need…you…now." She enunciated with each thrust of her hips, arching her back.

His response was to lean in and capture a jutting breast with his mouth and suckle.

Mmm, infuriating man. Frustrating man. Talented man.

She came again, harder, drawing his fingers into her.

He drew back. "I adore watching you respond to me."

She licked her dry lips. That was the most amazing

orgasm she'd ever experienced, yet she wanted more. Wanted him inside her in the most intimate way.

She boldly grabbed his cock and skimmed her hand along its hard length. So big and powerful, just like the rest of him. "My turn."

He leaned in for another passionate kiss, allowing her just that slight amount of time to play with him before he repositioned himself over her.

"Not fair," she whined.

"Another time."

She spread her legs to accommodate him and welcomed the full pressure inside as he slipped into her. For a second, he stayed utterly still. His manhood caressed every special place within her. She breathed rapids breaths. It was exquisite. Like nothing she'd ever known.

He groaned deeply, almost a growl, as beads of sweat dotted the skin of his face, his neck, his chest. His eyes glowed with emotion as they met hers, hungry and intense, and then he began to move inside her. He seemed so determined, so controlled, so powerful. *"Tu es à moi."*

With her limited French, she didn't quite know what he'd said, but she was too into feeling to allow her brain to function. His unrushed plunges demanded all her attention. And she gladly obliged, absorbing his thrusts, matching his cadence, scoring his back with her nails, and wrapping her legs around his hips, lifting higher, higher, faster, wilder while heaving breaths and then exploding into another feverish rush of magnificent sensation.

And following the crest of her orgasms, she felt his release.

He tensed over her, his muscular neck and shoulders straining, and after several forceful shudders, he collapsed, taking her with him onto their sides. Curling into each other, arms and legs entwined, he stroked her back lightly.

In her exhaustion, she let him pet her as long as he liked, as she savored the most incredible sex she'd ever had, never quite forgetting that she very well might never experience such again.

Yes, it could all end tomorrow.

The stars remained sharp and vivid on the horizon as Ian rose and slipped from beneath the sheets. Grace stirred. "It's okay. Stay right where you are," he whispered. With the creak of the mattress he leaned down and kissed her lips, then cheek, then nose. "Venn and I have business with the Divine Tree. I shouldn't be long. Go back to sleep."

To his surprise, she laced her hand behind his head, drawing her to him for a deeper kiss. "I'll be waiting," she purred.

"You're wicked, you know that?"

She gave him a sleep-tinged smile.

Though he really didn't want to, he spun on his heel and headed to the bathroom for a quick shower. He paused to glance in the mirror as he ran his hand over the stubble covering his jaw. He didn't look different, but he sure felt it.

He hadn't slept at all during the night. He'd listened to Grace's soft breathing, aware of every dip in the mattress, and her sweet floral scent tying his stomach in knots. A fierce protectiveness settled over him the instant he'd coupled with her. Now more than ever he needed to keep her safe from Death, from harm's way, from illness, from mortal hazards. Grace was somehow in his blood now. The question was, did he allow her to stay there or chase her away?

18

Underneath the massive roots of the Divine Tree, Ian and Venn were perching on the edge of a bench in front of a glowing knot of burl wood as it swirled to life in a three-dimensional display of shades of gold, green, and red.

The last time he'd sat in this spot, World War II had just ended. Very few automobiles rattled along the dusty roads. There had been a Congress of Guardians then. The conclave had been imperative after the death of their brother Euler and his Divine Tree.

Now Venn was parked by his side. He would have never imagined that.

The colors in the circular protrusion whirled faster, blending together until darker hues surfaced forming a clocklike pattern that settled into images of Ian's other brothers, nine more Guardians. The burl served as a huge computer screen and was Custos's communication mode, one they'd had from the start and Ian's only link to his brothers until recent years. The connection moved through the Divine Trees across the earth, circumnavigating the globe like a wind-borne weather pattern, but with lightning speed.

Behind Ian and Venn, tucked into an alcove was a tomb that held his brother Euler, the twelfth Guardian, who along with his Divine Tree had died during Hitler's vicious reign. The tree's death allowed the Dark Realm to unleash the Holocaust.

Disaster and violence followed the Dark Realm's debauchery. Every war and disease, famine and flood, had its roots started in that evil vessel. Millions of lives lost and hopes destroyed. Ian knew well the potential consequence if they didn't adopt a unified front. Death may not be set to kill him or the tree, but if he used information absconded from Custos, well, that could be enough for the black growth of evil to get a solid foothold. It was like the first inch of dirt moving to set off a mudslide. Once it started, it was near impossible to stop.

At once, the image of Njorth, the eldest brother, filled the circle. "I don't believe it," he said from his tree in Colorado. "All of us together. My eyes."

A hand squeezed Ian's heart as his brothers all began speaking at once. It had literally been more than a human lifetime since they'd all been together, even if it was only via the Divine Tree.

"Welcome," Ian said, his voice thick. He closed his hand on Venn's shoulder, glad to at least have one brother here in the flesh. He expelled a long, labored breath.

Another synchronous murmur spread through the space as the brothers shared their intense reactions. Given their unique abilities, Ian knew each could separate and distinguish every word and greeting in the same way sounds of the wind and brook were discernable from the scurry of a squirrel and snap of a twig.

Ian perused his siblings, all strong warriors thrust into modern times. He remembered the fights and brawls of their youths, how their fierce personalities collided—the commander, Njorth, clashing with enforcer Lachlan, and strategist Tristan. Everyone else seemed to choose sides after that, equally dominant in their own way. At least that's how he recalled the brothers of his younger days. So long ago. He sighed.

When the greetings settled, Njorth got straight to business. As much as they were joyous at the reunion, they all knew this sort of gathering meant one thing: something horribly wrong was going down. "What's the problem?"

Venn took the lead. "We've entered the Thousand Days before the Age of Atonement. Seth confirmed as much."

"Why don't the trees know this?" Tristan asked.

"Because the Divine Trees' existence are an internal one. They store and protect information, they don't reach out into the world…unless the world encroaches upon that knowledge," Rurik of England replied.

Aidan filled the screen, his long, dark hair gathered in a queue at his neck. He lived the most isolated existence of them all on an island off Japan. And yet, from what Ian could tell, he employed the most advanced technological equipment as a form of entertainment.

"How is that bedraggled archangel?" Aidan asked. "It's been a long time since I've seen his sorry ass."

"Consider yourself lucky." Venn gave a rueful shake of his head. "Wherever Seth goes, misfortune follows."

"Is he still drooling over the newest cooking shows?" Brandt interjected, his face a healthy bronze from the sunshine in Peru. Like Dustin in Africa and Graham in Australia, Brandt's complexion reflected his life in a warmer climate.

Usually stoic Colby, his tree in India, laughed at the running joke.

"Most likely," Ian said. "He's watching over Venn's place while he's visiting me."

"What? You're together?" Njorth bit out. "I never knew that would be possible. That's a boon for us all."

"Do you think that's wise with the AOA looming on the horizon?" Lachlan asked from Turkey.

Venn shrugged. "Seth is the one who suggested it. He should know the risks better than anyone."

"True," Lachlan admitted, but the hard set of his jaw indicated he wasn't convinced.

Tristan of Russia, stood and paced, occasionally traveling beyond the screen's view before moving back into it again. His shoulders were broader and thicker than Ian recalled. Tristan paused and leaned in closer to the tree's display. "Let's get back to the subject at hand. Explain what's happening there so we know what to expect."

Venn gazed into the knot, summarizing, "A few weeks ago, Io visited me and nearly killed my Divine Tree by using—and somehow twisting—the powers of my mate."

Rurik of England coughed. "What was that? Your mate?"

"You heard correctly."

Rurik jabbed a finger into the sphere. "You owe us an e-mail when we're done here." Moving his hands to his hips, he inhaled deeply, then nodded. "Go on."

"I was a breath away from death," Venn went on, "as was my tree. But thankfully, Emma managed to turn things around. My tree is but a sapling now, though, and is unable to communicate with any of you until it matures."

The fracas that broke across them could have outdone the roar of a jumbo jet engine, not that he'd experience that firsthand, but great pressure waves of sound certainly rolled over him.

"Quiet," Ian demanded.

The roar quieted slowly. When order returned, Ian continued taking the lead. "We're dealing with another issue here in France. Death is on a destructive path. I believe he's trying to save himself before the Atonement begins, beseeching Custos to restore him and return him to human life. This kind of rise in evil is to be expected leading up to Atonement. We need to stop it as best we can, and to prepare for more attacks on the trees. Whenever the Dark Realm succeeds, it will grow that much more powerful. Perhaps even to a point we can't contain it. Venn and I think we'll all be seeing more of the same. Every foul creature out there will be trying to save its ass before the darkness falls."

"Brothers," Venn jumped in, "you must fortify your guard now. One thousand days and we'll be tested like never before."

"I think it's already begun here, too," Aiden said. "A deadly tsunami struck Japan recently."

"Peru suffered an earthquake," Brandt contributed.

"There's an ebola outbreak in Africa," Dustin jumped in. "I didn't see a connection until now, but with all these things happening at once… Well, there's definitely something brewing."

"I had no idea," Ian said.

"We should stay in close contact," Tristan advised. "We should share the nature of such attacks as they happen and watch for other signs that the Dark Realm is gaining power."

The wind howled vigorously, shaking the oak. Ian frowned as he met Venn's gaze. It appeared he wasn't the only one who thought the gust implied more than the weather being bad.

"We need to go," Ian said. "Take close watch, Guardians."

The swirls within the burl wood changed to shades of very deep red, the color of blood. Was Custos trying to give them a sign?

Ian had relished meeting with all his brothers, but now he

was exhausted. Not physically but mentally. He had too much on his plate, as the modern saying went. Venn must have felt it also, because his brother excused himself for a while. To be with his wife, Ian figured.

The novel idea of having someone else to lean on and share life with appealed to Ian. In fact, he was somewhat jealous of Venn. Perhaps that explained his urge to seek out Grace. For the time being, she was his *someone*. He wanted to be with her, even if he couldn't share everything about the Divine Tree.

Although, at the moment, he knew he wasn't the best company. The whole AOA predicament triggered tension he rarely experienced, making him edgy and worried.

The quiet château amplified his unease as he tromped through the halls. With only a few sniffs, he picked up Grace's floral scent, which led him to the veranda. She was lounging in a chair, gazing over the vineyard, as he approached from behind.

He leaned over and planted a quick kiss on her lips. "I have to go to the winery. Would you like to come?"

She smiled up at him. "That would be lovely."

"I should check in with my winemaker, too. Is that too far for you?"

She rolled her eyes playfully. "I walk farther than that in a shopping mall."

He took her hand and held it as they proceeded down the walkway.

"How was your meeting with your brothers?" she asked.

He hesitated at the question, suddenly realizing how much she had already learned about his life. She knew more than any other person with the exception of Bernard, but he was an assistant, summoned to serve by Custos.

He massaged his neck with his free hand. "It went well."

"But you're not happy?"

"The unknown concerns me. There is much more than my vineyard at stake."

"I understand a fear of the future, believe me."

"That's enough talk about me." He pursed his lips, thinking, trying to lighten his attitude and mood. "Tell me, what is it you like most about France?"

"That's an easy one. I love the countryside, the vineyards, and the old buildings. In the States, our buildings don't date back nearly as far."

He enjoyed the dreamy, romantic tone in her voice.

"Because I live here, I overlook that, I suppose," he said.

"Have you ever traveled?" she asked.

"No. Guardians must stay near their Divine Trees. And besides, my vineyard is here. I have no need." Although he wondered if someday…

"Wait. But what about Venn? He is away from his tree."

"True. I guess he's what you call an exception to the rule. It's complicated."

They reached the winery, entered, and he guided her straight to his private rooms. "I'll get a bottle of your favorite."

"How do you know what's my favorite?"

"Your face, *ma chérie*. It tells the story of your life. I see everything here—" he swept the backs of his knuckles lightly around her brow and eyes "—and here." He brushed his lips over hers.

Then he left the room, spoke briefly with his wine master, snagged a bottle of the old wine that had made her eyes sparkle, and returned.

She'd made herself at home, as he knew she would, and had even opened the hidden staircase.

"Can we go up there?"

"Of course." He motioned the way to the elegant tasting room that he'd shown her before but that they hadn't entered.

"I love secret rooms. They…"

She turned sharply and looked at him with eyes full of desire. He set the bottle on the nearest table and pulled her to him. "They what?" he asked.

"They turn me on," she said honestly.

All the pent-up tension in him burst forth. He cupped her head with both his palms and drew her to him in a fierce kiss. A devouring kiss. A consuming kiss.

When he let her go, they were both panting. She reached for the buttons of his shirt and undid them. He kissed her temples and hair as she did so, inhaling her intoxicating fragrance. Then he felt her fingers splay out on his chest, flexing and bending, her nails raking ever so gently over his skin. His bear persona came unleashed, and he returned her play, helping her strip down to her panties.

He growled. She was so damned gorgeous.

"I don't think…" he began.

She rubbed her thumb over his lips and shook her head. "No talking."

He raised a brow but clamped his mouth shut. His jaw flexed as he fought for control as she undid his pants, pushed them down, and freed his manhood, which she stroked along the way.

God, her touch sent his pulse sky-high.

"You said another time," she tormented, fondling him with enjoyment.

"And for once you're following the rules?" he teased, nibbling her ear.

Drawing back, he looked around for a place to take her, noting the long table created from a thick slice of tree coated with polyurethane, its legs a branch of the tree. To one side hung a large mirror over custom-built shelves. The other three walls were covered with wine bottles. The room suited him. But with Grace here, he may have just found his new favorite place.

Kicking his clothes from his ankles, he guided her to

the table. She pushed her bottom lip out when she had to release him, but as soon as she could she was caressing him again.

He went to lift her onto the table, and she placed her hand on his chest and shook her head. With a wicked smile, she leaned over and took him into her mouth, rubbing her tongue up and down the length of him, teasing his tip. With a groan, he tugged her up and raised her bottom, setting her on the tabletop. He kissed her long and hard, and they melded together.

She spread her knees, and he wanted to tell her how beautiful she looked but he couldn't stop. He stepped into the space she'd made for him, tracing kisses along her neck and breasts. She scooted to the edge and welcomed him to enter, which set off a frenzy of pumping and thrusting and grinding until she threw her head back with her orgasm. With a final lunge, he joined her.

Grace curled into Ian, resting her head on his chest. His heartbeat thudded against her ear, so strong and forceful. The waves of pleasure rippled and pulsed in her groin. He was magnificent.

He stroked her back as he'd done before and held her until her body calmed. She lifted her head and found his mouth waiting for her. He kissed her tenderly, then drew back. "Am I allowed to speak now?" he asked in a rugged voice.

She smiled sheepishly. "Yes."

"Then slide back on the table and I'll join you."

For a second, she wondered if it would hold them. He was very big and very solid. But she trusted him to know the limits of the furniture. Yes, she trusted *him*. She inched farther up the table, far enough to allow him room.

He crawled up until his body covered hers. They rested

there, his heart beating against hers. Slowly, languidly, he kissed her once more. This time making love to her with the utmost of care. And she loved him in return.

The following morning, unease still hung over Ian, despite the amazing night he'd had with Grace. Restlessness churned in his gut, and at least half of the feeling had to do with the tug he felt toward her.

After breakfast, she wanted to stroll in the garden, so he escorted her. Death could be anywhere. Ian wasn't sure how close or how far, but he could sense the evil nearby and wasn't going to risk it.

"You seem distracted," she said as she ambled through the garden, admiring and touching the unfurled greenery and smelling the assortment of roses and other white and dark-pink potted flowers. She seemed to have a love for every growing thing. And was it his imagination that the plants perked up when she walked by?

His eagle's gaze fell on a frog poised to catch a fly. The morning unfolded with an eerie stillness as motionless gray clouds pressed down. A sense of unease that remained following the meeting with his brothers left him conflicted.

"You told me you like to shape-shift and run. Maybe you should do that. Sometimes when I exercise, it clears my head."

He glanced at her, knowing it was a good idea.

"Go on," she urged. "I don't mind."

The thought of sharing that part of his life with her proved alluring. He could use a good run, and he should have taken one last night but he'd enjoyed sleeping next to her too much to disturb her. "Perhaps you're right."

He stood, sprinted a few steps, and then transformed into his bear. Leaving her behind, yet not traveling so far as he couldn't hear her or return quickly, he tore between the vines, pushing his muscles hard, traversing every row and then along the perimeter of the property. After ten minutes or so, he headed back, passing by the Divine Tree. There he found Grace, sitting beneath the shade of the oak.

He started to turn away. "Stay," she said. She patted the ground. "Come lie down beside me."

He approached with extremely slow steps. Never had he exposed himself to a human as a Guardian like this before, up close and personal while in animal form. Only Bernard had interacted with him in such a manner.

As he came up beside her, he dropped to his belly, tucking his massive paws beneath him.

"It's okay," she said soothingly.

He rested his head on the ground, and she buried her fingers in his thick fur, then patted and rubbed his head and shoulder. The encounter insinuated a glowing sensation into his heart. He wouldn't say it was love, but it touched his very being in an extraordinary way.

"I needed to be close to Skylar," she admitted. She ran her hand down his forearm with long strokes. Reaching under his chest, she pulled out his paw and examined it, comparing its size to her small hand. Finally, she stood. "Venn and Emma should be awake now. We should head back."

He rose and walked along beside her. *A woman and her bear,* he thought.

Exiting the vines, he changed back into his human form. When they reached the garden again he urged her to pause and face him. Drawing her into his arms, he kissed her soundly. "Thank you."

"Anytime." She returned to fussing over the plants.

He and Grace had finished breakfast hours earlier by the time Venn and Emma got up. While his brother and his wife ate, Ian regarded Grace. He enjoyed watching her as she wound in and around the plants, sometimes bending to sniff a flower, her round bottom jutting upward in the most provocative manner. He suppressed a growl, resisting the urge to steer her back to his bedroom.

The layers of life confounded him the way the good and the bad existed at the same time. The Dark Realm threatened to take everything he loved, and at the same time, everything he loved was right here. His to protect.

She glanced over her shoulder, her smiling eyes meeting his. A crash of desire rolled through him. He set down his coffee, then trekked to her with long, quick strides.

She reached her hand out to him and he took hold of it. Oh, Christ, he was so attracted to her he hated letting her out of his sight. He could watch her for hours.

"You should have been a gardener," he said.

"Plants have a language all their own. I love it."

"They speak to you, huh?"

"Sometimes." She continued her stroll, moving away from him, humming a tune he didn't recognize.

He stayed put, allowing her room to roam, while still keeping an eye on her. His hands flexed and arms longed to wrap around her. After last night, he was being more cautious than ever. The reaper could be lurking behind the next tree.

He blew a heavy rush of air from his lungs, releasing tension.

A breeze gusted and flipped Grace's hair into her face. She peered at him across the flowers. Her eyes seemed to give him that "come here" look again. His feet moved without thought. Then, inexplicably, her gaze changed to one of a faraway look and she collapsed onto the bed of flowers. Her body twitched and thrashed.

"Grace!" With a stab of fear hitting him square in the chest, he took several leaps over the flowers, crushing the delicate plants beneath his boots in his frantic effort to reach her. "Grace!"

Venn and Emma must have seen what had happened because the next thing he knew, they were right beside him.

"She's having a seizure," Emma said.

"Yes," Ian uttered, his throat so dry he couldn't swallow. "How can I help her?"

"Gently turn her on her side so she won't choke," Emma advised and leaned over to help. "She'll come out of it."

He stared at her, anxious, a heavy hand clutching his heart. "Surely there must be something more I can do!"

Venn bent over them. "Slide her away from those rocks so she doesn't hit herself on them."

Instead Ian tossed the heavy granite boulders aside as if they were made of papier-mâché. He took hold of Grace's shoulders and carefully turned her so her head wouldn't strike anything and she wouldn't choke on her saliva. Her muscles tightened and jerked beneath his palms. It killed him not to be able to make this stop, or to at least scoop her up into his arms. When she was situated in a safe position, he rested his weight on his heels. "How long does this last?"

"I'm not an expert, but it shouldn't be much longer," Emma replied. But she was eying Grace worriedly.

Ian growled a horrible, wrenching sound. Venn grasped his shoulder and squeezed, as if his brother understood something Ian himself didn't.

Finally, the seizure ended. Grace curled her legs up into a fetal position.

"What happened?" she whispered, her expression confused as she stared up at the three people hovering over her. She frowned. "I... I had another seizure, didn't I?"

Grace eased to her elbows. The disorientation she

always experienced following a seizure was gradually fading. She blinked several times. Oh God, she'd just had a second episode since she'd been here. This was much too frequent. Usually they happened every ten weeks or so. She tamped down the scary thought as to what that meant.

Ian's brow lifted. "Let's get you inside."

"No." She sat, stretching her sore muscles. "I'll be fine in a minute." She arched her back and rotated her head from side to side.

"How long have you had those? Do you have them often?" Ian asked, his handsome face drawn and his dark brows pinched in concern.

Grace hesitated, wondering if she should tell them the truth. "They're recent," she lied, deciding that was the best tact considering she'd be leaving here soon and probably never seeing them again. Why make them worry?

She began to stand and Ian offered his hand, effortlessly pulling her to her feet. When he slipped an arm around her, she leaned against him. The sheer strength and power of him poured into her. Her ribs expanded and contracted in a controlled sigh.

"I'm fine. I have seizures sometimes," she admitted.

"Should we take you to a doctor?" Emma asked.

"That's not necessary."

Ian's spine straightened, seeming to grab on to the notion. "Wait. Perhaps we should. Emma, is that what you think?" He looked at Grace as he added, "I'm not used to dealing with mortal ailments, but I want to be safe."

"There is nothing they can tell you," Grace said.

"Do you have a walk-in clinic?" Emma asked Ian, ignoring Grace.

"Didn't you hear me? I'm okay."

Venn crossed his arms over his chest, seeming bemused as he took in his wife. "Apparently not."

Emma glared at him. "Look, you boys are immortal.

Grace is not." She turned to Grace. "I think we should have you checked out."

Grace took a step forward, forcing the three around her to open their protective circle and allow her to move to the walkway. Ian's hand never left her waist. She discovered she enjoyed his closeness despite the direction of the conversation. It was comforting.

"Are you on any medication? It can often control the seizures," Emma said.

"Not in my case." Grace looked each of them in the eye, hoping they'd drop it. "I'm good. Really. We were going to the vineyard, right? So if you're finished with breakfast, let's go." She tried to insert energy into her voice.

Ian had remained silent long enough that she felt the need to twist to search out his face. His lips were pressed together, his brow drawn down. *Oh great.* He was going to take a stance on this.

Ian and Venn seemed to share something with their eyes, a message of some sort, something she couldn't comprehend. To her dismay, the intimate tone of the morning had been broken, replaced by tension.

"Look. It's over," she said. "The best way to deal is to move on."

"I'll be right back with the vehicle," Ian announced.

Seriously? He wasn't going to listen to her about her own body?

"I don't need to see a doctor," Grace said adamantly. But he still just tromped across the ground without comment. "Emma, come on," she said, trying to appeal to the fellow female in the group.

"I'm sorry, but I agree with Ian." Emma tilted her head, and her auburn hair covered her eye. She brushed it away. "I recently lost my grandmother as a result of some weird stuff, so I don't take anything for granted anymore. There are things the Guardians deal with that we can't imagine. Maybe they can have a deadly effect on humans. I don't know." She flipped a hand in the air.

"Like a reaper?" Grace questioned, hugging herself.

"Exactly," Venn chimed in.

"It wouldn't take long to get checked out by a doc," Emma said.

Grace looked down at her feet. They were all against her. She knew they were trying to help, but it was frustrating. She didn't want to tell them why she was having seizures. She didn't want them to feel sorry for her. She didn't want for them to look at her differently. She didn't want for them to find out the real reason she was here…to try to save herself from dying.

Ian pulled up in the car then. He came around, opened the door, and waited. "Do want to ride into town or stay here?" he asked Venn.

Emma answered for him. "We'll tag along. You don't have a clue when it comes to human medical situations, remember?"

Again, Emma had made the distinction between human and immortal, and this time it penetrated Grace's brain, making her realize just how different they were.

With reluctance, she slid into the front seat. She shot Ian a steely glare as he shut the door. This sucked.

Ian glanced at her with worried silver eyes. "Are you okay?"

"Of course. I'm not going to flop like a fish again right here." Yet even as her frustration rose at his overreaction, his concern made downy warmth spread in her chest. She was falling for an immortal who was way out of her league. Oh, how she wanted to see if what she felt was more than one night's passionate lovemaking, to test where this growing affection for him could go. On the other hand, she knew they had no future.

But was he *the one*?

She was running out of time to find out.

19

Patience was not one of Death's stronger attributes. In fact, he had zero tolerance for waiting and watching. He was a creature of action, he thought with a snicker. *Take a life…with a knife.* Now that was something to write home about.

So watching the foursome eat, and talk, and socialize, and blah, blah, blah was almost enough to send him off a cliff and back to the fiery gates. Almost.

And those lovebirds were going at it every other minute they were alone. He wondered if Ian sensed that the sound of them banging the headboard and moaning turned him on. It made him imagine all the fucking he'd do once he was mortal again.

The more he thought about it, the angrier he got at the unfairness of it all. Here they were, immortal and living like kings, while all he got was a hot ass while he roasted in hell. Rage ignited within him, and he jabbed the end of his scythe deep into the earth. That Ian and Venn were fawning over Grace and her illness made him grind his teeth, too. It was like pouring alcohol on a wound, reminding him of another reason to force the Divine Tree to cough up the secret to making him human again.

Fed up with just sitting around waiting, he transformed into a vulture and flew south looking for a victim. He noticed the Dubois family in their sedan, turning off their drive and onto the winding road to town. Little Maely and her brother were in the backseat arguing.

Perhaps today was his lucky day, after all.

The silence in the car amplified Venn's thoughts and doubts as he drove. He could hear the leaves falling off the trees as they passed, with a rustle and whish of wind. Grace's seizure had scared the hell out of him.

Why did you have feelings for her to begin with? He scolded himself.

He shouldn't. Period. A woman in his life wasn't for him, dammit. They all left whether they wanted to or not.

He glanced at Grace. She turned her face away from him and stared out the window.

"I think I should go home tomorrow," she said. "There's nothing I can do for Skylar now if your tree won't help me. There's no reason to hang around at this point."

Emotion hit him square in the chest. He ignored it. Wasn't this what he'd been pushing for since the beginning? For her to leave well enough alone?

The gas pedal felt good beneath his foot. He pressed down harder, savoring the moment of control over something. Then it struck him, he couldn't allow her to leave. She knew too much about the tree.

"There are complications now," he said. "We'll discuss options when we return."

Ahead, a sedan became visible in the distance. As he

got closer, he recognized the car as belonging to Maely's family. Suddenly, the dark-blue vehicle swerved left, then right. It veered sharply off the road, out of control, then it stopped with several forceful, irregular jerks.

He slammed on the brakes, and the four doors of his Mercedes opened almost simultaneously.

Madame Dubois leaped out of the passenger door of their car. "Help me. My husband! You must help him!" she cried hysterically.

"What happened?" Ian asked as they rushed toward her.

"We were going to the village. All of a sudden he looked at me, gave a heavy grunt, and collapsed on the steering wheel." Madame Dubois words tumbled out in a panic. "I had to steer the car. I barely managed to get to the brake in time. The children…"

"You did a great job," Grace said, maintaining a calm tone. The children in the backseat watched her with round, frantic eyes.

Madame Dubois shuddered. "I think he's had a heart attack."

Ian opened the car door, and Monsieur Dubois slumped toward him. Venn stepped up and helped Ian get the man out and onto the ground. They exchanged a look. Their extraordinary senses told them both the same thing: *No heartbeat. Not breathing.*

At the same time, Maely came running around the car. "You must save Papa! You must!"

"We need to start CPR," Grace said in a shaky voice, even though she was obviously trying to hide it. "And we need to call emergency services." She pushed Venn aside. Kneeling, she tilted Monsieur Dubois's head back.

Ian noticed a brownish-red spot on the guy's neck. What was that? He focused, his heartbeat speeding up when he saw that the mark was in the shape of a crescent. It was faint and could be mistaken for a mole, but it wasn't. No, it was a reaper's mark, the mark of death. Ian's gaze darted about in search of the death angel.

Not finding the monster, he glanced to Emma as she comforted the children and Madame Dubois. The muscles along his back stiffened. He and Venn should get them to a safer place.

Grace overlapped her hands and placed them on Dubois's chest. She started pushing on him, using her weight in rhythmic compressions. Ian felt wretched that her effort probably wouldn't make a difference.

"Did you call?" she asked as she worked.

Ian checked his phone. "No service," he said, not surprised.

"When I tell you to, pinch his nose and breathe into his mouth, hard. It will force air into his lungs," she explained.

Ian was shocked at the way his free-spirited sprite took charge, so determined to save him. He knew of CPR but had no use for it, really. His job was guarding and saving the tree, not people.

She did about thirty compressions, then paused. "Breathe now. Twice."

He did, then rested back on his heels. She began the sequence again. Little Maely and her brother moved closer. Emma wrapped an arm around each child, pulling them against her. Madame Dubois looked on with the back of her hand pressed to her trembling lips.

They all watched as he and Grace worked. Ten minutes turned into fifteen with not even the slightest blip of the man's heart.

Monsieur Dubois was *not* coming back. Ian set his jaw and subtly shook his head. Madame Dubois let out a muffled shriek, and Maely burst forward.

"Nooo! Papa can't die." The child threw herself onto her father. Then she pulled back and stroked his cheek. "We'll take you to the oak, Papa. It will be all right." She looked to Ian, her eyes round and brimming with tears.

"We have to take him there. The tree will know what to do."

Ian's gaze met Venn's. His brother's expression communicated precisely what he'd expected: no matter how much he wanted to help this family, what Maely was asking simply was against the rules. "Custos won't be able to help, *petit agneau.*"

"Please," she begged. "We have to try."

Grace rested her palm on his arm. "What would it hurt to give it a shot?"

Maely grabbed hold of his hand then, her tiny fingers not even spanning his burly knuckles. "Please, Monsieur Hearst, please," she sobbed. "I would even go back to being sick if the tree would spare Papa."

Ian blinked. Why were his eyes wet? Why did looking at Grace and Maely make his chest tight? Why was he so tempted to concede?

Grace folded her arms over her chest with a demanding look in her eyes, clearly getting frustrated.

"It won't change a thing," Ian whispered to her. "Just because we *can* do it doesn't mean we should."

Grace stood, ignoring him. "Venn, help Ian get Monsieur Dubois in the car."

With immense hesitation, Ian joined Venn, placing Dubois in the family's sedan. He swallowed, not wanting to give this family false hope but wanting so much to help. "Drive the Mercedes back to the château," he told Grace. "You may all wait there while we see what we can do."

She must have realized how far she could push him, because she nodded, swept the family into the Mercedes, and followed him.

The last thing he saw as he drove away were Maely's imploring eyes looking out the window at him.

The anxiety lodged in Grace's chest reminded her of

packed dirt, so dense and hard even a spade couldn't break through. What was going on? Ian hadn't actually said so, but she suspected this was the reaper's doing.

"I'll drive," Emma insisted.

Grace conceded, knowing that she shouldn't be driving at all, especially so soon after having an episode. Though she felt fairly certain she wouldn't have another one so soon after the previous.

When they reached the château, she hastily escorted the Dubois family inside and turned them over to Bernard's care. She pulled the man aside and explained what she could of the circumstances. "I'm going to meet Ian at the tree," she added.

As she rushed for the exit, Maely flew over, grabbing hold of her hand. "I want to come, too."

"No, honey. Stay here with your maman."

A maturity far beyond her years eclipsed the girl's face. "I've been through this. I can help."

Grace couldn't see how, but the child did indeed have history with the tree. What would it hurt to take her?

Searching Maely's eyes, Grace relented. "Okay."

She shared the plan with the girl's mother to make sure it was all right. Madame Dubois was in such a state of shock, though, that Grace could have probably said she was taking Maely to Mars and would have gotten the same glassed-over stare and "whatever, I don't care" head shake. She turned to the son, who seemed to mature before her eyes as he consoled his mother.

"You're such a smart young man," Grace said to the boy.

He almost pulled off a firm, manly nod. But his eyes told the truth: he was frightened beyond words.

Bernard placed a hot beverage in front of mother and son. "I'll look after them," he said to Grace.

Outside, Grace paused for a second. Should she travel to the tree by foot or take the Mercedes? The car would be a lot quicker. She opened the back door for Maely. "Climb in."

Again, Emma assumed the role of chauffeur, easing behind the wheel. The simple act reminded her of Skylar. Her heart squeezed as anger, pain, and hurt swam inside her.

Dammit! She wouldn't allow Death to win!

Emma drove between the rows of vines, following the path Ian had taken in the Dubois' sedan. The car rocked back and forth over the uneven ground. On the right, the terrain sloped sharply toward the next row of vines on a slightly lower terrace of ground, making Grace a little uneasy that the car could slip off the makeshift path the maintenance vehicles traveled. But she assured herself that if Ian could manage it, so could they.

Ian and Venn knelt beside Monsieur Dubois. They had been discussing their options: take the man inside the tree where the tree of life may have the knowledge to revive him or deliver him to the morgue. So far, Custos had been of no help.

The rumble of a car engine made him turn his head. It stopped, and he heard the triple sounds of doors slamming closed. Dammit, he'd given them explicit instructions to wait at the château.

His body wrestled with his brain—attraction versus common sense. His beasts taking sides with his hormones. Ian released a growl.

"Why do you do that?" Grace asked.

She caught him off guard. "Do what?"

"Make that sound."

"It's the bear and the hawk getting verbal."

"Oh."

"This doesn't look like the château to me, by the way," he said chidingly. "What are you doing here?"

She knelt down beside him and leaned in close so Maely wouldn't hear. "Because I'm dying, too. In fact, I could very well be next. And Maely might be the key I need to change my fate."

Something slammed into him, as if the wind were being knocked out of him. He couldn't draw a breath. He drew back, searching her eyes. She had seizures, but what was this she was talking about dying?

"Monsieur Hearst," Maely interrupted before he could ask, "he's resting on the wrong spot. You need to move him over there on the roots." Maely pointed off to the side.

Ian had a difficult time shifting his thoughts. His mind was still fixated on Grace and what she'd just told him.

But Grace and Emma didn't hesitate. They grabbed the man's upper arm, ready to do their part in moving him. Venn and Ian supported the man's other limbs and they shifted Dubois so his torso was draped over the tree roots.

Maely nodded. "That's good." She gave a little-girl sigh. Then she walked over to the oak and placed her small hand on the bark. "You need to touch it, too," she said to Grace.

Grace gave him an innocent look, almost as if saying to him, *How can I resist?* She came around to stand opposite of Maely.

"Custos, please, Papa needs your help."

The tree remained silent.

"Please. I know you can save him," Maely begged, tears streaming down her cheeks. "Monsieur Hearst, maybe you should add your hand to the tree," she suggested through her sobs.

Ian and Venn peered at each other, bewildered, then looked at Emma. Kindness shone in her eyes as she said,

"You, better than any of us, know how it is with Divine Trees."

The two Guardians nodded and then all joined the vigil.

Ian knew his tree, though. It was inclined to go into a deep slumber, sometimes for days or weeks or months at a time. He couldn't fathom why Custos would do so now, with the harvest about to begin and with Death about and the Atonement coming so soon. He wondered at the silence. Perhaps this situation was beyond the scope of the Divine Tree.

Ian gave the tree a hearty shove with his hand, hard enough that the leaves shook slightly over their heads.

Guardian, there are other things to consider in this, Custos whispered in a deep rumble that only Ian and Venn could here.

Ian drew taller, his senses sharper. *She thinks you can save him.*

It is always an unknown, the tree replied.

Maely grew quiet and tipped her head. She looked straight at Ian. "The tree speaks to you, doesn't he? You hear him even now."

Grace's gaze shot from the child to Ian. He sensed something in Maely but couldn't put his finger on it. "The oak and I communicate, yes. It's part of my job as Guardian."

"Bring the father unto me." Custos spoke aloud this time so all could hear. "Child, go home, and have faith."

Maely instantly dropped her hand. "I will," she said with quiet determination. Without another word, she trotted toward the car, paused to glance over her shoulder, and waved Grace to follow.

As if with the change of the breeze, the tension dissipated. Grace seemed somewhat confused as she glanced at him. He couldn't blame her. He wasn't sure what was going on, either. But they assumed their roles, she and Emma escorting Maely back to the château, and he and Venn tending to Monsieur Dubois. He prayed they would all be safe and that the outcome would be a good one.

Ian hoisted the man onto his shoulder. "This way," he said to Venn.

When the women were safely in the car, he glided through the porthole into the oak. Venn fixed the lights so they could find their way down into the catacombs. When they reached the lower chamber, Ian deposited Dubois near Sklyar.

"This is crazy," Venn commented.

"Yeah... Our problems are multiplying."

Venn shook his head. "No. The oak is becoming more like a tomb than a tree of life."

It took a moment or two for her new predicament to sink in: the Dubois' vehicle blocked their way out and she didn't have the keys. The silence of the vineyard pressed on her, and the muscles along her neck and shoulders clenched. There was no telling how long Ian would be.

Grace met Emma's gaze. With the single-lane access, they either had to wait for Ian to move the car or put the Mercedes in reverse and back out the way we came. Which was a hell of a long way to negotiate backward. "Do you think you can do it?"

Emma looked back and nodded resolutely. "Sure."

"Is your seat belt buckled?" Grace asked Maely.

"Oui."

"Driving in reverse a long distance is not my forte," Emma said worriedly. After putting the car in reverse, Emma braced her right hand on the console, looking over her shoulder as she steered with her left. Easing her foot off the brake, the Mercedes rolled slowly backward. "I can do this."

From the passenger seat, Grace flashed a warm smile. "Of course you can."

Emma's face warmed with embarrassment. "Thanks."

Trying the gas pedal, she gave it fuel and the car picked up speed. She chewed her lower lip as the tires tugged her off course when she hit bumps and clumps of dirt.

Only about a mile to go.

Out of nowhere, something dropped in their path. It was huge and black as night. Emma gasped and slammed on the brakes.

Grace tipped her head to see better. Whatever it was moved unnaturally quick. "The reaper."

Maely jumped. "Where?" Her voice rang with fear.

Grace grimaced because she'd said that aloud. She hadn't meant to scare the girl. "Forward. Forward," she screamed to Emma.

Emma frantically tried to shift into drive, only managing to get it caught in neutral when the front passenger door jerked open, ripped right off its hinges. Death cast it aside as if it weighed nothing.

Oh God. Oh God. Oh God.

Her hand slapped against the seat belt buckle, fumbling at the latch. She glanced sideways, hoping to find Ian there, too, but instead, she stared into evil, endlessly black eyes. He was in human skin, almost handsome with bony cheekbones and a tapered chin, but it was merely a mask.

His lips curled into a sneer. "Gotcha."

His scythe descended.

"Maely, run!" she cried as the blade snared the strap covering her breastbone, precisely cutting the seat belt in two, freeing her. As she scrambled in the opposite direction, she was aware of Maely hustling out the back door on the other side of the car.

Good. Perhaps she would get away. Plus, Emma was helping the child.

A hand, unnaturally long and spindly, reached through the doorway and clutched her arm in a viselike grip. She tried desperately to escape but to no avail. Death dragged her to him.

"Let go of me," she screamed, landing a foot to his shin and a knee to his groin. He didn't even flinch. She clawed his face. "I'll scar you for life."

"And therein lies the problem... I have no life." He tucked her into the crook of his arm and carried her like a football around the back of the car. Then he was running after Maely and Emma, hauling Grace along with him.

He snatched Emma by the hair, gave it a jerk that seemed to render her unconscious, and then dragged her back to the car where he stuffed her in the trunk. All with one arm, all with little effort, all with vicious intent.

Grace couldn't even tell how he'd gotten the thing open, her main thought—he was stronger than she remembered. How was that? She fished through her knowledge of paranormal beings. With some, evil deeds fueled them. Did his kills make him more resilient, more powerful?

Still, she wouldn't give up. They had to get away.

She craned her neck to see in front of her, hoping the little girl was gone. But Maely must have injured herself during her retreat, for she was hobbling with a limp that slowed her down. With several enormous strides, the reaper closed the distance and snagged the child.

To Grace's horror, the fiend had one arm snuggly wrapped around each of them at the rib cage. He squeezed so they couldn't scream, couldn't even draw a breath. It seemed so effortless.

Maely's large blue eyes searched Grace's, as if asking, *What now?* Grace tried for a comforting smile to ease the girl's fear, even though she couldn't breathe, either, even though she was terrified herself, even though she was most certainly going to die today.

Grace fought with everything she had, jabbing her elbows into his torso. She kicked furiously as her panic rose. But his grip never loosened. The pressure on her ribs just grew. She couldn't expand her lungs even the tiniest fraction. She looked over at Maely. The little girl was passed out.

Is this it? she wondered. Was the last thing she saw to be a row of Ian's wilted, sick grapevines?

Can't breathe.

A veil of darkness descended as her eyes closed.

20

Death could have howled with joy. That is, if he could have felt that jubilant emotion. Which he couldn't. Oh, he remembered what those wonderful feelings were like—the sweet satisfaction of a superb cut of prime rib, the warm mellow glow of winning a card game, and the pleasurable burn after screwing some bitch out of her mind.

But that had been a damned long time ago and even the memories were fading. In his condemned-to-hell state, all he was able to experience was pain, or the absence of it. The hurt coursed through him at different degrees, like hot and cold water in a water pipe. Fucking boring, usually.

But right now he figured he was fire-hose material—all pressure and snap.

After rendering the females unconscious, he'd brought them to his makeshift quarters at an ancient, dilapidated, underground building on the outskirts of Ian's property. He had Grace and the girl locked up in the room next door so he didn't have to look at them and resist the temptation of killing them now.

He chortled to himself. They were his bargaining chips. A little demonstration to drive home just how serious he was, and make them see that he would stop at nothing until he was reinstated in his human form once more. The tree knew how to accomplish the task; of that Death was certain. It simply needed a little persuasion.

Frankly, he was looking forward to the big reveal. What was the secret formula? Would the Divine Tree perform some magic spell?

Whatever. As long as he got what he needed, it didn't matter. Otherwise, Grace and Maely would suffer excruciating pain. And the blame…the blame would rest with Ian Hearst.

Venn rubbed the back of his neck as he looked down at Dubois and Skylar, then turned to Ian. "I think we're delaying the inevitable."

"Hush," Ian whispered. "Did you hear that?" He snapped his head around, listening for the sound that came from far off, aboveground.

Venn jerked up, straightening his back. "A scream?"

The brothers scrambled for the aboveground entrance. As they exited the porthole, their feet striking firm ground, they shape-shifted almost simultaneously. Wolf and bear sprinted side by side framed by more and more dying vines until they came upon the abandoned Mercedes where they shifted back to human form.

"Grace?" Ian shouted, not quite sure what was going on.

Silence.

Ian called on the homing skills animals naturally possessed, even in his human form his sense of smell and hearing were sharp and acute. They split up as they approached the front of the vehicle. He checked the ground and sniffed the air, worried since the scents were detectable, but not strong. No, not nearly as robust as they should be.

Panic seized Ian's chest when he saw the car door ripped from the vehicle, the metal a twisted clump among the vines. The work of Death, he had no doubt. Oh fuck.

Venn halted, a growl tearing from his throat when he arrived at the trunk. His muscles tensed. He didn't budge but for a miniscule tilt of his head and the flare of his nostrils. Ian recognized he was following a scent.

In a move far more frenzied than what he'd been doing seconds ago, Ian's brother clawed at the trunk and punched the clasp in frantic repetition. "She's in here. Emma! Emma, I'm coming!"

Ian dashed to the driver's side and popped the trunk release. Through the rear windshield, he glimpsed the hood angle up. Then he ran back to see, hoping beyond hope that Grace and Maely were also there—and that he'd find them alive.

Venn lifted a limp Emma from the well of the trunk, cradling her in his arms. He gave a sharp exhale of breath and buried his face in the crook of her neck, choking out a sob. When he pulled back, his eyes brimmed with tears.

"Is she…?"

"Breathing," Venn said.

"It was the reaper." Ian stated what they both knew. "Nothing else could have done this."

"Agreed. And for whatever reason, he didn't kill her. Thank God."

Ian sighed in relief for Venn and Emma. It would have been awful if something happened to them on his watch. However, his own fear for Grace and Maely twisted like a tornado inside him.

"What was I thinking?" Ian tipped his head back,

allowing self-loathing to settle over him. "I shouldn't have left them alone."

"Don't panic," Venn said as he curved Emma tighter against his chest. "They might have gotten away on foot."

"Or Death has taken them somewhere else."

Ian's emotions felt like a wine cellar during an earthquake, with bottles crashing and breaking and sending shards of glass in every direction—some piercing his heart. "Look for signs of where they went."

Ian instantly changed to eagle form to look around from above. Venn trod a loop around the vehicle.

Emma moaned. She blinked her eyes several times before actually looking at Venn. "Where are they?" she whispered hoarsely.

"I don't know," Venn managed to somehow get out. "They're gone."

Ian flew in a circle. Ian and Grace and Maely were nowhere in sight. He could easily make out Emma and Venn below.

Emma tried to rise from Venn's arms. Her gaze swept the area as if she didn't believe him. "The reaper struck me. That's the last I remember."

"I'll make him die a dozen times over," Venn ground out.

Ian landed returning to human form. "After me, brother."

"I'm sorry. I don't know anything. Before I knew it, I was unconscious. The last thing I remember, Grace and Maely were running," Emma said.

Ian scanned the area again, looking for some sign of what had transpired and which direction he'd taken them. If he'd carried them off, then he'd had to travel by foot. Near the lower tier of vines, the ground was gouged. It seemed as if someone had scrambled to get away, only to be dragged back, fighting. Three sets of prints turned into one.

Where would Death have taken them? Ian inhaled for a scent of Grace.

"I'm going to take Emma to the house," Venn announced. "Then I'll catch up with you."

"I think he headed south."

Ian transformed as muscles and tendons popped and enlarged and reshaped into a powerful bear. *The better to hunt down a monster.*

He followed the single scent lingering on the grasses— the stench of old blood. *Death.* The evil creature made no effort at all to camouflage his trail. Which meant he wanted—and expected—Ian to follow him.

Grace's eyelids felt as though they had elephants sitting on them. She raised her brows in an effort to open them, seeing through the merest slit. Then with greater effort, her view widened to take in the dim, cave-like structure.

She was immediately transported back to the memory of her first MRI, when she'd declared she wasn't claustrophobic with cavalier certainty only to realize, moments later, that she wouldn't be able to withstand the crushing closeness. Her heartbeat thudded in her ears now as it had then, her palms growing moist and one of her fists pressing against her chest. Only this time she couldn't tap out. Struggling for control, Grace inhaled a long, calming breath and let it out.

Then she felt Maely's limp body pressed against her arm.

Grace coughed, flinched, blinked. The child was still alive. The pale-pink color of her cheeks and warmth of her skin, slight as it was, told her that much. But the little girl remained out cold.

Not a bad thing.

Rotating her head a little bit, her gaze swept the dim room. Where were they? The place smelled of stale, damp earth—musty, kind of reminding her of mushrooms. On the other side of the room, a single candle flickered. Light danced and swirled over walls constructed of rock and mud.

Please let this place be on the winery grounds. Please let Ian be close by. Please let him find us before it's too late.

Her eyes adjusted to the darkness, and she realized she could make out a few details. They seemed to be in the back corner of the room, and a narrow doorway let in a hint of sunlight.

Grace swallowed and tried to scratch her nose—it itched from the moldy odor—but she couldn't move her hands. They were tied securely behind her. She squinted, trying to make out what held her as it seemed to drape off to the side. Not metal. No, the binding seemed like rope, or a vine, she realized.

For a second she considered if they could be inside Ian's oak tree. Given the state of her surroundings, the idea repulsed her. Could Custos be working with the reaper? The tree hadn't helped Skylar and wouldn't even let Grace see Skylar's body.

A shadow of a figure altered the faint glow of the candlelight as the air moved slightly. She held her breath.

"I know you're awake." From the shadows, Death's gravelly voice grated on her nerves. Every night terror she'd ever had as a child flashed through her mind as if he'd had some control over that. She pressed her spine against the hard, rough stones and, with fierce determination, shut him out of her head.

It worked. Her heart rate began to calm.

The reaper howled in anger.

"Let us go," she said, "and maybe Ian won't kill you."

A nasty laugh echoed through the chamber, reverberating off the walls. Involuntarily, her feet moved, digging into the earth. They didn't realize there was nowhere else to escape.

Maely stirred. Grace could tell the moment the child came fully awake for her thin arm twined around Grace's, which meant if she was bound, it was in a different manner.

"I want to go home," Maely said unhappily.

"I know, sweetie. Me too." She didn't have a clue how she was going to thwart this spawn of the devil. She only knew she had to. Somehow.

Death's skeletal shape stole in and out of the light. Maely cringed and leaned closer. Grace bit her lip in thought, then taunted, "Why don't you go fetch Ian? I'm certain you'd love to rub his failings in his face. I mean, you did seem to take us right from under his nose."

"I did, didn't I?"

There was a long silence. The scrape of dirt beneath footfalls indicated the reaper moved closer, but she couldn't make out anything, not a glimpse of bones or movement of clothing.

Without warning, a gaunt hand gripped her throat and pinned her head against the rock behind her. The lightning strike of adrenaline zinging through her chest hit her breastbone in a surge of pain.

"Don't toy with me," Death ground out, moving his face closer to hers.

Her gag reflex worked as his foul breath fanned over her cheek. Blessedly, she couldn't see those cold eyes. "Wouldn't dream of it," she croaked.

He held on to her longer, his skeletal fingers digging into the tender flesh of her neck. Air became scarce as his grip tightened.

Why had he brought her here just to kill her? *No*. There had to be another reason.

Abruptly, he released her, and she sucked in precious air.

Seeming pleased with himself, he spun around and exited.

Maely stroked a delicate hand against Grace's face, and as she did, Grace drifted back from the dreadful place she'd been, a place so close to death.

21

As Ian tore down the vineyard rows, the earth shook beneath the weight of his bear's great paws. He came to a crossroad of scents, halted, and lifted his snout. Swinging his head left, then right, and back, he sniffed. Death had traversed this intersection of vines many times. His stench was everywhere. To separate out the most recent trail, though, was key.

In bear form, Ian's sense of smell was more than two thousand times better than a human's, yet somehow the scents were jumbled. What game was Death playing?

Ian paced, then held himself utterly still, tamping down his fear and digging deep, trusting the skills he knew he possessed but hadn't needed to rely on for centuries.

Then it came to him, he had to go beyond the immediate perimeter, expand the boundaries past his estate. He should be able to capture Grace's scent for many, many miles; all he had to do was reach out. With renewed effort, he loped outside the labyrinth the reaper had created, then inhaled. From far away, her sweet floral bouquet drifted to him. It was laced with the pungent aroma of fear.

As he followed her scent, he wondered if he could bluff his way out of this and convince Death that Grace didn't matter to Ian and force the reaper to play his hand.

To imagine her terrified, injured, and dying summoned the beast within him. Rage, hot and vicious, filled every fiber of his being. He plowed through the vines and leaped over the earth in massive strides until he came to a screeching halt.

Death blocked the path.

Ian rose to a hulking stance on his hind legs and snarled, fierce and low. Peeling back his thick lips, he flashed sharp fangs, ready to tear the reaper apart. But Death stood his ground as he raised his scythe.

"Guardian, halt," he bit out.

Ian had no choice but to obey. Besides, he was dying to know what the plan was here. Dying... *right,* he scoffed. The hilarity of the thought wasn't lost on him. He returned to his human state simply for the pleasure of facing the reaper man to man, asking, "Do you have the balls to kill a Guardian?"

"Ha! Your soul doesn't interest me."

"That's good. Because you can't have it."

Death laughed. "Cocky bastard." He lowered the blade to angle it in front of his thin, lanky frame. "I want what only a Divine Tree can give me... the recipe for life."

Ian forced himself to scoff. "Good luck with that."

"And you're going to help me get it."

"Not. A. Chance."

"You will if you want the woman and girl."

Ian's hands closed into tight fists. "Harm them and hell will seem like a fucking picnic."

Death laughed in his face.

Ian stretched tall, a solid mass rooted in place. Obviously, the reaper didn't detect the extent of the relationship between Guardian and Divine Tree. Otherwise he'd have changed tactics.

"Here's the deal. You get me the formula on how I can become flesh and blood, alive once more"—Death's voice grew excited at the prospect—"and I give you back your measly humans."

Inwardly, Ian cringed at the thought of Death near Grace even for a second. "Amazing how you insult the very thing you long to be."

The reaper shrugged. "I don't intend to remain small and meaningless."

"Take me to the females," Ian ordered.

With a flick of his wrist, Death retracted his scythe into a small, fork-sized rod. Son of a bitch, Ian had never seen the soul collector do that before; didn't even know it was possible.

The new trick caused tension to twist along his spine one vertebra at a time until his neck seized. Beads of sweat dotted his brow. What else wasn't he privy to?

"Not so fast, Guardian. We haven't yet come to an agreement."

Ian's anger rose as he stared at Death, making it difficult to come off disconnected and bored. Still, he inhaled deeply as he crossed his arms. He couldn't allow the reaper to know how terrified he was for Grace and Maely. This was the most important poker game of his immortal life.

"I'll think about it," Ian muttered. Out of the south, he caught a whiff of Grace's scent. He jumped in that direction, ready to bolt. There was no backing down. He had to rescue Grace and Maely.

Once again, Reaper obstructed his path. "Out of the way," Ian snarled.

"You will do my bidding. Or else,..." Reaper paused as

if trying to make a decision. "I will serve you her head on a platter." He raised a black brow.

Ian retreated a single step. He wasn't the least bit sure Reaper would spare her life, regardless of what Ian did for him. Even so, Grace's and Maely's best chance of surviving this ordeal included allowing Death to *believe* he was in control and calling the shots.

And fuck it all, right now he was.

"Okay," Ian conceded. "I will consult with Custos. But I can't promise I can get you what you're looking for."

"If you don't, well, I can't assure you that Grace and the girl will live to see another sunrise."

22

Together, Grace and Maely worked at their bonds, trying to free themselves. At first it appeared as if Death had been foolish by tying Grace's hands and Maely's feet. Grace surmised they could simply undo each other. The twine didn't look that strong, but that turned out to be deceiving. Perhaps it was even a form of torture on the reaper's part, allowing them to think they could get away.

Grace tugged and pulled at Maely's cord until her fingers bled. She tore at it with her teeth, spitting out the nasty bitter taste it left behind and swiping the back of her hand across her lips. Not so much as a single fiber broke. Worse, the cord seemed to disappear into the earth and was somehow fixed there, as if it was rooted in the soil.

Grace breathed hard. They weren't going anywhere.

She sat back, resting. The candle flickered and danced a taunting dance. She was as tied to this place as the flame was to the wick. She groaned and closed her eyes. Flicking her tongue over her dry lips, she realized how thirsty she was. They needed water.

Opening her eyes, she searched the space. "Maely, maybe your eyes are better than mine. Do you see any bags or trunks or anything tucked into a corner?"

The child perked up given this new task. Her gaze swept the room, as did Grace's. "I don't see anything. Only the candle."

"Neither do I."

Which meant Death didn't plan to keep them here long, since he hadn't brought any provisions. Was that because he lacked the memory of what people needed to survive or because he had no intention of letting them survive?

Oh shit.

Even though he wanted to go straight to Custos and get the answers he needed, Ian took the long way into the tree. He couldn't be too careful where Death was concerned.

He changed into his eagle and soared across the vineyard to a centuries' old storage shed, formed by rocks, was cut into the landscape. There were many such entrances to the underground passages, but unless one knew the layout, it would be like getting lost in a cave. Inside, and at the back of the cave-like dwelling, nestled within a clump of large rocks, was a hole just big enough for a bird of prey to wiggle through. Ian entered the underground tunnels, then altered into his human form.

His muscles adjusted quickly, and he moved in long powerful strides as he pressed on toward the Divine Tree. At first, darkness enveloped him. As he went, he drew on the sight of the eagle to help him navigate the pathway.

Eventually his eyes adjusted into night vision sharpness.

At the underground entrance to the oak, he completed the anointing ritual, then entered. His breastbone ached as if someone were scrubbing knuckles over it. Tension coiled in his chest. He dropped into his oversized chair in the center of the seating area, rested his elbows on his knees, and cradled his head in his hands.

Damn. What a mess. He threaded his fingers into his hair and raked them over his scalp.

He had some recourse, though, didn't he? Because Death hadn't just immediately killed Grace and Maely. Ian had a chance for negotiations, and if that didn't pan out, then he wouldn't stop until he found them and stole them back.

"What is troubling you, Guardian?" Custos asked.

Ian had learned over the years that the tree's interest was predominantly turned inward, focusing on the greater aspects of the universe over that of humans. "The reaper has taken Grace and Maely captive. He's given me an ultimatum. Either I get you to reveal how he can become mortal once again or he will kill them."

"Indeed." The oak creaked and groaned in the long pause that followed.

"Do you have a solution to my problem?"

"This is something I cannot reveal."

"I was afraid of that."

"However…"

There was another pause. Ian could hear his heart pounding in anticipation.

"There is a way to stop Death. And you must! The child must not die. She has another purpose."

"The child? What about Grace? She is my true love. I can't let her go now that I've found her." Ian rubbed his chest.

"I see. Then you need to steal the reaper's scythe. Without it, he can't do his job and will be extradited back to Hell where he'll receive a penalty for its loss."

Ian shoved himself to his feet. "Then thwarting Death *is* possible." The Divine Tree might as well have told him to drag the moon from the sky, but by God, he would do it. Anything to save Grace and the girl.

Slowly, as if waking after a hibernation spell, he realized a painful truth: he wouldn't be able to accomplish this task alone. He would need help. One did not steal a reapers scythe without an element of distraction.

On a lamented sigh, he shoved his hands into his pockets.

"But Guardian, do not get yourself killed. I need you."

Grace closed her eyes as her imagination began to work overtime. She saw herself on a job, interviewing clients about the disappearance of a woman and child. She pictured entering the cave-like structure with cameras in tow, of the film footage revealing the bones of a woman and young girl tied together where they had died.

She sucked in a sharp breath.

"What's wrong?" Maely asked.

"Nothing." She blinked several times to get the image out of her mind. "If we could only get free of these binds, we could make a run for it." With renewed effort, she tugged at the ties at her wrists and feet. The smooth ropelike vine slid through her fingers, a little moist, reminding her of a living plant. When she pulled again, it seemed to tighten so she changed her tactic. With soft, light strokes, she massaged the woody cord, hoping it would stretch. In an unexplainable phenomenon, tiny shoots of green sprung forth all along the base and even at spots along the cord encircling her wrists. Those shoots grew, sending out more and more new growth. Within minutes, both she and Maely were surrounded by green vines, climbing over their legs, around their waists, and up over their shoulders.

Grace moved her hands away and clutched them together. At this rate, the plant would overtake the entire room.

Back at the château, Venn was in his room, most likely tending to Emma. Ian knocked on the door, and it opened. His brother stood on the other side of the threshold, his brow furrowed.

"How is she?" Ian asked, taking in Emma lounging in a chair by the fire.

"She's had a shock. I didn't want her to catch a chill," Venn said, explaining the fire. "Plus, this will keep Death from slipping down the chimney again. I had Bernard unseal and light all the fireplaces.

Ian nodded. "That's fine. But… I need your help."

Venn turned to Emma. "Will you be—"

"I've told you, I'm fine. Go on." She waved Venn away with the back of her hand.

"The balcony," Ian instructed, indicating the direction. Outside at the rail, he said, "I have a plan but need your help to distract the reaper. I believe he's holed up in a small shelter at the edge of my property. We need to surprise him and, according to Custos, take his scythe."

"I've never seen him without one," Venn pointed out.

"That's why I need your help, brother. Be creative. And I will get the scythe and the girls."

Venn frowned. "The last time I followed your directive, it landed me into fighting a barghest, teaming up with an angel, and ultimately receiving a Guardianship. Seems to me your plans are questionable."

Ian glanced over his shoulder. "Hey, you have your soul mate, don't you? I'd say you got a pretty good deal."

"I did, indeed." Venn glanced back in the direction of his mate and then looked out over the vineyard. "We going to fly?"

Ian nodded and then took the lead, shape-shifting into his eagle form and flying across the vineyard. A second later, Venn was at his back. Based on the tracking his bear had done earlier, he'd positioned Grace in the southernmost quarter of the property.

Ian flew just above the grapevines, noting with sad apprehension the growing number of dead vines. The malady encompassed several rows now, despite his efforts to eradicate the unknown disease. Then he realized that they'd started dying the same time Death had appeared.

The destroyer.

Ian circled over the edge of the vineyard where the property bordered a series of small rocky hills. There were several old storage huts built of rock and dug into the earth like the one he'd used earlier, as well as a wooden shed. His bet was that the reaper had his hostages housed in one of those.

He landed in human form near the shed first, his boots digging into the ground. He'd begin here and work his way around to the other locations, hoping to find them by process of elimination, if nothing else. Using precautions so as not to be seen, like a soldier on a mission, he stayed close to the wall as he listened, checked for scents, and scooted around to the interior. He knew the place was empty by the time he rounded the doorway. It was too quiet, and Grace's scent was missing.

The next possible hiding spot, a dugout, was over a small hill and close enough that it didn't make sense to expend the energy to shape-shift in and out of form. He repeated the stealth procedure, dipping inside the second structure. He held his breath, wanting so much to find Grace and free her from this nightmare.

Nothing.

Shit. Venn grit his teeth.

It was infuriating to miss once, let alone twice.

As they moved on to the next building—or pile of rocks with an entrance—he thought Grace's scent floated to him on the breeze. Ian stopped and snapped his head around. "No, not that place. She's this way." He led Venn off to the right, over another hill.

Now the smell of her clean flowery fragrance mixed with human sweat wafted to him, and his whole body reacted. His muscles constricted, his palms grew moist, and his pulse escalated, heart beating hard against his ribs.

"Game time," he whispered over his shoulder.

23

With stealth movements, Ian inched to one side of the entrance, Venn to the other. These storage buildings didn't have doors, just an exposed arched entry formed of rocks. The brothers paused to listen, their gazes meeting across the space. Grace's and Maely's voices flowed through the opening.

Ian released a shaky breath. They were alive. At least Death had upheld that part of the bargain. *So far.*

"Need to be quick," Venn advised.

Ian slipped past the doorway, searching the interior. Damn, he wished his vision would adjust to the dim light quicker. What if the reaper was hiding just behind the entrance?

Squinting, he scrutinized the area. He took the fact that nothing immediately knocked him on his ass as a good sign. He moved deeper within, stepping toe to heel, traveling cautiously so as not to disturb loose rocks and give away his presence. He certainly didn't want to risk the females' lives with a rash move. Venn followed closely behind.

As Ian's sight grew clearer, he was shocked to find half the room covered in green vines. No sign of Death, though.

"Grace?" he called.

"Over here," she yelled back. The vines shook. "We're tied up and can't break loose."

Ian peered through the mountain of green before him, trying to glimpse Grace. It wasn't until Venn tore at the vines that a slip of white showed through. Grace's shirt, maybe?

"We'll get you out of here." Ian's voice cracked as the tension in his gut relaxed at having found them alive.

Still, they weren't in the clear yet.

Ian pushed the greenery down, tramping it beneath his feet until he finally got to Grace and Maely. "Where did all this come from?"

"I have somewhat of a green thumb, apparently," Grace said.

Ian shook his head. "That can't be the reason for all this. There has to be another explanation."

"Well I don't know what it is," she replied. "I was trying to get these off—" she held up her wrists for him to see "—and it just sprouted and grew."

"Wow," Venn said.

Each Guardian whipped out a knife and helped to cut Grace and Maely free of their binds.

Ian helped Grace up while Venn had sawed through the cords at Maely's ankles and lifted the girl into his arms.

"Are you all right?" Ian asked Grace.

"Yes. Just…scared."

"Understandable." He dragged her up against him and kissed her. "We need to get going before Death returns." With his arm around Grace's waist, he gently chucked the little girl's chin with his free hand. "How about you, *petit agneau*? Are you ready to go home?"

"Oh oui."

Stepping high over the vines, they scooted through the doorway and into the fresh air one at a time. A chorus of audible sighs dissipated on the wind. They'd done it.

A sickly, croaking laugh rumbled over them. "Going somewhere?" Death hurtled from a nearby elm, landing in front of the group. He wielded his scythe in the air. "I think not."

A natural reflex, Ian shoved Grace behind him. "Go to hell," he growled at the reaper.

An evil smile split across Death's face. "I've been there. It's highly overrated." He moved closer.

Ian tipped his head toward Grace, whispering, "Stay close to me."

"No problem there."

Ian didn't take his eyes off the reaper as he traveled as far around him as he could. Way beyond the reach of that sharp, sickled blade. Not that it mattered. The ugly monster was capable of traveling at enormous speed and could reach them in the space of a heartbeat.

"No, no, no. You're going the wrong direction," Death intoned.

"I'm going home," Ian said. "I suggest you do the same."

The reaper clucked his tongue. "A bargain is a bargain. Do you have what I asked for?" He didn't move. He merely twisted around in order to follow their progress as they put distance between them.

Then with a crack of a twig, all hell broke loose. Death dashed across the earth in a streak so fast, he was invisible for a moment, and the next thing Ian knew, Maely was clutched in the reaper's skeletal arm, resting against his hip, and Venn staggered backward from the forceful contact, barely maintaining his balance.

"What the fuck!" Venn bellowed.

Death ignored him. "Ian, you have a choice—Maely or

Grace. But know she's destined to—" He nudged his head at Grace. "Oh never mind. You'll find out soon enough."

Ian felt every ounce of blood within him drain to his heels. Death was asking him to choose who would live and who would die.

As his red eyes burned into Ian, Death nodded his head. "Choose."

Venn took a step forward.

The scythe swung down, striking the earth at his feet.

Maely's face was as white as her teeth as they sank into her bottom lip. The girl was trying to be brave and doing an admirable job of it.

"Wait. Custos didn't say what you're asking *couldn't* be done." Ian folded his arms over his chest, struggling to control his anger. He hated that he couldn't solve this on his own. Even the idea of depending on Custos was painful. But not as agonizing as watching either Grace or Maely die. "I think we should all go to the Divine Tree and see if we can get an answer."

A long silence passed as Death seemed to consider the idea.

Ian didn't want to give him the luxury, or the time, to think of another plan. "Come, I'm sure Custos will indulge us. But if you harm them, you will remain as you are. That I promise you."

Ian could tell the moment Death's insatiable desire to be human again won over. The red of his eyes glowed brighter. With care, Ian started to walk, taking Grace with him at his side.

The reaper followed along, still carrying the child.

"I can walk," Maely announced with fervor.

"No. You'll run away."

Ian smiled to himself. True. She'd already done that. He looked into her big blue eyes and saw a mixture of fear and determination. And then, like a practiced child fighting to get what she wants, she began to wail and pitch a fit, kicking and crying at the top of her lungs.

And the angel of death didn't have a clue how to handle her.

Venn immediately came to the rescue. "I'll take her."

Relief such as Ian had never seen swept across Death's pitiful face. He handed Maely to Venn. As predicted, she instantly hushed.

"No funny business or I'll strike you both down," Death said.

Venn gave a sharp nod.

En masse, they trudged between the vines until they stood before Custos, the orange glow of the setting sun dipping behind the horizon as their prospective executioner balanced his scythe over his shoulder.

24

Grace worried that the amount of anxiety ricocheting through her would tear a hole right through her heart. She was starting to accept that she loved Ian beyond measure, and there he stood, all handsome and protective of her. But he didn't realize her fate was to die regardless. She didn't think he believed her when she'd told him earlier.

She trembled, and with good reason. If memory served her, she stood in almost the very spot Skylar had fallen. "Man, this was the worst paranormal experience I've ever had," she whispered to Ian. "And I didn't even get it on tape."

He frowned.

Yep, she even loved the way his brow scrunched. Too bad. Too damned bad she wouldn't have more time with him.

She'd come to a decision back in the cave, that if it came down to it, she'd fall on Death's blade in order to save the child. Now she watched closely as the Guardians seemed to have some communication thing going on with the tree.

The reaper shuffled his feet in a side-to-side dance.

Finally, Ian stepped toward the tree then turned to face Death. "Okay. Custos may have the ability to do what you want, but it's never been done before."

"But he'll try?" The excitement in Death's voice was unmistakable.

"He will." Ian moved closer to the tree. "You need to put both hands on the oak's trunk while we create a circle, closing in you and the Divine Tree."

"And I will be human again?"

"You will be changed." Ian motioned for Venn, Grace, and Maely to join him. "You must place your palms on the bark like this." Ian demonstrated, bracing his hands against the tree.

Death didn't hesitate. He propped the scythe beside him and performed the movements exactly as Ian had instructed.

"Good," Ian said. "Now we form a circle around you." He stretched out his arms wide, taking hold of Grace's hand on one side and Maely's on the other. Venn took the position on the opposite side.

Since the tree was so large, their arms barely reached around, but they held on, pressing Death against the tree. "How long does this take?"

"It's not done until you feel something," Ian said.

Suddenly, it was as if a bomb exploded. Venn pushed in, grabbed the scythe, and ran full force in and around the vines. Death tripped and crawled across the ground after him. He scrambled up and began to track Venn.

"Run!" Ian yelled to Grace and Maely.

Grace took the girl's hand and fled several steps, then halted. She hugged her and then cupped Maely's face in her palms. "Your mother and brother are at the house. Go to them."

Maely turned and sprinted toward the château.

"What are you doing?" Ian grabbed her shoulders so that she faced him.

She smiled, "Staying with you."

"No. I want you safe."

With a loud growl, Death appeared to have lost it. He thrust himself at Ian, sliding off his arm. As the reaper lost his balance, he seized hold of Grace and took her down with him. She tumbled, scraped her knee against the tree, and landed on that repulsive bag of bones.

Ian yelled her name.

If Grace was injured, he'd dislodge every rattling bone in Death's body. Ian reached to help Grace up. "Are you all right?"

"Yes." She backed away from Death.

"Where did he go?" the reaper demanded.

"Like I'd tell you." By now Venn should be deep inside the Divine Tree, out of reach.

"You lied," Death sputtered.

"No, you believed what you wanted to believe. I said you'd be changed. And you shall."

Realizing his fate, that without his scythe he'd be returned to Hell and have to start all over again, his fury erupted. He tore through the vines, screaming and howling the most horrid of sounds, a high-pitched wail. In his rage, he swiped his hand along perfect grapevines, turning them to ash, leaving nothing but a few dead leaves clinging to the supported runners.

Abruptly, he halted, a look of horror etched on his face. Then as if something tugged him by the ankles, he quickly sank into the earth. When he was gone, a cloud of dirt settled.

"Oh my." Grace staggered backward. She wiped the back of her hand across her forehead. "What happened?"

"I think the Dark Realm snatched him back into hell."
He shrugged. "But that's just my guess."

Ian opened his arms, and she stepped right into them.
"You were so brave," he said. When she tilted up her face,
he kissed her, long and hard and with everything he felt for
her. Admiration. Wonder. Love.

"I love you," he said, not caring anymore that she was
mortal.

She threaded her fingers into his hair and drew him
back to her mouth. With her lips brushing his, she
whispered, "I love you more."

He smiled against her mouth. "That's not possible."

He held her to him, knowing how close he had come to
losing her forever. Then he recalled what Grace had said
earlier about humans dying and realized that it still would
be their fate, whether from illness or old age. Anguish
seized his heart.

"Where did Venn take the scythe?" she asked.

"Inside the Divine Tree."

"One of these days, you're going to have to take me in
there," she said, raising one eyebrow slightly.

"If I'm allowed."

She gave a small laugh, and he took hold of her as they
strolled toward the château. She paused mid-stride. "Oh,
Ian, your poor vines."

"There's always next year."

She rested her cheek on his chest. And despite the
disaster his vineyard was now, he was the luckiest man—
or, um, Guardian—in the world.

Her eyes shone even in the dim light as she gazed at
him. Then her face assumed a stricken expression, as if she
realized or experienced something excruciating. She
grabbed hold of her head and collapsed in his arms.

"Grace. Grace." He swept her up and held her to him.
She wasn't breathing. He heard no pulse or whisper of life.
"No. No. No. Nooo."

Cold dread slammed into his chest. Life without her would be bare and empty and meaningless. He stood frozen, holding her, lifting her close so he could press his lips to her still-warm throat.

Slowly, a hot breeze washed over him. He turned his head and there was Custos, seeming larger than ever. The sensation brought him to what he needed to do. Without much thought, he had trekked to the Divine Tree instead of the château, and now he entered the secret porthole, still carrying Grace. He progressed into the catacombs.

"What happened?" Venn asked when he saw them.

"She...she died. I don't know...but she just d-died."

In my arms.

"She has a growth in her head, a tumor. It was her time," Custos said sadly.

"No," Ian wailed, on the verge of falling apart. He'd grovel and plead, anything to bring her back. He rested her limp body on the wood floor. "Custos, help her. You can heal her. I know you can."

"It's not that simple."

"Please." His voice raised in anguish as his eyes filled with tears.

"*If* I can heal her, she will not be yours to keep. She may not remember you or what has happened." He paused a beat. "Ian, you will have to choose between saving Grace's life and giving her up."

25

"Heal her," he said without hesitation. "I want her to live and be happy, even if we can't be together." He knelt over her, placing his hand over his heart.

Custos's sigh sounded like a long roll of thunder. "Venn, bring the girl to me."

Venn sprinted toward the underground passageway.

Ian waited for what seemed like forever, considering Skylar and Monsieur Dubois at the same time. Such a waste. At least his Grace might live again. Mixed emotions warred within him. He imagined her expressive face as she scolded some other man, laughed with someone else. And he would be alone, as he'd always been.

It was as it should be.

He wasn't even thinking anymore when Venn returned with Maely. He was simply numb, because otherwise…otherwise it hurt too much.

Custos gave a rustling command. "Child, you will help me. You have the gift of healing within your hands.

Together as I direct my special energy, we may undo the damage."

Maely nodded.

Ian wondered what the girl could possibly have to do with this healing, but she seemed to know exactly what was required of her. Standing at Grace's head, she placed her palm on her crown. Ian watched, heart racing, as Maely breathed in and out in exaggerated breaths, as if she was doing it for Grace, too. Then Ian noticed the rise and fall of his love's chest and the rosy color returning to her lovely skin. A glow danced and hovered over Grace's temple, and then flitted through the air and into the wood of the tree. Maely stepped back, a pleased expression on her face.

Grace's eyes fluttered several times and then she looked at him blankly. He leaned forward, pulling her to him and cried. For the first time since he was a child, he bawled like a two-year-old. *"Tu es à moi."*

"You are mine?" Grace repeated in a questioning, hoarse voice. She placed her palm on the center of his chest and pushed him away. "Give me some room." She tried to sit up on her own, then fell back and passed out.

"Grace? What's happening?" he asked, worried. "Custos? She didn't recognize me. Is she all right?"

"The rush of blood was simply too much for her. She'll come around again," Custos said. "However, I warned you. Her situation is different. She died because it was her time. Bringing her back has altered things."

"Is the…tumor gone?" Ian asked, hoping she was truly healed.

"Yes. She is ill no longer."

Maely knelt at her father's head next. "Can I?" she asked Custos.

"Go ahead, and we shall see."

Maely repeated the process with her father, this time placing her hand on his chest, over his heart. She waited calmly, and then repeated the same breathing technique she'd done with Grace. The white glow of energy hovered above his sternum, then shot into the tree. Like a car sputtering to life, Monsieur Dubois bucked and coughed, and then his breathing became regulated with his daughter's.

"It's…a miracle," Ian said, moved by this turn of events more than by anything the Divine Tree had done before.

"I could not have done it alone," Custos told them.

But it didn't matter how the miracle had happened. Grace and Monsieur Dubois had another chance at life. *That* was the miracle.

Maely hugged her father. Then Ian glanced over to the side. "What about Skylar? Can't we do the same for her?" he asked Custos.

Only the Guardians were privy to the Divine Tree's answer. *It isn't the same. She died by the scythe. Her soul was affected. Perhaps with some time that may change. I will monitor her.*

"Did the tree answer?" Maely asked.

Ian nodded. "There is nothing that can be done for her now. But perhaps over time." He looked to where Grace rested, eyes closed, oblivious to what had just transpired. She would be so disappointed that they couldn't help her friend.

Ian pressed his lips to her forehead.

Take them home, Custos said wearily to the brothers.

The room possessed a glow that seemed brighter than it had a minute ago. Ian placed a hand on a knot of golden wood and pushed to his feet. He lifted Grace—still passed out but breathing—and led the way to the exit.

Venn hefted Monsieur Dubois and carried him toward the arched doorway. "Come child. Help me with your father."

They filed out behind Ian. And even though he held Grace tight to his chest, he was worried she had already slipped from his grasp. She hadn't recognized him. So she couldn't be his. Wasn't that what Custos had told him? Not his love. Not his wife. Not his mate.

It struck him what a curse this was.

Regrettably, Ian couldn't simply stay in the bedroom with Grace. He had to attend to matters downstairs and see the Dubois family got home. So he tucked Grace beneath the covers, hoping that when she awoke she'd be fine. And that she'd remember him.

"Good morning," Bernard said when Ian entered the kitchen.

Ian glanced out the window. Sure enough, dawn had broken. The passage of time was a strange thing, and what had transpired last evening must have taken the entire night. He hadn't even realized.

"Venn, will you and Emma escort the Duboises home? I don't want to leave Grace," Ian asked.

"Sure."

Maely held her brother's hand, asking, "Will Maman and Papa remember what happened?"

"No, petit agneau. I don't think they will. Custos has a way of controlling that."

She squinted her eyes, saying with pride, "I will, though."

"Yes. You have a unique connection with the tree, and you possess a special gift. One only time will reveal," Ian said.

Maely tilted her head. "Grace has a special gift, too. You'll see."

"Run along. The car is outside." Ian watched from the doorway as the children hopped in the rear as Venn held the door. With the click of the shutting car door, he turned. Bernard shoved a tall tumbler of bourbon at him.

"Thanks. I certainly need that."

"I thought you might."

Ian stood at the window, looking out for a long time, nursing his drink. He didn't think, or analyze, or consider the future. For the time being, he simply existed.

Finally, when he reached the bottom of his glass, he turned and traipsed past his assistant, who took it from him. Ian nodded his thanks. "If you need me, I'll be upstairs."

Ian stood in the shadows of the kitchen, observing Grace on the dining patio as she sipped her morning coffee. She sat in the very chair where he'd bandaged her arm and introduced her to Chêne Sacré wine. He'd learned on that day how determined she could be and how she didn't sensor anything that came out of her pretty mouth. And he had to admit, he'd been a little smitten even then.

"She seems to be doing well," Bernard said.

"Yes. Except she doesn't remember anything about the past week." Including the relationship they'd formed. She didn't recall Skylar's death, or the reaper, or their incredible times making love. He stretched his neck at the pull of tension there. He had told Bernard the whole story of how Grace died and Custos revived her.

From where he stood, Ian could easily overhear Grace's attempt at calling her friend. "Skylar. Pick up. I've texted you three times. Where *are* you?" She paused. "I think the tumor has created a gigantic gap in my memory. I don't know." She blew a sigh. "Anyway, I've determined there isn't as much paranormal activity here as I originally thought. Actually, I don't know why I chose this winery in the first place. Call me when you get this message. We should head home."

Ian met Bernard's troubled gaze. "Do you know what

happened to the young woman's cell phone?" Bernard inquired.

Ian straightened. "It may still be on her. Who knows if it's even still charged." Turning from watching Grace, he headed for the tunnel door. "I'll go find out."

When he entered the kitchen again a short while later upon returning from the Divine Tree, Grace was strolling toward the house. He opened the door for her as she approached. Damn, being this close to her and unable to draw her into a hug was excruciating. He pushed his free hand into his pocket, resisting touching her and stepping aside to allow her entry.

She held up her phone, a hint of exasperation animating her face. "I finally got a text from Skylar."

"That's good," he said, his eyes darting to Bernard and then back to Grace.

"I'm not so sure. Evidently she's experiencing a bit of French culture with the young man she met at your gala." She shook her head. "Which again, I can't remember. She said she'd meet me in Paris. If not, then she's fallen in love and would live here forever."

"Romance, it is the French way," Bernard commented with a chuckle.

Ian hid a smile.

"Geez, the youth of today." Grace walked on by, heading in the direction of her room.

When she was gone, Bernard winked. "Nice work."

He gave a weary shrug.

"Are you going to encourage her to remember?"

"No. I would not have her go through that trauma again." Better to let her go.

26

A week later, Grace had her belongings laid out on the bed, as she put her things in a suitcase. A soft rap sounded on the door. Ian angled his head in past the opening.

"You're awake," he said.

"Yes. And I feel terrific this morning. Better than I have in ages. Except…" She paused, tugging her hair over her shoulder. "Except I don't quite recall some things. My memory is fuzzy. But my work is done here, I think."

"And you're packing?"

"I do appreciate you're hospitality, Mr. Hearst."

His handsome face flinched as if he'd been struck.

She took an involuntary step closer. "Is everything okay? I hope I haven't put you out."

"No. No. It's fine. I've enjoyed having you here."

She touched her forehead. "Funny. I don't remember much about my stay." She looked around. "But your place is beautiful."

"Thank you."

She closed her suitcase, zipping it with finality. It was time to go home.

"I'm making a quick trip to the winery. Bernard is downstairs if you need anything," he said.

"Okay. Thanks for letting me know."

He nodded and left.

She hauled four boxes onto the bed. Bernard had brought them to her room earlier at her request. Better to transport her equipment safely. She frowned at the scratches and dents she found on the video recorder and tripod as she place the items within a box. Strange, she couldn't recall how they'd gotten so beat up. Looking around, she realized Ian's assistant had not given her tape and a marker to finish the job.

With a shrug, she headed downstairs to get the items from Bernard. At the bottom of the stairs, she paused and listened. A rattling of dishes came from the kitchen. She followed the sound.

Bernard stood on a ladder, putting large serving platters on the top shelf.

"I sorry to bother you, but I need packaging tape and a marker."

"I'll be finished in a minute and will be happy to get the items for you."

"No, I can get them. Just tell me where to look."

He stared down at her, frowning.

"Come on. I'm a big girl, I can handle it."

Gradually, his mouth lifted at the corners and his eyes crinkled. "You should find whatever you need in the desk in the study. Bottom drawer on the left."

"Thanks." She turned with a swing of her hair. "Carry on."

As she walked down the hall, she wondered if Ian would mind if she took some pictures of his place with her cell phone. She wanted to remember it and all of its beauty. When she got to the desk in the study, she paused.

Had Bernard said the left or right lower drawer?

She opened the right side and peered in. Nope. No tape or markers. But sitting within a sectioned off box was one of her video memory cards. What the heck? She knew it was hers because she marked each paranormal video card with a color-coded stripe. This one had a slash of orange across the corner. The color designated for the French winery investigation.

Puzzled, she lifted the card and slipped it into her pocket. Geez, that was a three hundred dollar high-end card. When she got back to the room, she'd pop it in the recorder to make sure it was hers.

Glad she'd chosen the wrong drawer, she fished in the left drawer finding the tape and marker she'd originally wanted.

Back in the bedroom, she went straight for the recorder and loaded the memory card. Bothered by the condition of the recorder and not able to recall how it had been damaged, she pressed the "on" button and hit "rewind." If she went back a little, it might show her what had happened. Maybe she'd fallen.

The images caught her off guard. She couldn't breathe, couldn't utter a sound. Shape-shifters, a vulture, Ian, Skylar, Death, and his wicked scythe. She dropped the camera onto the bed as if it were molten lava and cried out.

Then Ian was there, wrapping her in his strong, protective arms. She hadn't heard him enter the room, but that was understandable given what she'd seen and the horrible memories the video sparked. Now, she recalled the events with undeniable clarity.

She clutched Ian to her. "Oh my God. I remember."

"I'm sorry. You weren't supposed to see that. I had taken the card so you wouldn't."

"I… I found it while getting packaging tape." Her voice sounded thick, on the verge of tears.

"But you remember now?"

"Yes. Everything." She hugged him tighter.

He smoothed her hair tenderly around an earlobe.

She shut her eyes, letting the images she recalled float over her mind. Vivid images that weren't caught by the camera. "The walls inside the oak were the most beautiful polished wood I've ever seen. Was it real? Was I inside the Divine Tree?" Her gaze slid up to look into Ian's eyes. She'd find the truth there.

Oh, it was real all right, as was the skip and flutter of her heartbeat.

He leaned in and planted a firm, solid, this-was-not-make-believe kiss on her mouth. She kissed him back before she had to pull away. Something was gnawing at her about her memories.

"I had died. How did you bring me back?" she inquired.

"It helps to be acquainted with the source of the secrets of the universe," Ian replied.

Grace didn't know what to say to that. But she was thankful, very thankful indeed. But…

"Ian," she said, "I need to go back and see Skylar."

"I understand. How about we give it a few days? I want to make sure you're fully recovered."

She nodded. She knew it was the best offer she was going to get.

As promised, Ian took her to the tree four days later. They'd spent nearly the entire time in his room, where he'd pampered her, loved her, and made her rest. She had to admit, she felt so much better. Ready to live again.

They went into the oak via the same tunnel they'd taken when Custos had turned her away. Her stomach tightened as they approached. "Will he allow me entrance this time?"

"I think so."

His muscular arms reached out, his movements beautiful as he performed the same blessing ritual he had performed the last time. Grace waited in nervous anticipation. After what felt like an endless moment, the arched door marked by swirls and growth rings swung open.

"I'm pleased you are well, Grace." The rough, raspy voice of Custos wrapped around her.

She gasped, eyeing Ian. The Divine Tree spoke so she could hear. Ian nodded.

"Thank you," she whispered.

Ian led the way through several rooms, and she had the sense they were going down deeper underground until they stopped in the largest room of all. Slowly, she took in her surroundings. At last, she shared the Divine Tree experience. At least that she could remember.

A weak smile curved her lips. "Exquisite," she whispered.

She glanced over to where Skylar's body rested, off to the side in a small alcove. Her hands overlapped on her middle, not posed but close. She looked…peaceful. "She reminds me of Sleeping Beauty."

"Venn said the same thing."

"Why couldn't the Divine Tree bring her back?"

He ran a palm over the stubble that covered his chin, and his silver eyes met hers. "When Death slayed her with the scythe, he separated her soul. That's part of the power of the blade. Custos can't revive Skylar right now because her soul is in limbo."

"Some of the ghosts I encounter are like that."

He lifted a shoulder. "My understanding is he must find a way to bring her mind, body, and soul together as one again before she can return to us."

"Can he do that?"

"I'm not sure. In time. Perhaps."

She nodded, wishing her friend pleasant dreams.

"Until then, she will remain here, safe and protected."

Grace swallowed, hard. "Good. This is a beautiful place."

"We should go meet up with the others," he said. Placing a hand beneath her elbow, he helped guide her out of the tree. "I invited the Dubois family for lunch. I decided it's better to foster good relations rather than to remain so isolated."

"Will I be able to come back down here again?"

"That's up to Custos."

Grace allowed her gaze to sweep the room, trying to take in every detail, just in case.

Ian cradled his arm around the small of her back. He urged her toward the doorway. "How do you feel?"

She thought about it. "Quite well actually. Almost as if I'd had a couple cups of coffee along with a handful of vitamins." She kissed his cheek. "Thank you."

"Remember, we must keep the Divine Tree's secrets."

"Always."

Ian encircled her in his arms, and lowering his head, he took her mouth in a toe-curling kiss.

He drew back. "I was never so scared in my life. I thought I'd lost you. Don't ever leave me again."

"I won't. Now kiss me, Guardian. Harder."

"Bossy, aren't you?" But he seemed more than happy to oblige.

With trembling fingers, she brushed the tousled hair from his brow. Then she hesitated. "Do you think my tumor is gone?"

"Definitely."

"Good." She smiled and wiped the mist from her eyes. Going through that once was enough. "I'm hungry," she said, licking her lips.

His eyes were filled with desire as they roamed over her face, and then he cocked a brow in that sexy way he did.

"Me too. Should we have dessert brought to our bedroom after the meal."

Grace smiled and nodded eagerly. She liked the way he said *our*.

It seemed Maely had some plan worked up and couldn't wait to get Ian and Grace alone. So while Bernard entertained the others, the little girl dragged them outside. Ian was getting used to the child grabbing hold of his hand and tugging him along.

"I've been thinking about this since the other day." Maely paused, making sure she had their attention. She raised her brows and tilted her head in an impish manner. "You know, I have an idea… Grace can make the vineyard well."

"What are you talking about?" Grace asked with a puzzled smile.

"Come, I'll show you." Maely led them deep among the vines. She didn't stop until they reached the rows of sick grapevines.

A sea of dried, brown vines stretched out before them, lifeless, with shriveled dead fruit. His stomach churned and rebelled. He could only hope that the trunks and roots weren't affected and that eventually new shoots and tendrils would grow. Otherwise, his life's work was destroyed. Many of his vines were almost as old as he was. And as with humans, health could have a lot to do with where one lives. He could only hope that the proximity to the Divine Tree may have healing effects.

Ian peered at Grace and Maely as the girl coaxed Grace to move farther from him. He knew Death was gone, but he couldn't help the pang of uncertainty and anxiety that hit him.

Maely tugged Grace down to her level and whispered

in her ear. Then Grace stood, saying, "It's worth a shot."

She walked over to the nearest vine and bent at the waist, rubbing the tree's trunk and shoots. Just as the plant had in the cave, the miracle of life took over, turning the vine green and lush. The phenomenon spread down the row, and to the next row, and to the one after that until, in wave of green as if part of a time-lapsed film, the acres of vines were filled with plants tendering green leaves and sumptuous, ripe fruit.

He lifted Grace's feet off the ground, hugged her fiercely, and kissed her. Maely squealed with joy and clapped her hands.

"Amazing." Ian couldn't believe his eyes. He knew she had a way with plants, but this was beyond his imagination. He tickled Maely's neck. "*Petit angeau,* you were magnifique. And so grown up."

Grace looked on and stroked the little girl's back before the three of them made their way back to the château among peals of Maely's laughter.

Venn and Emma came out to see what the commotion was about.

"Look!" Maely exclaimed. "Grace revived the vines!"

"Unbelievable," his brother said, eyes wide. "Everything is green and thriving again."

"Beautiful," Emma added.

Venn hauled Emma into a sideways hug. "It's good to know we'll be leaving on a high note."

Ian kissed Grace's brow, cheeks, and nose, finishing on her lips.

For some reason, this made Maely laugh, and he brought his head up, smiling at the child. "I should kiss you, too, for being such a fine helper."

She blushed and shrugged her little shoulders. Then she ran and threw herself into Ian's arms. He had no choice but to hold her as she kissed his cheeks four times in rapid succession.

"That seals it," Venn said. "Now you'll have the best of luck."

Ian clasped Venn's hand and hit his shoulder to Venn's, saying their goodbyes. "I wish your visit could be longer, but I know you have duties, as well. And I doubt if Seth will last much longer down on Earth." They both chuckled as they parted.

Ian wrapped an arm around Grace's waist and they both waved as Bernard drove his brother and sister-in-law down the drive and away to the airport.

The hike to the vineyard's epicenter progressed uneventfully, even though Ian worried that the distance might be too much for Grace. "Maybe we should take a truck so you don't have to walk that far."

"I'm fine."

The rain held off, as Ian thought it would, with the sky actually peeking out from between clouds. The sun promised to burn even brighter by the time they would reach the ancient oak. Which was good for his grapes.

They resumed plodding along. "Tomorrow you experience your first vendange."

Grace flipped her hair over her shoulder, finger-combing it for a second. "Vendange?"

"The grape harvest. The picking crew has arrived, and they will begin early in the morning, when the grapes are perfect. It's the most exciting time at the vineyard."

"Do you use machines, or is it done by hand?" she asked as they entered the vines.

Ian's lip curled with disapproval. "By hand. The old way is the best. A machine can't determine between perfectly ripe clusters and moldy fruit."

Grace poked him in the rib. "You're too much the perfectionist. OCD is what they call it in the States."

"Can you live with that?" he teased.

Her lively, expressive face showed her mixed emotions, but then she said, "Oh, no, the question is can you live with me, with all my imperfections? A flighty, ghost-hunting, out-of-control mess who used to have a brain tumor but is now thrilled to experience true love." She'd said all that in one breath so she inhaled a rapid puff of air to recover.

"Hmm, guess we'll have to see."

"Oh, you." She plucked a grape off the vine, popped it into his mouth, and kissed the sweetness from his lips.

THE END

Thank you for reading *Awakening Touch*. If you enjoyed this story and want to stay up-to-date on my next book and release dates then sign up for my newsletter. (I promise your email address will never be shared and you can unsubscribe at any time.)

https://larissaemerald.wordpress.com/contact/

Did you know that one of most awesome things you can do for an author is post a review? It doesn't need to be long, just a few lines will do, but a review goes a long way to help authors achieve visibility. So, if you enjoyed the book, share the news with a friend and take a few minutes to leave a review!

Stay tuned for the next book in the
Divine Tree Guardian Series

AWAKENING STORM

to be released in Spring 2017.

Excerpt from

AWAKENING STORM
by Larissa Emerald

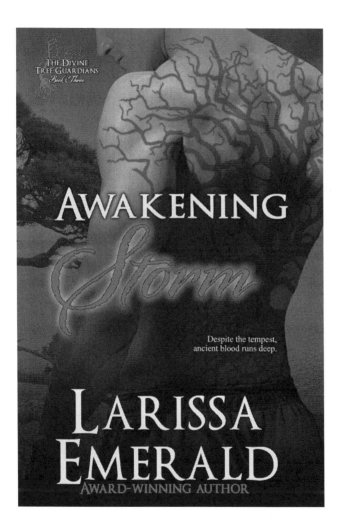

THE DIVINE
TREE GUARDIANS
Book Three

AWAKENING

Storm

Despite the tempest,
ancient blood runs deep.

LARISSA
EMERALD
AWARD-WINNING AUTHOR

1

October 6

The pup tramped in a happy circle. Even with the slap of the surf against the hull, Aidan's superior hearing distinguished the clacking sound of the dog's nails over the fiberglass deck. Pup snapped his head around and peered at Aidan with trusting chocolate eyes. After three failed attempts to jump onto Aidan's lap, the animal finally pawed his way up, resting on his thighs. He hung his gigantic front feet over Aidan's arm as it draped over the steering wheel, guiding the sailboat's passage.

"I can't keep calling you 'Pup.'" Aidan stared across the thrashing waves, thinking. "Takeshi. You will be Takeshi. *Fierce warrior.*" He let the name roll over his tongue, pleased with the symbolism. It reminded him of the early days in Scotland, when he and his brothers protected the moors from invaders, in the time before they became Divine Tree Guardians.

Good God, that had been ages ago.

He could use a warrior at his side to help fight the current rise of evil that preceded the Age of Atonement. His brothers had revealed as much during the Guardian Congress last month.

He stroked Takeshi's brindled, salt-dampened fur, allowing his gaze to sweep the ocean as far as the eye could see. His remote island, the place where his Divine Tree resided, was about six hundred miles east of Yamada, a fishing town in Japan. It was uninhabited except for him. He would sail a full twenty-six hours to reach his island home, a trip he made about three times a year.

Takeshi barked at the flap and crack of the sails. A gray and windy day loomed before them. A series of storms had been predicted. The waves peaked higher the farther he navigated into the Pacific, away from Japan and Yamada, where he had a house—a home base of sorts. Naoki, his *delegato*, or assistant, resided in the modest home and kept Aidan supplied with everything he could want or need. Hence the Akita pup to replace the dog he'd lost in July. He stroked Takeshi again. He had lost many animal friends over his centuries as Guardian. He still remembered and treasured every one.

Takeshi licked Aidan's face and then wagged his tail with pent-up energy.

"When we get home, we'll run the entire island," Aidan told him. "And I'll introduce you to the tiger and eagle."

In the middle of leading a Pilates class, Rhianna Singleton lifted out of plank position to discover a handsome, toned man, standing in the doorway along with her business partner. Terri wore a giddy smile as she waved Rhia over.

What was going on?

"Joy, will you lead the class in a cool down, please?" Rhia asked her assistant.

As Joy came to the front, Rhia headed to the rear and followed Terri and the stranger into the hallway. It was then that she noticed the cameraman filming.

What the...?

Her mind raced to fill in the blanks. The man looked vaguely familiar.

"Rhianna Singleton?" the man asked with a practiced voice. "I'm Dillon Savage from the reality television show *On Your Own*, and you're our next adventure-trip winner! So drop everything and let's go!"

She stared at him, shocked and unprepared. But that was the point, wasn't it?

Another cameraman stepped closer off to her right. Here she stood, in her exercise garb, and she was expected to drop what she was doing and take off?

For a few seconds, she numbly perused Dillon Savage. He was shorter than she'd expected and not nearly as handsome as he appeared on the show.

Terri bounced on her toes and clapped, bringing Rhia back to the here and now. "This is so exciting." She grabbed hold of Rhia's shoulders and gave them a shake. "Go. Go. I'll take care of everything—your apartment, your plants, the business. Don't worry about a thing." She finished by wrapping her in a big hug.

Rhia squeezed her back, then stepped away, smoothing her hair with nervous fingers.

She lifted her chin, determined to see this through. Yes, she'd auditioned for the show—not so much because she was a survivalist but because she was intrigued by the location where this episode would be filmed—the very island off the coast of Japan where her great-grandfather had vanished, never to be heard from again. She'd longed to travel there and experience her heritage. Her ancestors on her father's side had been samurai warriors, and she'd traced her line back to the Nabekura Castle in northeastern Japan. And then…nothing.

But trying to discover more about what had happened to him was now just part of the reason she'd signed up for the show six months ago. Now, more than ever, striking out with something new would do her good. She needed excitement. She needed to prove to herself that she was strong and resourceful and her own person. Her ex-fiancé kept saying she couldn't make it without him. He was wrong.

Plus, she wanted the trip around the world that she'd win if she managed to stick it out the prescribed thirty days.

She took a deep breath. "Okay, Mr. Savage. Let's go."

"We must leave immediately," he said, following her to the entrance, allowing the camera crew to trail behind.

"And we will. However, I believe I need my passport."

She gave him a wink, and he laughed. "Ah yes. That's right."

She traipsed into the parking lot with Savage and the cameramen following behind her. Terri and some of her students followed, too, and hurried forward to line the walk.

"Have fun," Terri called with a wave. The others joined in.

"I will!" She blew kisses to them with both hands and then slid into the back of the designated black SUV.

Her hands shook a little as she settled into the seat and watched her support group fade from view out the window.

Twenty minutes later, she and Dillon Savage were in her kitchen. She glanced around, grimacing at the still-dirty omelet pan and breakfast dishes in the sink. How could she possibly just walk out of her life like this? And for an entire month!

Savage cleared his throat. "The passport?"

"Yeah." She retrieved it from her desk in the corner and briefly showed it to him, letting him know it was up to date.

While Savage waited at the door, Rhia jotted down a few notes for Terri. She set the list on the table.

"Any chance I can change into fresh clothes?" she asked.

He shook his head. "Nope. But you should have a bag packed for after the survival challenge."

She did, as per the instructions she'd received during the audition. "I've got one. But honestly, I figured I had as much chance of being selected for the show as winning the lottery."

She grabbed her purse and jacket. From being a fan of the show, she knew they'd allow her to take what she could wear in with her. Evidently that didn't extend to a change of clothes. A jacket would come in handy, though. This time she didn't ask as she slid it on.

"Well, today's your lucky day."

Four days later, Rhianna braced herself against the onslaught of the next gust of wind. It pitched the helicopter off its mark by several feet. The pilot circled around and made adjustments on the decent. Below, the waves slapped against the finger of sandbar that jutted off the south end of the island and was surrounded by shallow water. She was to be dropped off here. Evidently, it was the only section of solid ground devoid of trees and dense vegetation.

"Are you sure you want to head out today? Can you

handle the weather?" the helo copilot asked, seeming far more concerned about her welfare than the TV show's director and host had seemed.

"Yes," she answered, adjusting the waterproof GoPro camera on her head. The camera and a satellite telephone would be her only contact to the team and the outside world once they dropped her off. She inhaled a deep breath, her heart tripping in her chest.

Thirty days. Alone.

The touchdown was far more controlled than she'd anticipated. The copilot slid open the side door of the helicopter. She got her first view of the island. *Swiss Family Robinson* come to life. Savage slid to the edge to help her out and so he'd be in the picture frame.

"Okay. Out you go," Savage said.

Her heart raced faster. Scooting to the edge, Rhianna quickly climbed out. Her feet sank into the sand as water gushed across her shins in waves exacerbated by the helicopter's gusts.

Savage thrust a canvas satchel toward her. "Here's your survival bag."

Her arm sagged as she accepted it. "My goodness it's heavy."

"It includes the extra batteries for your electronics and a solar recharger so keep it dry in the waterproof bag," he ordered. "You'll get a replacement bag each week."

She nodded. Man, she hadn't recalled those details from the show. What else had she missed?

The next thing she knew, she ducked her head and hustled from the chopper, following the sand. A few seconds later, it was flying away, back toward the mainland. She stood transfixed and watched it disappear.

Eventually, all she could hear was the whoosh of the wind and lap of the surf. Which was quite a foreign sound for a Kentucky girl who had only been to the beach once in her life. She turned and tromped along the sandbar to the shore, her running shoes creating a sucking *kerplop* sound with every step.

Reaching the shore, she took stock of her location. She'd have to make it back here for her pickup when her time was up. Better remember where it was. However, the sky was completely covered with nasty-looking clouds, making it impossible to determine the placement of the sun to get her bearings.

Knowing she had to find shelter before the rain started, Rhianna found an opening in the foliage. In the midst of the enormous trees, there were several open areas where she could make camp. Later, she would explore and find the perfect, more permanent spot, but for tonight, she chose a group of fallen trees near a deep ledge.

She was preparing to take a closer look when a dog's bark ripped through the wind. She turned toward the sound but saw no one. She could have sworn it had been a dog…

She flinched as her satellite phone rang. Pulling it from the satchel, she answered it. "Rhia here."

"Hi, sweetheart," Savage greeted her. "Just double-checking the equipment."

"It's working. Thanks."

"Good. Good. Then I'll—"

"Savage, wait," she interrupted.

"Yes?"

"This island is supposed to be uninhabited, right?"

"That's right."

She paused as she considered telling him about the dog she'd heard, but then again, she didn't want to seem like a wuss less than thirty minutes after landing.

"Well, good luck," he said before the phone went silent.

"Thanks," she whispered to herself, clicking the "off" button.

For a second time, she heard a dog bark. This time she

was sure of it. When she had researched animals on the islands, there had been no mention of dogs. They had to be wild, she thought with a shiver. *And probably hungry.*

As she prepared her camp and gathered wood to build a fire, she also found a long, straight stick that would make for a decent spear in case she needed protection. The question was, did she have what it took to use it if the time came?

AVAILABLE SPRING OF 2017

ACKNOWLEDGMENTS

Many thanks to my fabulous team of professionals:

Cover design: The Killion Group, Inc.

Interior formatting: Author E.M.S.

Editor: Karen Dale Harris

Copyedits: Daniel Poiesz, Double Vision Editorial

ABOUT THE AUTHOR

Larissa Emerald has always had a powerful creative streak whether it's altering sewing patterns, or the need to make some minor change in recipes, or frequently rearranging her home furnishings, she relishes those little walks on the wild side to offset her otherwise quite ordinary life. Her eclectic taste in books cover numerous genres, and she writes sexy contemporary romance, paranormal romance, and futuristic romantic thrillers. But no matter the genre or time period, she likes strong women in dire situations who find the one man who will adore her beyond reason and give up everything for true love.

Larissa is happy to connect with her readers. Stop by and say hello at her website, Facebook, Twitter, or send her an email: larissaemerald@gmail.com.